Henry Wilcox

Dakken Haes

Dakken LLC

To the men walking through the quiet shame of job loss—
may you know, deep in your bones,
that your worth was never measured
by a paycheck, a title, or a business card.

This book is for your courage in waking up anyway,
for the love you still give your families,
for the dreams you're afraid to say out loud.

May you find here a reminder:
you are not alone,
you are not a failure,
and this is not the end of your story.

Chapter 1

Henry Wilcox

Henry woke before dawn, not because he wanted to, but because sleep had grown into a kind of stranger.

His body ached, toes swollen and stiff from gout, his knees creaking when he swung his legs over the edge of the bed. The room was dark, except for the blinking light of the modem in the corner. His wife lay on the other side, turned away from him, her breathing steady but distant, like she was already somewhere else.

He sat there for a while, hunched, elbows on his thighs, palms pressed together. The carpet beneath his bare feet was threadbare, flattened in spots where he always stepped. He could remember a time when the mornings had felt alive with purpose—early trains to catch, meetings to lead, people waiting for his decisions. Now, the only thing that waited was the glow of the computer screen in the dining room and another day of unanswered job applications.

He walked through the house carefully, each joint reminding him of age and of neglect. The refrigerator hummed louder than it should. He poured himself a glass of water and swallowed the pills lined up on the counter.

From the window he could see the neighbor across the street, a younger man with a trim waistline and a confident stride, jogging with earbuds in. Henry turned away before the man could look back.

The neighbors didn't say much directly, but he'd caught their smirks.

The sideways glances at his yard when the grass grew too long. *Look at his yard. Even the dandelions have given up.*

Or the whispers about his failures in the job market. *The executive that wasn't*

But what was most painful was the way his wife friends constantly questioned why she was still with such a failure.

Henry was a joke to his whole neighborhood, and he knew it.

Ignoring the physical and psychological pain, Henry powered up his laptop. The screen lit the dim room, highlighting his sagging features reflected in the glass. His inbox was mostly spam, newsletters he hadn't unsubscribed from. No replies from the companies where he'd applied.

He'd sent out over a thousand résumés, each tailored and adjusted. Each one felt like tossing a stone into an ocean and listening for the splash. Nothing ever came back.

He thought about the job fair last week, the one his wife had convinced him to attend, lined with eager recruiters and bright-eyed recent graduates. He had walked through the aisles in his best suit, the one that fit too tightly now, sweat dampening the collar. Every table he approached, every handshake he offered, he saw the flicker of recognition in their eyes—not admiration, but pity, or worse, dismissal. He was fifty-two, washed out of the industry, carrying a résumé that once shone like polished brass but now looked like rust.

The memory of that humiliation pressed down on him like a weight. His wife had tried to smile afterward, tried to soften it with small talk on the drive home, but he could hear the strain in her voice.

She hadn't touched him in years, hadn't leaned her head on his shoulder in comfort. Whatever tenderness they had shared once had curdled into a kind of silent endurance.

He closed his eyes, and the present dissolved into memory.

I used to walk into an office where people straightened their backs when I entered. VP of the IT division, pulling in two hundred and fifty grand a year, more with bonuses. The numbers never felt real at first. I'd open my paycheck, see the deposit, and laugh out loud in my car on the way home. I remember the leather smell of the seats, the new BMW, the way the dashboard lights glowed blue in the night. I thought it would last forever. I thought I had cracked the code of life.

The first-person voice in his head startled him sometimes, so different from the hollow third-person shell he inhabited now.

He leaned back in his chair, let the images play.

Back then, his days were a rhythm of power. Meetings with clients where he could feel the deal tipping in his favor, conference calls where his voice commanded attention. There was a sharpness in his mind, a speed to his decisions. He knew systems, networks, the architecture of IT like the back of his hand. Younger men wanted to be him; older men envied him. His salary bought dinners downtown, weekends on the lake, vacations where he and his wife would drink wine at sunset and laugh until their sides hurt.

She used to look at me like I was someone extraordinary. I'd walk through the door, loosen my tie, and she'd be there with that smile.

God, that smile.

We used to dance in the kitchen sometimes, music spilling from the little speaker on the counter, her hair brushing my face when she spun. I can still feel her hand in mine, warm, trusting.

How did we get here?

The present clawed back in—the dim light, the silence of the house. He pressed his palms to his eyes until spots danced in the dark.

Outside, the jogger had looped back, sweat glistening on his temples. Henry turned away again, focusing instead on the clock on the wall. The minutes dragged. His wife would be up soon, preparing for her day at the nonprofit where she worked as the VP of Operations.

She had a reason to leave the house.

She had colleagues.

She had purpose.

Henry shuffled to the sink, rinsed his glass. He caught his reflection in the window: thinning hair, lines etched deep around his mouth, shoulders slumped. A man he didn't recognize.

The uninvited flashbacks came again.

College, the rink, the sharp cold of the air biting my lungs. I was a hockey player then. Not NHL material, maybe, but damn good. Defenseman, broad shoulders, quick on the skates. I remember the crash of bodies against the boards, the roar of the crowd when I landed a clean hit.

My teammates clapped me on the back

Shouted my name.

There was sweat, blood, adrenaline—it made me feel invincible. I carried that same energy into the boardroom years later. It was all connected. Hockey taught me to keep my head up, to see the ice, to anticipate. Business was no different.

He rubbed his knees absentmindedly, as if the memory of the ice still lingered in his joints.

From upstairs, the sound of water running in the bathroom. His wife beginning her day. He stayed rooted to the spot, listening. Once upon a time he would have joined her in the shower, hands sliding along her back, laughter echoing against the tile. Now, he didn't even walk upstairs until he heard her leave for work.

He returned to his laptop, clicked through job postings. Each description blurred into the next—requirements stacked high, years of experience demanded, younger titles dressed up as senior roles but offering half of what he used to make. He applied anyway, filling out forms, attaching his résumé.

The futility of it gnawed at him, but he couldn't stop.

His wife entered the room, dressed in a neat blouse and slacks, hair pinned back. She nodded at him, offered a polite "Morning," and poured herself coffee. The space between them was filled with everything they no longer said.

He wanted to tell her he remembered—he remembered the nights they stayed up talking about dreams, the way she had believed in him when he was starting out. He wanted to say he was still that man, somewhere beneath the sagging skin and the failures. But the words clung to his throat, heavy, useless.

She kissed the rim of her coffee cup instead, slung her bag over her shoulder, and left with a brisk, "See you tonight."

The door closed.

Silence.

Henry let out a long breath. He pressed the heels of his hands against the table and whispered, "I used to be somebody."

The whisper startled him—it was the truth escaping without permission.

He sank back into the chair, staring at the glow of the screen. He closed his eyes again, let the first-person memories crash through him.

We were in love. Really in love. I can still see her at twenty-five, standing in the bleachers at one of my college games, cheeks flushed, eyes wide. She told me later she liked the way I moved on the ice, that I looked unstoppable. When we married, I thought that was it—the perfect story, the perfect ending. House, career, vacations, laughter. And for a while, it was. I swear it was.

The ache in his chest was worse than the gout in his feet.

Soon his self-pity was broken by the kids getting ready for summer camp, a boy and a girl 10 and 8, already teenagers, taking care of each other, while he was struggling to take care of himself.

Bounding down the stairs, Henry quickly got up and made them breakfast.

Soon the kids thundered in, Henry scrambled to make breakfast—oatmeal with blueberries and toast. His culinary masterpiece, if you counted "not burning the toast" as culinary mastery.

"Don't forget it's pizza night," Henry announced with mock authority.

"Yeah, awesome, pepperoni only. No fruit!" Thomas said, glaring like pineapple was a war crime.

"Oh its late, bus will be here soon." Said Henry.

Then quickly pulling the lunches out of the refrigerator, he made them the night before, he kissed them good bye as they headed out to the camp bus.

After Henry kissed them goodbye and sent them to the bus, he felt oddly proud. At least the kids thought he was useful—for food, if nothing else..

Now was the bad part of the day.

The morning passed like so many others: the steady hum of appliances, the dull ache of his body, the blank screen waiting for him to write something persuasive about himself that no one seemed to want.

By noon, he'd given up on applications and stared out the window instead, the branches of the maple tree scraping against the glass like the hand of time itself.

The silence pressed on him until it fractured into memory again.

Hockey. God, the sound of it—the skate blades carving into ice, the whistle of the puck as it left the stick. I was never the fastest skater, never the flashiest, but I had weight, presence. Defense was my territory. No one got past me without paying for it. I can still feel the thud of my shoulder against an opponent's chest, the crowd exploding when he crumpled to the boards. It wasn't just violence—it was discipline, it was strategy. Hockey taught me to keep my head steady, even when chaos erupted around me. That ice was my first office. I was good at it. I was proud.

It was in those years, during the blur of practices and classes, that he first saw her.

She was standing in the bleachers at one of my games. Red scarf, a wool hat pulled low, cheeks pink from the cold. She wasn't cheering like the rest—no waving arms or shouting. She just watched, steady and intent, like she could see something in me the others didn't. I remember skating off the ice, heart hammering, trying not to look but failing. I knew, even then, that if she looked at me like that once, I'd chase that gaze for the rest of my life.

Her name had been on everyone's lips—she was known for her sharp wit in seminars, her bright essays, the way she commanded attention without even trying. He was a hockey player with muscles and bruises; she was the one professors singled out. It could have been cliché, but when they finally spoke, it wasn't.

Third-person Henry sat in his dining room, but inside, he was back on that night after the game, sweaty hair sticking to his forehead, mustering courage to approach her at the campus coffee shop.

I asked if she'd seen the game. She smiled, slow and knowing, and said, "I saw you body-check that poor kid so hard he looked like he'd swallowed his own tongue." I laughed, embarrassed, but she kept watching me with that steady gaze. Not impressed, exactly—interested. And that was worse. Or better. Or both.

They talked for hours that night, the coffee cooling, the world shrinking until it was only the two of them. Henry remembered leaning forward, listening harder than he'd ever listened to anyone, and thinking, this is it. This is the woman I will marry.

Back in the present, he closed his eyes and rubbed his forehead. He could almost hear her laugh, a sound that used to be his reward at the end of a long day. Now, the memory felt like a cruel trick.

But the flashbacks surged again, relentlessly.

We were in love. Not just the easy, youthful kind, but the real thing. The kind where you fight and forgive, where you share everything—dreams, fears, failures. I thought it would last forever. I thought we were unbreakable.

Henry opened his eyes. The dining room was still, the screen on his laptop dimmed to black. He ran a hand over his face, weary. He wondered when exactly it had changed—when the laughter had stopped, when the closeness had thinned into silence. It hadn't been one moment but a thousand small ones, piling up like snow until they couldn't see each other anymore.

He stood, joints stiff, and moved to the kitchen. The cupboards were full but uninspiring. He remembered the dinners they used to cook together—complicated recipes, bottles of wine, flour dusting her hair when they made bread from scratch. Now he microwaved leftovers, ate standing at the counter.

Today he leaned against that same counter, staring at the tile, letting the weight of those memories crush him. In them, he was still young, still powerful, still loved. In the present, he was a man with swollen feet and an empty inbox, a man whose wife barely looked at him anymore.

And yet—beneath it all, in the marrow of him—Henry still carried the echo of who he had been.

But time, like a slow leak, began to wear him down.

Time was his enemy at work. The industry shifted. Cloud technology, younger managers with newer degrees, startups running leaner, hungrier. Henry had grown comfortable, confident in his position, and while he adapted at first, the edges began to fray. Meetings grew tense. Projects missed deadlines. He worked longer hours, trying to claw background, but the energy that once surged through him felt diluted, stretched thin.

At home, the long hours turned into absences. She would wait up sometimes, book in hand, but the warmth of those nights of laughter and dancing in the kitchen dulled. He didn't notice it at first. He thought love was permanent, immune to the erosion of time.

I should have seen it. The way she stopped looking at me when I came through the door, the way her smile dimmed around the edges. I thought money was enough. I thought if I just worked harder, climbed higher, it would fix everything. But money doesn't kiss you goodnight. Money doesn't laugh at your jokes. I traded hours with her for hours with a screen, and by the time I realized, she was already somewhere else in her heart.

Henry rubbed his temples. The silence of the dining room felt heavier now, thick with all the things unsaid.

Then came the collapse. The layoffs rolled through the company like a storm, executives with decades of service shown the door. He was one of them. The shock of it had gutted him. For weeks he wandered the house like a man stunned, clutching the severance letter like a death certificate. He remembered telling her, voice shaking, and the way she nodded, lips pressed thin, as though she had been expecting it.

At first, he thought it would be temporary. A man like him, with his résumé, his experience—he would land somewhere else quickly. But weeks stretched into months, months into years. The résumés piled up, the rejections came—or worse, silence. The industry he had helped shape seemed to have no room for him anymore.

His body betrayed him, too. The long years of stress and neglect settled into his joints, his stomach, his skin. Gout flared, knees stiffened, sleep grew thin and restless. The mirror became an enemy, reflecting back someone bloated, sagging, unrecognizable.

He thought of his neighbors again—the way they smirked, the half-hidden amusement in their eyes. They knew. Everyone knew. Henry, the once-proud executive, now a man trimming coupons, wearing worn-out shoes, his wife drifting like a planet into a separate orbit.

Henry pressed his palms against the table, knuckles white. The contrast between then and now threatened to split him in half.

The golden years had been bright, yes. But they had also been fragile. He had thought himself invincible, and that belief had blinded him to the slow corrosion. He had been a hockey player who forgot to watch the ice, a businessman who forgot to anticipate the shift. A man who forgot his wife. And now here he was—jobless, unloved, mocked, aching in body and soul.

The clock ticked on the wall. Afternoon slid toward evening. His wife would return soon, tired from her day, her eyes already looking past him.

"I used to be somebody."

The words hung there, fragile, breaking against the silence of the room.

Chapter 2

Backward Cap Man

The first laugh arrives like a dropped glass in an empty room—clear, brittle, and a little too loud to have been accidental. Henry hears it through the screen door before he sees anyone, a bright peal carried by the slant of late afternoon. He's at the sink, wrists wet, a plate balanced on his palm. Soap slips, the dish tilts, then settles as he steadies himself against the counter. He doesn't move for a moment. He just listens.

The front porch has been a stage these past months, though he would not have used that word if anyone had asked. Not a stage—just a place where voices happen. The younger men from down the block seem to orbit their cul-de-sac like well-groomed satellites: lawn-mowers, strollers, jogs that end in easy stretches and story-swapping; the loose apprenticeship of neighborhood life. They've taken lately to lingering by his front walk, because his wife, it turns out, is good at conversation. She is good at most things when she wants to be.

Another laugh, softer. Then her voice—his wife's—composed and buoyant, summer-smooth.

He turns the faucet off. Water tapers to a thin metallic thread and ends.. His gaze drifts to the window over the sink—trees framed by the screen's fine grid, the corner of the porch barely visible if he leans left. He leans. In that sliver of view: her forearm, the curve of her cheek, one strand of hair blown forward and tucked behind her ear with the same absent grace she once used on him in crowded rooms.

When he finally sets the plate down on the drying rack, his hands are too careful. Care has become a way of walking through his days—care not to bump the furniture, not to leave crumbs, not to claim space. He wipes his hands on the towel and stands there, listening to the choreography of voices he cannot quite bring himself to join

"—no, seriously, it was like that big," says one of the younger neighbors, amusement tightening his words, as if the joke has a size it must be measured to.

"Stop," his wife says, laughing. A small, bright refusal that means continue.

The screen door to the porch is cracked open; pale rectangles of sun lie like quiet animals across the hallway floor. Henry walks toward them. The air is warmer near the door, a cozier, lived-in warmth, freighted with summer grass and someone's cologne and the faint coppery note of the grill two yards over. He tells himself he is just going to look. He tells himself he is the homeowner and it is his porch and that is reason enough.

From the doorway, he sees the scene in its whole arrangement, and it is somehow worse than he anticipates for how casual it is. Two of the young men— he has names for them, but in his head they have gradually become types: Marathon Shirt; Backwards

Cap—stand at the railing, drinks in hand. His wife is between them, a triangle of attention. She is animated, weight balanced lightly over one hip, her eyes moving from face to face, making each man feel, he recognizes, focused on, validated. She was always good at that: the democratic distribution of charm. His throat tightens with an old pride he cannot fully separate from the ache that follows it.

Behind them, the block is doing what blocks do at the good end of a workday—children on bicycles sketching bright cursive down the pavement, training wheels clicking a tidy metronome; a sprinkler whipping rainbows across a front lawn; someone's radio far away, set to an optimistic station. His kids—his kids—are among the riders, small helmets bobbing, one of them standing on pedals, daring and imprecise, the other humming to herself between breaths. He feels the instinctive double tug—inward, toward the house where he has retreated so reliably; outward, toward the porch, the sidewalk, the life with its motion.

"Hen?" his wife says suddenly, but she isn't calling for him. She's using his name as a prop in a story, something he recognizes like a picture of himself taken ten years ago. "—and then Henry says, 'I'm not going to eat pizza without proper plates,' and he brings out the good ones, like he's hosting a gala. We were in sweatpants." More laughter. It is kind laughter, generous, and yet his skin hears only its geometry: exclusion wears the same pitch as affection once did.

He wants to speak and cannot. He wants to say: I brought out plates because you were tired and I wanted it to be special. Instead, he watches the way one of the men leans in to share, and how she leans, too, not a rebuttal—an echo. He notices the slope of her shoulders in a blouse he has never seen; he notices the quickness with which she gestures, the way she exaggerates the shape of a story with her hands as if language alone cannot carry it.

Then it happens. The gesture is so fluid he will later doubt he saw it correctly. Backward Cap says something he can't hear, pats his own stomach hard enough to make his drink slosh. The group laughs. His wife, unthinking, does it back—lifts her arms out from her sides and rounds them forward, a pantomime of a belly. Big. Playful. The shape she makes is unmistakable: here is a circumference, here is the room it takes. She rolls her eyes as though to say, "What can you do?" and then closes her lips into that thin line of mock agreement—our private joke about the body. She does not look toward the door. She does not check the space where he stands with one foot on sunlight, one in the dark.

He feels the air change pressure inside his chest. For a moment, nothing in the world moves. Not the bicycles, not the strip of sprinkler-rain, not the drops spilling from the drinks. He hears his own breath the way you hear thunder when lightning hits very nearby—not as a sound, but as an event.

I was fast once, Henry thinks, the thought arriving in his voice, first-person, unfinished, as if it has been waiting on the stairs for months and has now decided to come down. I was fast and I held the line. Boys who weighed as much as small cars came at me and I met them at the boards and the collision echoed so loud my mother covered her mouth in the stands. I knew where my body ended and the world began. I respected the perimeter. I respected myself. When did I start letting the world draw the line around me?

On the porch, the moment is already over. These are the small evaporations he has come to recognize. Laughter becomes another topic becomes another slant of body toward a different story. His wife's hands have returned to neutral. Marathon Shirt glances down the block at the kids on their bikes and calls out some affable warning about the end of the street. A car turns the corner slowly, like a patient animal. One of the smaller riders bounces her wheel into a crack and steadies herself, triumphant, radiant with the dumb luck of balance.

Henry steps back from the door. The sound of the hinge is almost nothing, but he still holds his breath. He does not want to be seen not because he is ashamed to watch, though he is, but because he wants to control the direction of his own face. Inside, his face can sag. Inside, the muscles around his mouth can exile themselves from dignity for a few seconds. Inside, he can lean his shoulder against the hallway wall and feel the paint cool against his skin.

There is a moment—brief, elastic—when he almost turns on his heel and strides onto the porch with some version of how he used to enter rooms: a joke so well timed that it stitches everyone together in its wake, a kiss to his wife's temple that reads ownership without offense, a nod to the young men that makes eye level into a treaty. He can almost feel the wind of that other life, the one in which he still possesses a center of gravity. Instead, he straightens, relights the old algorithm of composure—chin parallel to floor; shoulders back; stomach—he presses a palm there and feels its indignation, the proof of years the boys have not yet counted.

He drifts to the window that faces the street. From here, he sees the porch at an angle that makes everyone look like they are slightly turning toward him, though they are not. He lifts two fingers and parts the curtain just enough to make a keyhole. Through it, the world is framed small enough to endure.

His children vanish and reappear as they loop the block, the older one cutting the corner so tight his left pedal nearly skims the curb. The younger child sings—a made-up refrain that falters on the high notes and then insists on itself with fresh authority. Their bodies do not yet seem like adversaries to them. The joy in their motion arrives to Henry as a rescue and an accusation. He tells himself that he will oil their chains this weekend. He tells himself he will jog—no, walk—no, stretch—around the park tomorrow morning before the heat. He traces the path of their circling in his mind like a chalk diagram: here is where the maple roots buckle the sidewalk, here is where the neighbor's lab leaves paw prints in damp cement, here is where you could be better if you began.

A peal of laughter lifts from the porch again, then words fall in shapes he cannot catch. Backward Cap flicks his eyes down the street then back to Henry's wife with the amused composure of a man who has learned without trying that his age and jawline grant him a base level of credit. Marathon Shirt—his real name is Brandon, Henry recalls; he taught the older child to throw a spiral last spring on the stretch of grass between stoops—makes the small bow you make when you say goodbye to someone you hope to see again soon. They are all so easily vivid to one another. That is what stings. The effortlessness.

She used to lean on me, Henry thinks, and this time the first-person is a corridor with pictures hung close. She used to put her hand at the small of my back when a room made her nervous, and the heat of her palm would say don't move and also don't you dare leave me here. We went to parties where I knew no one and she would tilt her head to listen to me and all of a sudden I knew everyone. We were a door we opened together. That's the memory I kept. Not the last two years. Not the separate beds or the separate spoons in the drawer that somehow knew which side to fall to.

He realizes his jaw is clenched and moves his hand along it, as if to polish a stubborn thought. The boys on the porch linger. The sun changes angle so the rail casts a thinner shadow. His wife swats at a fly that has mistaken her for sweetness. He is the one who put the citronella candle out there two nights ago and turned it with a match until the black wick brightened, the smoke moving in a deliciously unpretentious ribbon into the evening. He had been out there alone then, the porch an island. Tonight it is a country and he does not have a passport.

He imagines, for a feral instant, walking onto the porch and striking the railing with the flat of his palm. Not hard enough to be violent—just enough to make the hollow wooden sound that says remember I am here. He lets the image evaporate. He has made a private ritual of refusing his own worst theatrics. The calories he saves go nowhere good. They hover under his skin.

The kids come into the frame again. The older one skids to a controlled stop in front of the porch and looks up as if taking attendance. "Mom, watch!" he calls. She looks. He launches himself forward and stands on the pedals again, this time for longer, legs piston-quick, body tilting into a thrilling near-fall before correcting, exultant. The younger follows, wobbling, concentrating in the absolute way the young concentrate: whole face dedicated to a single act. They pass Henry's field of vision and vanish toward the end of the block, where the street humps slightly and the asphalt glitters with embedded stones. He wants to be out there to warn them about the glitter—that it's beautiful because it's sharp.

When he glances back to the porch, he catches the tail-end of another gesture. He cannot tell its content; he only sees the ripple of complicity—three adults held briefly in the geometry of a shared joke. His wife's hand is still in the air. She isn't cruel, he tells himself. She is— lonely. She is like a plant finding light. If the window were opened and he said her name in the tone he used to use, she would turn to him with that startled softness he misses and he would see, even now, that everything isn't lost. The thought is a bruise he presses and presses.

He retreats from the window and moves through the house with the restless carefulness of someone who does not want to invent an excuse to go where he is not wanted. In the living room, the couch has a shallow collapse where he sits most evenings. He passes it with the dignity of ignoring your own imprint. On the far end table is the photo in the silver frame he keeps forgetting to move. Their wedding day: a square of captured confidence. His tux is a little too slick, his hair a little too shiny, but the eyes are and will always be honest. She is leaning into him, head tilted with that unmistakable look of not just love but certainty. He cannot remember what joke the photographer made to get that expression, or if it was not a joke at all, but something that began behind her eyes and ended at the edge of the picture.

He lifts the frame. Maybe he will put it in the den. Maybe he will put it face down in a drawer and call that mercy. The glass has the faintest scatter of dust. He breathes on it and uses the hem of his shirt to rub a circle clear, which of course makes the ring more obvious. He sets it down again, defeated by the implication that some objects have decided where they live.

In the dining room, the laptop's screen saver is a field of Antarctic blue. Penguins on an ice shelf stare unconvincingly at a horizon. He touches the trackpad and the birds vanish into a grid of boxed certainty—folders with names like "Tailored Resume—InfraSec," "Cover Letter—Enterprise PM," "Follow-Ups." He knows now which companies will never answer. He knows the weight of the air that descends in the seconds after you click "submit." He watches the way his cursor trembles slightly and blames the machine. The last email he sent this morning vibrates there in its polite, terminal optimism. He has learned to be apologetic about his own experience, to phrase the sentence in which he used to announce power as a timid inquiry. He closes the laptop slowly, like laying a hand over a bird that is not yet dead.

From the porch: "We should do a block thing," Marathon Shirt says. "Like a chili cook-off. Or trivia night." Then his wife's voice, obliging, warm; she is very good at the temperature of agreement. He tries not to calculate how many weeks the phrase "we should" includes him by default. There was a time when he would already be planning the teams and the scoreboard and the playlist and the prizes—the self-appointed commissioner of neighborhood joy. Now he does not make plans that require others to choose him.

He is halfway back toward the kitchen when his older child barrels in through the back door, reprieved from gravity, helmet askew. The boy stops short at the sight of Henry, as if caught in a net he did not expect. His face is open; Henry tries to match it. A father's knowledge is a strange instrument—you can tune it to fear too easily.

"Water?" the boy asks, already reaching for the cabinet with his quick animal certainty. Henry nods, steps aside. The boy pours sloppily with the competence of youth, gulps, breathes in a dramatic, appreciative whoosh, and then looks up at his father—really looks, a sonar ping. "Can you come watch?" he asks, and the five words open something in Henry with a blade's quietness.

"I can," Henry says. The answer arrives clean—no flinching. He is already moving toward the back door when the other thought starts, the one that begins with unless. Unless your mother... unless the neighbors... unless you look slow beside their speed. He steps over it like a crack he has learned not to test.

On the porch, three adults turn like flowers tracking light. His wife's face registers surprise and then relaxes. She smiles, genuinely, at their son. For a small instant, nothing else is asked of anyone. Marathon Shirt lifts his drink in a neighborly salute. Backward Cap says, "My guy," to the boy. Henry stands on the threshold, not yet stepping into the tiny society that has formed, and makes two choices at once: he lifts a hand to greet the men in a gesture that neither promises nor denies anything; and he keeps his gaze on his son.

"Show me," he says.

The boy launches. His bicycle is a bright blue comet with scratches along the frame where bravery has already left its autograph. He veers into the street with more confidence than safety would recommend, but the afternoon is forgiving. He stands and pumps and stands again until he is a stitched seam of speed, then drops back to the saddle and coasts into a grin that pulls both corners of his mouth into declarations. The younger child follows, determined, tongue at the corner of her lips like a scholar.

Henry watches—and lets himself be seen watching. He feels the men's attention slide off him and onto the children, which is a mercy. He feels his wife's gaze touch his cheek and flutter away, like a small bird who has learned to keep moving. When the boy passes the porch again, he calls, "Dad! Did you see that?"

"I saw," Henry says. "I saw all of it."

The boy disappears down the block for another loop. Henry lets his arms fall. He becomes aware again of his body in the way a person becomes aware of a room after an argument: nothing has moved, and everything is different. He is about to step forward, to join the rail and the candle and the smiles with something like a companionable ease, when Marathon Shirt, without malice and without much thought, says to his wife, "You two doing the lake thing this weekend? You could paddleboard. She killed it last time."

His wife laughs and shakes her head. "Oh God, no. Not with my balance. I almost fell in like five times." She makes a small show of wobbling at the waist. It is harmless. It is a kind of capitulation to the angle of conviviality.

Backward Cap grins. "He could," he says, jerking his chin in Henry's direction—not quite looking at him; somehow that would be too much. "He looks like he could use it. No offense." Then the quick, empty chuckle men use to salt the casual cruelty. "Get a sweat on, you know? Cut a line across the lake."

The porch waits for the joke to settle into a category—banter or offense. Henry feels a taste flood his mouth that is neither metal nor salt; it is simply old. He can almost see himself on the board for a second, legs planted by memory, chest tall, the calm slide over water, the unbroken line between his shoulders and the horizon. Then the picture sours, flickers, recalibrates to the present with the ungenerous fidelity of cheap video. His wife, to her credit, says lightly, "We're more patio people these days," and taps the railing with her knuckles like a cymbal. He cannot tell if she has defended him or dismissed him. Perhaps both; perhaps that is the modern compromise.

He does not trust his voice to handle the word "maybe." He nods instead, a polite tilt that costs him something he cannot name. Then he addresses the space beneath the comment by speaking to his daughter, who has cruised up to the step with the solemn air of an envoy.

"How many laps?" he asks. She holds up a hand and then remembers she needs a number and chooses five, which she repeats with the gravity of law. He tells her she's faster than the wind. She declares that the wind cheats. There is laughter. For a moment, it is a family sound.

He does not stay long on the porch. He finds a reason to step back inside before his body must remain in the grammar of collegiality one second longer than it can bear. In the hallway again, halfway shadowed, he exhales so fully his chest trembles. The pressure that had built there releases—but not harmlessly. It leaves a soreness, the way a thumb pressed against a bruise leaves behind the echo of its shape.

In the kitchen, his glass of water is still where he left it. Condensation has made a neat circle on the table. He places his fingertip in the puddle and draws a small ring inside the ring, then wipes it all with the cuff of his sleeve. He imagines—quixotically—doing pushups right here beside the oven until his arms wail, until some absent tribunal declares him absolved. He imagines opening the back door and running until his lungs find their old size. He imagines unloading the basement weight bench and conceding that every decision that mattered lately has been a decision not to begin.

You were a defenseman, he tells himself in the private second person he reserves for pep talks and rebukes. You did not let the puck through. You were the last clean line. Get to your skates. The metaphor is both too much and not enough. He lets it hang in the air and then watches it drop, quietly, as metaphors do when they are asked to carry a body.

The voices on the porch soften; the choreography of departure begins—the subtle shifts of weight, the feints toward the steps, the "we should"s that are promises to the moment more than to the future. He hears the hinge; the screen door eases open and the porch becomes again the porch, relinquishing its specialness like a stage after curtain. His wife lingers, talks to the children briefly, sends them on one more lap, and then he hears her footsteps in the hall.

He does not flee. He stands at the counter and pretends to be indifferent to the arc a droplet of water takes down the side of a glass. When she walks in, her face is softened by air and attention. She looks younger, he thinks, when she has spoken all her words for the hour.

"Hey," she says, and the syllable is benign.

"Hey," he says back. He considers the math of asking how it was, as if she had been somewhere, returns to the algebra of small talk. "Bikes are getting a workout."

"Mm," she says, opening the fridge. The interior light reaches for her cheek. "They're happy." She takes a bottle of something citrus and leans on the counter to drink. He sees a faint smudge of sunblock by her ear and has to deliberately un-remember the intimacy of the gesture it would take to wipe it away with his thumb.

"They are," he says. He wants to say I heard you laugh. He wants to say I heard the way my name sounds when it is not for me.

Instead: "Need anything for dinner?"

She thinks for a second. "I can start something later," she says. Then, as if realizing the words might be read as a claim about territory, she adds, "Or we can order. Up to you." She smiles in a way that cedes a choice while reminding him the stakes are small. The smile is not unkind.

He nods. "I'll look," he says. It is a promise to find something solvable. It is a truce that neither enjoys winning.

She sets the bottle down, its base making the quiet thock of glass on wood, and taps the counter once with her knuckles, that tidy, neutral signal she uses to release herself from a moment. Her footsteps move down the hall. He stands still until he hears the bathroom door close and the sink run, a small choreography of privacy.

Chapter 3

The Call

The rhythm of the summer is simple, it is easy. Freedom, warmth, family, friends and neighbors.

Well two out of five ain't too bad. Henry thought to himself.

Outside, the bicycles pass again, their shadows long now and comic. From the neighbor's yard, someone calls a name that sounds like a bell rung twice. The house reinhabits itself: the ticking clock, the friction sigh of the air conditioner, the soft internal weather of a family. Henry turns his phone over where it rests facedown on the table. The black screen is a strict mirror. He sees the shape of his shoulders in it, the slope of his neck. He props it against a salt cellar, absentmindedly, so it will not look so much like a closed eye.

He is still standing there when, a minute later, the phone lights and vibrates against the wood—once, twice—its bright rectangle startling the kitchen into attention. He looks down at the name blooming on the screen. He blinks, surprised by how quickly he recognizes it and by the warmth the recognition carries.

He wipes his hand on his shirt, as if he might have left sweat where he will touch and reaches for it.

"Henry! You old bastard."

The voice on the line carried laughter in it, an immediate familiarity. For a second Henry forgot how to breathe. It was Mark, his friend from the hockey team—

defenseman too, heavier, but always quick with a story. They hadn't spoken in almost a year. Maybe longer.

"Mark," Henry said, and heard his own voice stretch thin before it found shape.

"You sound like you swallowed a church bell," Mark chuckled. "Listen, I and putting a trip together. You and I. Two weeks from Friday. Up north—canoes and tents, you know the drill. A couple of nights, some fishing, some drinking, pretending our backs don't hurt when we sleep on the ground. You in?"

Henry pressed the phone to his ear as if it were something fragile. He glanced through the window at his kids circling the block, their bikes wobbling in long shadows. His chest stirred—fear, excitement, disbelief.

Camping. Christ, when was the last time? Ten years? More? But I remember it. The crackle of fire, the smell of pine, the stupid way we tried to out-drink each other under the stars. I remember feeling like I belonged to something. Like I was still made for it.

"I—" He hesitated. His instinct was to retreat, to invent some excuse, to say he wasn't up for it. But the silence on the line carried Mark's certainty, and Henry realized he wanted, more than anything, to believe he could still say yes.

"I'm in," Henry said.

The words escaped before he had weighed them. But once they were out, he felt lighter.

"That's what I'm talking about," Mark said. "I'll text you the details. Don't bring too much crap—just the essentials. And maybe that old flask, if you still have it."

They said their goodbyes, and Henry hung up. He sat there, phone in hand, feeling the echo of what he had just done. For a long moment he just let himself smile— small, private, but real.

His wife entered the kitchen just then, hair still damp from washing, soft wisps clinging to her temples. She looked at him with curiosity.

"Who was that?" she asked.

"Mark," Henry said, trying to sound casual. "He invited me on a camping trip. Couple weeks from now."

Her eyebrows lifted. For a heartbeat he thought she would frown, tell him it was childish, tell him they didn't have the money or the time. But instead, her face brightened.

"That's wonderful!" she said, and her voice carried something he hadn't heard in months: relief. "You should go. You need to go."

Henry blinked. "You think so?"

"Yes," she said firmly. "Honestly, Hen, it'll be good for you. And for me, too. I'll take the kids to my parents. Grandparents weekend they'll love it. Me and the girls, will have this place to ourselves." She smiled, and it was the kind of smile that reached her eyes, rare and startling.

Henry felt heat in his chest. She wanted this for him. She wanted him to step out of the shadow he'd been living in. He nodded, unable to keep the awkward grin off his face.

"That's… great," he murmured.

"Go get your gear," she teased. "Make sure the sleeping bag hasn't rotted in the basement."

Henry chuckled, embarrassed, and shuffled toward the basement door. Dust rose when he flicked the light on, the old pull-chain swinging overhead. The gear was there in a corner—duffel bag, camp stove, lantern, and his old sleeping bag rolled tight with faded straps. He picked it up, a wave of nostalgia washing over him.

I remember this. nights zipped up tight, listening to rain patter the nylon. I remember her curled against me, back when she came along. She used to say she liked the smell of smoke in my hair, that it made me smell like the woods themselves. God, she used to look at me like I was enough.

Henry carried the gear upstairs. His wife was waiting in the kitchen, arms crossed, smiling faintly. He dropped the sleeping bag on the floor, crouched, and unrolled it. The nylon rasped against the tile. He slid his legs inside, pulling it up past his thighs. Then he tugged harder. It stuck at his hips.

"Damn thing shrunk," Henry muttered, tugging again. The zipper groaned, teeth straining.

His wife laughed—real laughter, sharp and sudden. "Hen, it didn't shrink," she said. "You grew." She made a round gesture with her arms, miming a belly. The same gesture she'd given the neighbors earlier. Only now it was aimed directly at him.

Henry's cheeks flushed. He tried to laugh it off, but the sound caught in his throat. He wriggled, trapped, before finally giving up and peeling himself out of the bag. He sat on the floor, breathless, heart pounding with embarrassment.

"Guess I'll need a new one," he said softly.

She smirked, shaking her head, and patted his shoulder as if he were a child who had failed a simple task. Then, without malice but without tenderness, she turned away. "I'll put the kids down," she said. "Don't stay up too late."

He watched her go, her figure retreating up the stairs, her voice drifting as she called for the children. He stayed on the floor for a moment longer, staring at the empty sleeping bag, the nylon darkened by the sweat of his effort.

I used to fit. I used to belong in everything I owned. Now even the objects remember me better than I remember myself.

Henry stood, folded the bag clumsily, and shoved it back into its straps. He turned off the kitchen light. Upstairs, the house murmured—the creak of floorboards, his wife's soft voice reading, the children giggling before settling. He climbed the stairs slowly, one hand on the railing.

When he entered the bedroom, she was already in bed, the lamp on her side switched off. Her breathing was steady, deliberate. Henry changed quietly, slid beneath the covers. The sheets were cool, impersonal. He lay on his back, staring at the ceiling, listening to the sound of her sleep.

He whispered into the dark, so low even he could barely hear:

"I'm going camping."

The words felt both like a promise and a plea.

Chapter 4

Dropping the Ball

The garage smelled faintly of oil and pine. Henry had pulled the extra tent bag down from the rafters, spread it half across the concrete floor, and was sorting through poles that always seemed one piece short until the last second when, like magic, the missing segment appeared behind a cooler or beneath a duffel bag. It was late afternoon, one of those Midwest evenings that held the faint shimmer of summer fading toward autumn. The air had that bite—cool enough that the sound of kids playing outside carried sharper, cleaner.

He was supposed to be "getting gear ready," at least that was how he'd described it to his wife, though if anyone had peeked in, they might have accused him of merely moving piles from one corner to another.

The Boundary Waters trip was a sacred thing, something he'd been doing since he was young enough to carry only a paddle and half a pack, back when older men in his life took responsibility for all the logistics. Now he was the older man, the one supposed to check for missing stakes, untangled fishing line, bug dope that hadn't dried into useless gunk, and tarps that still shed water.

The kids' voices floated from the yard, bright and uneven like wind chimes in a gust. A thunk followed by laughter. Henry glanced through the open garage door. A group of neighborhood kids were tossing a football back and forth. Among them was the man Henry thought of only as "backward cap guy"—mid-thirties, built like someone who once played high school ball and never let go of the look. Always in a sleeveless shirt, always with that cap spun backward as though time had stopped for him around 2010

Henry bent over his pack, stuffing sleeping bags into stuff sacks that refused to be small enough. That was when the ball skidded into the garage. It bounced once, smacked the cooler, and rolled to a stop against his foot.

He looked down at it. A Wilson, slightly scuffed, leather worn from too many driveway games. The kids shouted, "Mr. H, throw it back!"

Henry scooped it up, feeling its laces. Muscle memory tugged at him. He hadn't thrown a ball in years, not really—not since backyard games with his own kids before they'd decided their father was more embarrassing than fun. He squared his shoulders, raised the ball, and for a second pictured himself making the perfect spiral, sending it arcing gracefully into backward cap guy's waiting hands.

The throw left his hand wrong. Too high, too slick, his palm sweating from wrestling with the tent earlier. Instead of sailing in a neat spiral, the ball sliced sideways, wobbling like a wounded bird. It didn't just miss backward cap guy—it went nowhere near him.

The ball smacked directly into the side of his wife's lawn gnome.

The gnome had stood sentry by the flower bed for nearly a decade. A squat fellow with a blue hat and a fishing pole, he had survived rain, snow, and the occasional mower mishap. He had watched over tulips, petunias, and weeds alike. Henry had never liked the thing, though he'd never said as much—it was one of those household objects you learned to ignore. But now, fate had chosen this moment for its downfall.

The football cracked against it, sending the gnome toppling sideways in slow motion, like a soldier falling on the battlefield. Its hat chipped, its fishing pole snapped, and it landed face-first in the dirt.

For a moment, silence.

Then the kids burst into laughter, high-pitched, unrestrained. One of them doubled over, slapping his knees. Another shouted, "You killed him, Mr. H!"

Even backward cap guy chuckled, that low masculine laugh meant to signal camaraderie.

Henry stood frozen with his throwing arm still extended, hand empty, body locked in a ridiculous pose like a quarterback statue gone wrong.

From across the yard, his wife's voice rang out, sharp with that particular mix of embarrassment and irritation. She was standing with a cluster of neighborhood women near the patio, all of them holding plastic wine cups. They had been mid-story—her hand gesturing, eyes sparkling—when the gnome fell. Now she stopped mid-sentence.

She looked at Henry, then at the gnome, then back at her friends. With the subtlest flick of her wrist, she made a gesture, not quite dismissive but certainly not supportive. A little shake of the head, a roll of the wrist that said, What can I do? That's Henry.

The women laughed politely, eyes darting between her and Henry. One of them covered her mouth, another sipped quickly at her wine. His wife turned back to them, her voice rising an octave as if to redirect the story, as though by ignoring the fallen gnome she could erase the spectacle.

Henry bent down, picked up the gnome, brushed dirt off its cracked face. He could hear the kids still laughing, backward cap guy tossing the football casually from hand to hand. "Nice arm, man," he said, not unkindly, but not kindly either.

Henry forced a smile. "Guess I'm out of practice."

Inside, his stomach tightened. Outside, he set the gnome back upright, its hat chipped, its fishing pole gone. He muttered, "Sorry, buddy," under his breath.

The kids ran off, chasing the ball again. Laughter moved down the block. The moment passed for everyone else. But Henry stood there in the garage doorway, gnome askew beside him, wife's gesture still burning in his memory, the sound of laughter echoing longer than it should have.

Henry was still brushing flecks of dirt off the gnome when a shadow fell across the driveway. He didn't have to look up. Only one man in the neighborhood cast that particular silhouette: broad shoulders, tank top, baseball cap spun backward as if locked in permanent rebellion against the forward-facing world.

Backward Cap Guy.

"Hey, champ," the man said, voice pitched in the casual authority of someone who assumed familiarity. He strolled up the driveway, football tucked under his arm like he was perpetually en route to a highlight reel.

Henry straightened, setting the gnome carefully beside the flower bed, hoping maybe if it stood upright no one would notice its hat was chipped. "Hey," Henry said, trying for neutral.

"Nice toss earlier," Backward Cap Guy grinned, winking like they were teammates sharing a private joke. "You know, if that gnome had been running a slant route, you'd have nailed him perfect."

Henry forced a laugh, though it came out more like a cough. "Yeah, precision passing—that's me."

Backward Cap Guy slapped the football against his thigh. "So listen, your wife mentioned you're headed up to the Boundary Waters. Big trip, huh?"

Henry nodded, already feeling the conversation shifting into dangerous waters. "Yeah, few days. Just trying to make sure I've got everything in order."

Backward Cap Guy stepped closer, eyes roaming the garage like a coach scanning a rookie's locker. "You got a good stove? I've got one of those jet-boil setups if you need. Real slick. Boils water faster than you can say ramen."

Henry gestured vaguely to the pile of gear at his feet. "I've got my old WhisperLite. It still works fine."

"WhisperLite?" Backward Cap Guy repeated, like Henry had just admitted to using dial-up internet. "Man, that's vintage. Classic. I mean, respect. But you sure it still works? Don't want to be out there sucking on cold beans, right?" He laughed, then elbowed Henry in the shoulder like they'd shared years of inside jokes.

Henry took the nudge, wobbling slightly, and pretended to adjust a duffel bag. "Yeah, I test-fired it last week. It's good."

Backward Cap Guy leaned against the garage frame, casual as if he owned the property. "Alright, alright. Hey, you got a bear canister? Because let me tell you, I've got the Cadillac of bear canisters. Thing's like Fort Knox for granola bars. You could park it outside a 7-Eleven and not even the raccoons would crack it."

"I've got one," Henry said quickly.

"You sure?"

"Yes."

Backward Cap Guy grinned again. "Okay, man, just offering. Don't want you coming back skinny."

Henry muttered, "That'd be a first," under his breath, but not loud enough to be heard.

From the patio, laughter floated over—his wife and the other women still mid-conversation. Henry caught a glimpse of her hand fluttering in that way she did when she was telling a story. She looked relaxed now, like his gnome fiasco had been neatly filed under just another Henry moment.

Backward Cap Guy followed Henry's glance. "Speaking of," he said, lowering his voice just slightly, "your wife told mine—well, not really mine, I mean my girlfriend, but she's over a lot—she told her that she's planning to hang with your wife while you're gone. You know, keep her company, girls' nights, that sort of thing."

Henry turned back, raising an eyebrow. "Oh?"

"Yeah," Backward Cap Guy said, nodding. "Don't worry, man. I'll keep an eye on the house. Watch over the girls, you know what I mean?"

Henry blinked. "The girls?"

"Yeah," he gestured toward the patio, where his wife and the neighbors were sipping wine like suburban royalty. "Them. I'll make sure nobody messes around while you're gone. Not that anyone would, but hey—you never know. Strong male presence, right?"

Henry just stared at him. The words "strong male presence" floated in the air like a bad cologne.

Backward Cap Guy seemed oblivious to the weight of his own statement. He flipped the football up and caught it one-handed, smirking like a man who had never missed a layup in his life.

"Don't worry," he repeated. "You go paddle your canoe, I'll paddle the ship here. Keep the ladies entertained, if you catch my drift."

Henry's first instinct was to laugh it off, pretend he hadn't heard the undertone. His second was to visualize the gnome hurling itself at Backward Cap Guy in a noble act of vengeance. His third was to say something— anything—that reestablished dignity.

What came out was: "Uh, thanks."

Backward Cap Guy slapped him on the back, nearly knocking him into the cooler. "That's what neighbors are for, man!"

Henry forced a smile that felt like holding a plank position for too long. "Appreciate it."

"Anytime."

The man's grin widened, teeth too white in the waning sun. He spun the football in his hands, then cocked his head toward the patio. "You ever notice how they all laugh louder when they're together? Like, one glass of pinot and suddenly it's a comedy club. Cracks me up."

Henry half-shrugged, wishing desperately to retreat back into his gear piles. "Yeah, I've noticed."

"They're good girls," Backward Cap Guy said, as if Henry needed reassurance. "Real good. I'll make sure they stay that way while you're gone."

This time, Henry couldn't even muster a fake smile. He bent down, busied himself with a sleeping bag strap, tugging it tight as though the fate of the entire trip depended on its precise roll.

Backward Cap Guy, oblivious, continued. "So, Boundary Waters. You excited?"

Henry straightened. "Yeah, I am."

"Good, good. Man, I haven't been since college. Brought a whole case of beer once. Big mistake. You paddle with that weight and you start thinking, 'maybe I'll just drink it all now and lighten the load.'" He laughed at his own story, pounding his thigh.

Henry gave a polite chuckle, though inside he was counting the minutes until this interaction ended.

Backward Cap Guy leaned closer, conspiratorial now. "So, uh, if you do end up short on gear—you know, stove breaks, tarp rips—you just holler. I'll swing something over. Don't want my boy Henry out there roughing it."

Henry thought about correcting him—we are not friends, you are not my boy, and I do not want your bear canister—but instead he just nodded. "Sure."

Backward Cap Guy gave him another hearty slap on the back, then jogged off, tossing the football to himself. "Strong male presence, brother!" he called over his shoulder, laughing.

Henry exhaled slowly, long enough that his chest ached. He glanced at the gnome again, its hat cracked, its fishing pole gone. The gnome seemed to look at him, face chipped, as if to say, Really? That's the guy you're leaving behind to watch things?

Henry muttered back, "Tell me about it."

From the patio, his wife's laughter rose again. And Henry, standing there with his half-sorted gear and his fractured dignity, thought: This trip better be worth it.

Henry dragged the duffel into the mudroom, shoulders tight from the encounter with Backward Cap Guy. Every time the phrase strong male presence replayed in his head, he felt a small shiver of secondhand embarrassment crawl up his spine. The gnome's cracked face, his wife's dismissive gesture, the kids' laughter—it all seemed to travel with him like extra weight strapped to the pack.

"Finalize the packing," he muttered under his breath. He wasn't even sure what he was doing, still miffed about the encounter with the *girls savior*, he was lost in the packing.

The Boundary Waters checklist was taped to the fridge:

Tent ✓

Sleeping bags ✓

Pad ✓

Stove (Working? Maybe?) ✓

Food bucket (to be filled)

Paddles (two, scratched but serviceable)

Maps, compass, GPS (overkill, but he liked redundancy)

He scanned it like a student trying to memorize for a test. Everything looked familiar. Everything looked incomplete.

He set the duffel down beside the washer, opened it again, and frowned at the contents: socks, tarp, bug dope, extra headlamp batteries. Why did he always feel like he was missing the most obvious thing?

"Finalize," he muttered again, pulling the zipper halfway closed.

He should have gone back to the garage. Should have checked the tent poles once more. But his back ached, and his head was still buzzing with the echo of neighborly laughter. Instead, he drifted toward the kitchen, then toward the living room where his laptop sat open on the desk.

Just a quick check, he told himself. Nothing serious. Just email, maybe the news. A small break before he wrestled with gear again.

The laptop hummed awake, screen glowing. Notifications bloomed in the corner: two shopping ads, one forwarded recipe from his wife's sister, and an email with a subject line that made his chest tighten instantly.

"Update on Your Application – IT Project Manager Position."

Henry's hand hovered over the trackpad. He had been waiting for this one. Not just another résumé flung into the void—this was the interview he'd thought had gone well. The call where the hiring manager had nodded at all the right points, even laughed when Henry made that joke about legacy systems being like stubborn uncles at Thanksgiving. The follow-up email that had felt encouraging. For the first time in months, he'd thought: This one could work. This could be it.

He clicked.

The message was short.

It always was.

Dear Henry,

Thank you for your time and interest in the IT Project Manager role. After careful consideration, we've decided to move forward with another candidate.

We appreciate your efforts and wish you the best in your future endeavors.

Regards,

Talent Acquisition Team

Henry stared at it. The words blurred, but the meaning was sharp, immediate. Another rejection. Not just any rejection—the rejection.

He slumped back in the chair, exhaling through his nose. For a moment, all he could hear was the distant laughter from outside—the women's chorus of wine-sparkled amusement, Backward Cap Guy shouting "Go long!" to a kid in the yard.

The timing of it made him laugh. Not a full laugh, not even a chuckle—just a small burst of air that sounded more like a bark. "Of course," he muttered. "Of course today."

He rubbed his face with both hands, pressing against his eyes until the rejection email vanished behind bursts of color. He tried to think of what to do next—reply? No. Close the laptop? Maybe. Pretend it hadn't arrived? Definitely.

The cursor blinked at him, taunting.

For years, Henry had built projects out of chaos. Vendor negotiations, system upgrades, training sessions that had gone sideways—he had been the guy who kept it all taped together. Now, the only thing he managed was moving gear piles from garage to mudroom to living room and back again. His résumé told one story; his inbox told another.

He clicked the email closed. For a few seconds he stared at the desktop wallpaper—a stock photo of a lake with canoes gliding across calm water. It looked suspiciously like the Boundary Waters, though cleaner, emptier. Idealized. A place where nobody laughed at you, where no gnomes fell, where job rejections didn't follow you like shadows.

The irony wasn't lost on him. Tomorrow he would be paddling across the real thing, carrying real weight, sweating under real sun. And maybe—maybe—that would be enough.

But right now, all he felt was tired.

He pushed away from the desk, stood, stretched. His back popped. The duffel in the mudroom still waited, zipper half-closed like an accusing mouth. He shuffled over, sat on the bench, and pulled out a dry bag. Inside it was the food kit: oatmeal packets, trail mix, instant coffee. He checked them as if counting calories could distract from the email still lodged in his chest.

"Finalize," he muttered again, louder this time, as though by repeating it he could turn packing into a spell, a charm against failure. "Just finalize the damn thing."

He shoved the oatmeal back in, crammed the zipper closed, and felt a small jolt of victory.

One bag done.

A minor win.

The back door opened. His wife's voice carried in, light but edged. "Henry? You almost ready in there?"

"Working on it," he called back, trying to sound upbeat.

She stepped into the mudroom, wine glass in hand, cheeks slightly flushed from laughter. "You've been working on it all day."

"Yeah, well," Henry said, patting the duffel, "it's a process."

She sipped, studying him. For a second he thought she might ask about the laptop, might notice the tension still clinging to his shoulders. But instead she said, "The gnome's hat is ruined, you know. I told you years ago we should have moved it."

Henry opened his mouth, then closed it. There was no winning that conversation.

"Anyway," she continued, "I told the girls we'll do a movie night when you're gone. Maybe some wine tasting. Alex said you two talked, and he might bring over his projector for the patio."

Henry felt his jaw tighten. "Oh?"

"Yeah," she said breezily. "It'll be fun. Don't worry about us."

"I'm not," Henry lied.

She smiled, a small, sharp smile, and went back outside. The sound of laughter rose again, carried through the open door.

Henry sat there with the duffel half-zipped, the taste of rejection still bitter in his mouth, the words don't worry about us echoing like a taunt.

He tried to laugh at himself. Really, he did. The image of him winging a football into a gnome, followed by Backward Cap Guy promising to be the "strong male presence" while he was gone, and now this email—it all had the makings of a sitcom. If his life had a laugh track, this would be the moment the audience roared.

But sitcoms ended after thirty minutes. His evening stretched on.

So he did the only thing he could: zipped the duffel, stood up, and prayed his gout would not act up while in the boundary waters.

Chapter 5

Long Drive Ahead

Henry woke before the alarm, heart thudding in the quiet house. For a moment he lay still, staring at the dim ceiling. The day had come. The trip was no longer a circle on the calendar, no longer a plan scribbled on a yellow pad by the laptop. It was here.

He swung his legs out of bed and winced. His toes screamed with the dull fire of gout; his knees resisted, stiff and swollen from years of neglect. He sat a long moment at the edge of the bed, steadying his breath.

I used to spring up, lace skates in seconds, hit the ice before anyone else. Now I sit here waiting for my joints to negotiate with gravity.

The thought stung, but he stood anyway.

Downstairs, his gear was already laid out in awkward piles: the new sleeping bag still in its wrapper, the duffel bag bulging with clothes, the camp stove that smelled faintly of propane. He began checking each item with the nervous diligence of a man who had failed too often lately and couldn't risk another.

Flashlight. Batteries. Compass. Knife. He placed each on the table, muttering under his breath. He wanted to feel prepared, competent, like the man his friend Mark expected to see. But his hands betrayed him—fumbling zippers, dropping a lighter, spilling a bag of trail mix that scattered like marbles across the floor.

He knelt to pick it up, breath heavy, back complaining.

I carried canoes heavier than this gear. I carried them through mud and over rock, laughing at the burn in my shoulders. I was proud of the pain. Why does it feel so different now?

By afternoon, he had repacked everything twice. The house smelled of coffee, his mug cooling untouched on the counter. He checked his phone compulsively: no word from Mark yet. He paced the kitchen, listening for the crunch of tires in the drive.

Then the doorbell rang.

His wife's friends arrived in a chorus—three of them, arms full of overnight bags, voices bright and overlapping. They spilled into the hallway like color, perfumed and laughing, their chatter bouncing off the walls.

"Girls' weekend!" one of them cheered, tossing her purse onto the bench.

Henry hovered at the edge, awkward. His wife emerged from the kitchen, hugging them, her face lit in a way he hadn't seen in years. The sound of their laughter filled the house, pushing him further toward the shadows.

"Oh, Henry," one of them said when she spotted him by the gear. "Big trip, huh? Don't forget sunscreen for that bald head, or the top of your head will be red."

The others laughed. His wife smirked, shaking her head. "I've been telling him that for years," she said.

Henry forced a smile, touching the crown of his scalp as though to confirm its exposure. He muttered something about packing it already, then busied himself with straps and buckles.

The women swept past, carrying wine bottles and groceries for their own weekend. They filled the living room with chatter, cushions sinking under their weight. He caught fragments of conversation—work, kids, husbands, neighbors.

Then the name came, low and conspiratorial: "Alex" aka backwards cap guy.

He froze, listening.

One of the women whispered something that made them all giggle. "She's so lucky," another murmured, her eyes flicking toward Henry's wife. "Seriously, you always have the most fun."

His wife laughed, soft and pleased. She didn't deny it.

Henry bent lower over his duffel, his hands trembling as he adjusted a zipper that didn't need adjusting.

Lucky. That used to mean me. She used to tell her friends she was lucky to have me—my job, my shoulders, my plans. Now it's him, the guy with the cap and the easy smile. Christ.

The front window rattled faintly with wind. Henry imagined Mark's truck turning the corner, imagined escape. He straightened, rolling his shoulders, trying to shake off the sting. The laughter from the living room continued, light and careless, as though he weren't there at all.

He glanced at the clock. Any minute now. He told himself to breathe, to focus. The Boundary Waters waited.

The clock ticked louder than it should have. Henry paced between the piles of gear, double-checking straps, rearranging items that were already arranged. From the living room came bursts of laughter, the lilting cadence of women in easy company. He caught fragments of their chatter, words carried down the hall like crumbs: "Alex... oh, you're lucky..." He ground his teeth, but his face stayed neutral when he passed by the doorway, pretending not to listen.

Outside, the neighborhood was alive. A cluster of younger men had gathered at the corner—beer bottles glinting in their hands, their voices raised in carefree argument about nothing. They leaned on each other's shoulders, slapped backs, swore at a ball game streaming from someone's phone. Henry recognized two of them—Marathon Shirt and Backward Cap himself—and the others were the same type: fit, casual, hair cut sharp, arms tanned from hours outdoors. Their laughter carried too easily down the street.

Henry opened the front door. Warm air pressed against him, thick with the smell of mown grass. He bent, lifted the duffel bag, slung it across his shoulder. The weight wasn't enormous, but it settled into his joints with cruel precision. He winced, straightened, and stepped carefully onto the porch.

From the corner came a cheer. "Hey, Henry!" one of the men called, his voice dripping with mock camaraderie. The others laughed.

Henry forced a smile and lifted a hand in half-hearted greeting. He moved down the steps slowly, his knees trembling under the load.

I carried heavier. I carried canoes twice this weight over trails littered with rock and root. I was strong, damn it. This should be nothing. Why does it feel like everything?

The bag slid against his back. He adjusted the strap with a grunt, sweat already dampening his collar. His wife's friends had drifted onto the porch now, wine glasses in hand, their voices softening into amused murmurs as they watched. One of them pointed at him, whispered something, and laughter bubbled again. His wife shushed her half-heartedly, but her own mouth curved into a grin.

Henry's ears burned. He reached for the next piece of gear—the sleeping bag rolled in its tight cylinder. He balanced it under one arm, grabbed the camp stove with the other. His arms ached immediately, his grip uncertain. Still, he pressed forward, step by step toward the driveway where Mark's truck would soon appear.

At the corner, the younger men had noticed his struggle. One mimed a wobble, staggering in exaggerated clumsiness. The others howled. Backward Cap lifted his beer in salute, his grin sharp.

Henry clenched his jaw, focusing on the sidewalk. One step. Another. His breath came harsh.

Don't give them the satisfaction. You're still capable. You're still a man.

Then his foot caught on the uneven lip of the walkway. The duffel slipped sideways, the sleeping bag lurched, the stove banged against his shin. For a second he fought for balance, arms pinwheeling. Then he went down hard.

The impact echoed—a dull thud against concrete, the metallic clatter of the stove skittering across the driveway. Pain shot up his knee. He groaned, rolling onto his side.

The porch gasped in unison. One of his wife's friends covered her mouth, eyes wide. Another whispered something that turned into a stifled laugh. His wife called his name, but her tone was half-concern, half-exasperation, like she was scolding a child for falling off a bike.

At the corner, the men erupted. Cheers, whistles, mocking applause. One mimed tripping, arms flailing in parody. Another gyrated his hips obscenely, the motion obscene and exaggerated. Their laughter carried sharp as glass.

Henry's face burned. He struggled to his knees, hands scraping against the pavement. His gear lay scattered, humiliating in its sprawl.

Then the low rumble of an engine approached. Mark's truck turned the corner, gleaming under the noon sun. It rolled to a stop in the driveway, the engine cutting with a confident growl.

The door opened, and Mark stepped out—broad, bearded, his presence filling the space like a shield. He took in the scene—Henry on the ground, gear spilled, neighbors laughing. A grin split his face, but it wasn't cruel.

"Well, hell," Mark said, striding forward. "You starting the trip without me?"

Henry managed a weak laugh, relief flooding his chest. Mark bent, hauling the duffel with one easy motion, slinging it over his own shoulder. He grabbed the sleeping bag in his other hand, scooping the stove with his foot as though it weighed nothing.

"Still traveling heavy, I see," Mark said, his voice warm. "Some things never change."

Henry staggered upright, brushing dirt from his jeans. His wife appeared at the porch steps, her friends clustered behind her, their smiles strained. "You okay?" she asked.

"I'm fine," Henry muttered. He avoided her eyes.

Mark clapped him on the back. "Course you are. Let's get this loaded."

Together they hefted the gear into the truck bed, Mark cracking jokes the whole time, his laughter loud enough to drown the jeers from the corner. Henry forced himself to smile, though his cheeks ached with shame.

When the last bag was in place, Mark leaned against the truck, wiping his forehead. "All set?" he asked.

Henry nodded. His wife hovered at the edge of the porch, arms crossed. Her friends whispered, their laughter quieter now but still present. The younger men at the corner had returned to their beers, though one kept miming a stumble every few minutes, to renewed chuckles.

Henry climbed into the passenger seat of the truck. Mark started the engine, gears grinding briefly before settling into a steady hum. As they pulled away, Henry glanced back through the window.

The men at the corner raised their bottles in mocking salute. One exaggerated a trip, stumbling dramatically, while another thrust his hips in a lewd gyration. Their laughter echoed, cruel and careless.

Henry looked away, jaw tight.

Let them laugh. I'm leaving. Out there, the only thing that matters is whether you can carry your weight. I'll show myself I still can.

Mark drummed his fingers on the steering wheel, humming along to the radio. "Boundary Waters, here we come," he said. "Best damn therapy there is."

Henry nodded, eyes fixed on the road ahead.

The truck rolled forward, gravel crunching under its tires. Henry sat rigid in the passenger seat, his hands folded in his lap, knuckles pale. He could still hear the echoes of laughter behind him—sharp, jagged sounds that clung like burrs. He kept his eyes on the road, refusing to look back.

Mark hummed along with the radio, tapping the steering wheel with easy rhythm. He glanced sideways at Henry and grinned. "Don't sweat it, man. Those clowns back there? They've never slept a night without Wi-Fi. You and me? We're going where cell service dies and the stars still show up."

Henry forced a smile. "Yeah," he said quietly.

Inside, his chest still smoldered. They laughed. They saw me fall. Christ, my kids saw it too. My wife's friends whispering, her smirk—like I'm a joke at my own send-off.

He pressed his palms against his thighs, grounding himself in the rough denim. The truck engine hummed steady beneath them, a sound both familiar and foreign.

Mark chuckled. "Remember that trip back in '92? You dropped your whole pack in the lake. We had to fish your socks out with a paddle."

Henry blinked, startled by the memory. A laugh escaped his throat—small, but real. "Yeah. They smelled like mildew for a week."

"Smelled better than your boots," Mark teased.

The banter loosened something in Henry's chest. He leaned back against the seat, letting the rhythm of the road soothe him. Houses blurred past, each one framed by neat lawns and neat lives. He imagined the men at the corner still watching, beers in hand, their laughter spilling down the street. But distance grew with every turn of the wheels.

Let them laugh. Out there, they won't matter. Out there, the only voices are the loons and the wind.

The truck turned onto the main road, the neighborhood receding into memory. Henry exhaled, long and heavy, as though releasing something clenched inside him.

Mark reached for the cooler behind the seat, fishing out a soda. He popped the tab with one hand, handed it over. "Drink. Hydrate. We've got a long drive."

Henry took it, the cold can sweating against his palm. He sipped, the fizz sharp on his tongue. It grounded him, simple and clean.

They drove in companionable silence for a while, the landscape shifting from suburban blocks to open fields. Henry watched the sky widen, the horizon stretching. He imagined the lakes waiting beyond—Knife,

Basswood, Moose—names he had studied late at night on glowing screens, now calling to him with a voice older than rejection emails, older than shame.

The image steadied him.

But humiliation lingered like a bruise. He couldn't shake the sight of his wife's friends on the porch, wine glasses in hand, their eyes bright with amusement. The way one whispered, "You're so lucky," to his wife. Lucky—for what? For Backwards Cap's grin, his easy muscles? For the spectacle of Henry stumbling in his own driveway?

His stomach turned. He pressed the can harder against his lips, draining half of it in one gulp.

Mark broke the silence. "You know what I like about these trips?" he said. "No resumes. No titles. Nobody gives a damn what you make or what car you drive. It's just: can you paddle, can you carry, can you laugh when it rains? That's it."

Henry nodded slowly. His throat tightened. "Yeah," he whispered.

That's all I want. To be measured by something real again. Not by numbers on a screen, not by kids calling me fatty, not by neighbors with beers who'll never know what it means to portage thirty rods with a canoe on your shoulders.

The truck surged forward, eating miles. The younger men's laughter faded into the rearview, their mock gyrations dissolving into distance. Ahead, the road stretched open, a ribbon pulling Henry north.

He closed his eyes for a moment, letting the hum of the tires lull him. In the darkness behind his lids, he saw the lakes again—vast, glittering, patient. He heard the splash of paddles, the crackle of fire, the wild, lonely call of loons.

When he opened his eyes, the horizon was wide and waiting.

For the first time in a long time, Henry believed there might still be a place for him in the world.

Chapter 5

What's Tik Tok

The road narrowed into gravel, the truck tires rumbling across ruts and ridges. Mark leaned forward over the steering wheel, his broad shoulders flexing with each adjustment. Beside him, Henry pressed a hand against the dashboard, eyes fixed ahead.

They were close. The signs had told them so—Boundary Waters Canoe Area Wilderness, Entry Point—each one like a drumbeat, tightening Henry's chest. He'd imagined this approach for days, even weeks. In his mind, the parking lot was nearly empty, a handful of dusty pickup trucks scattered across gravel, their beds laden with canoes. He imagined stepping out into silence, the only sound the wind in the trees, the cry of a distant bird.

But as the road curved into the final stretch, sound hit them before sight did. A low roar, the churn of many voices layered together, laughter, shouts, cheers. Then, over it all, a woman's bright voice amplified through a portable speaker: "Hey guys! We just arrived at the Boundary Waters, and guess what? Yes—we have cell service out here now, thanks to my sponsor. I'm going to be giving you hourly updates on what it's like to survive in the wilderness with only the essentials—plus, like, some fun extras!"

Mark slowed the truck. "What the hell?"

They turned the corner and stopped.

The parking lot was jammed, wall to wall with vehicles—trucks, SUVs, even a gleaming new van wrapped in bright decals, the name of a brand plastered across it in looping script. The van's doors were thrown open, revealing cameras, lighting rigs, portable chargers stacked like ammunition.

At the center of it all stood a young woman in neon hiking gear, hair perfect under a spotless cap. She grinned at a phone mounted on a tripod, her voice chirping as she narrated. Arouncd her clustered other young people, each with their own devices, each talking at once. Some pointed their cameras at the crowd; others at themselves, narrating every movement.

And the crowd—good God, the crowd. At least two hundred people, maybe more, pressed shoulder to shoulder in the lot, cheering, waving signs with usernamhildrees written in glitter, phones lifted high to record. They blocked the trailhead completely, a wall of bodies between Henry and the wilderness he had come for.

Mark let out a low whistle. "Jesus. It's like a damn rock concert."

Henry said nothing. His throat tightened. He pressed his palm harder into the dashboard as if to steady himself against the sight.

This was supposed to be mine. Quiet. Trees. The first step into silence. Not this carnival, not this... this invasion.

The woman's voice soared above the din: "Don't forget to like and subscribe! We're going to show you what REAL camping looks like—hourly updates, twenty-four-seven wilderness content, baby!" She winked at the camera, then struck a pose with her hiking pole.

Mark snorted. "Hourly updates? In the Boundary Waters? That's not camping. That's performance art."

Henry's eyes stayed locked on the crowd. His chest felt tight, not just from anger but from the rising panic of logistics. Where would they even park? How would they carry their gear through that mob?

"Keep going," Henry muttered. His voice cracked. "Maybe there's space further down."

Mark shifted into low gear, the truck crawling forward. They passed rows of cars parked crookedly along the shoulder, the overflow stretching far down the gravel road. Fans milled everywhere—teenagers with backpacks, couples in brand-new hiking boots, middle-aged men holding selfie sticks. Some wore shirts with slogans: Camp Queen, Wilderness IRL, Team #NatureGirl.

Henry stared, jaw clenched. His palms sweated against his knees.

This isn't wilderness. This is spectacle. This isn't the place I remember, the place I came back for. Out there I was strong, I was capable. Out there I wasn't a joke. But how do you walk past this? How do you carry yourself through two hundred people pointing cameras, waiting for you to stumble?

Mark grumbled. "No way we're parking here. We'll have to backtrack, find a pull-off."

The truck rolled past the main lot, the crowd swelling around the van. Someone spotted them, a teenager in a baseball cap, and pointed. "Hey, more campers coming in!" A ripple of phones turned toward the truck. Henry flinched, ducking slightly though he knew it was useless.

Mark pressed the accelerator, pulling them clear of the main lot, tires spitting gravel. The roar of the crowd faded slightly, replaced by the steady thrum of engine and the occasional distant cheer.

Half a mile down, Mark spotted a dirt pull-off, just wide enough for the truck. He swung in, cut the engine. Silence fell heavy, but not the silence Henry had longed for. This was the silence of being displaced, forced aside.

Mark sat back, drumming the wheel. "Well. Half a mile isn't bad. We'll haul the gear. Once we're past the circus, it'll be fine."

Henry nodded, but his stomach knotted. Half a mile with gear was nothing to Mark. But for him—feet already aching, knees stiff, gout a ghost waiting to flare—it was something else entirely. He imagined the duffel digging into his shoulder, the sleeping bag slipping, the stove banging his shin. He imagined every step a test, the crowd watching, laughing if he faltered.

I used to run miles on skates. I used to carry weight without thinking. Now half a mile feels like a sentence. What if I can't do it? What if I fall again?

Mark clapped him on the arm. "C'mon. We got this."

Henry swallowed hard. He opened the door. The air smelled of dust and pine, faint but real. Somewhere far beyond the noise, the wilderness waited.

He stepped down slowly, knees twinging. The gravel crunched under his boots. He looked toward the direction they'd come, where the crowd's roar still echoed faintly. He imagined the two hundred bodies, the cameras, the bright young faces. He imagined threading himself through them, each step a humiliation.

His chest tightened. He pressed his hand to the side of the truck for balance.

Mark came around the back, already pulling gear from the bed. He grinned. "Let's get it loaded up. We'll show those TikTok kids what real campers look like."

Henry forced himself to nod, but inside he thought only one thing:

God help me.

My feet.

Please, not today.

Mark hefted the duffel onto one shoulder and grabbed two smaller bags in his free hand, as if they weighed nothing. Henry bent for his own load, the new sleeping bag awkward under his arm, the stove box clanking against his knee. He tugged at the strap of his duffel until it settled, though it dug into the tender notch between shoulder and neck.

The gravel bit at Henry's boots as they started down the road. Every step sent a dull throb up his feet, the familiar warning that gout still lurked, waiting to strike. He clenched his jaw, forcing rhythm into his stride. Mark walked beside him, steady, unbothered, talking casually about maps, routes, lakes.

But Henry only half-heard. His mind replayed the roar of the crowd they were walking toward, the amplified voices, the endless glow of phones. His chest ached at the thought of all those young faces turning as he stumbled past.

The noise grew louder as they approached the lot again. The gravel shoulder narrowed, forcing them closer to the mass of bodies. The van gleamed like a stage prop, its decals bright: Wilderness IRL! A tripod camera swiveled toward the incoming hikers, capturing each arrival.

Henry's pulse jumped. He felt the eyes before he saw them—hundreds, it seemed, tilting their heads, raising their phones.

"Whoa," someone shouted, pointing. "Check it out—vintage campers!"

Laughter rippled through the crowd. A young man in neon sneakers mimed an exaggerated limp, hunching over like an old man with a cane. "Don't worry, guys, we'll rescue you if you don't make it past the parking lot!"

Phones lifted, capturing the imitation. A chorus of chuckles followed, some sharp, some casual. Henry's ears burned.

They're looking at me.

Not Mark, me.

Old man, slow man, the one who might not survive a mile.

They don't see the games I played, the ice I cut across, the boards I slammed. They don't see the man who carried aluminum canoes over rock. They only see this—this limp, this sweat, this belly.

Mark glanced at him, face tight for a second, then barked a laugh. "Hey, if you're lucky, he'll out-paddle all of you," he called back. His voice was confident, easy, carrying just enough humor to blunt the edge.

The TikTok star—Nature Girl, Henry overheard someone call her—swiveled her camera toward them. She spoke brightly into the mic, smile flawless. "See, guys, this is what's so great about the Boundary Waters. You get all kinds of campers—young, old, experienced, beginners. Some might need rescuing, but hey, that's part of the adventure!"

The crowd roared with laughter, phones raised like weapons.

Henry stumbled, caught himself. His chest burned.

Rescuing. I don't need rescuing. I came here for silence, not to be someone else's punch line.

Mark leaned close, his voice low, private. "Ignore them. Eyes forward. Trees are just past them. Once we're in, it's ours again."

Henry nodded, but his eyes blurred. He focused on his boots, on each step. The gravel shifted underfoot, sending fresh jolts through his joints. His hands trembled around the stove box.

They edged along the side of the crowd, pressed so close Henry could smell perfume, deodorant, the sugary tang of energy drinks. Fans jostled, eager for better angles. One girl in a pink hoodie pointed directly at him. "Look at Grandpa Camper!" she shouted, giggling.

Henry kept walking, shoulders hunched.

Mark shouldered ahead, carving a path with his broad frame. "Coming through," he said firmly. The crowd parted grudgingly, muttering, still recording. Henry followed in his wake, each step a trial, each laugh a dagger.

At the edge of the lot, the trailhead sign rose like salvation: Welcome to the Boundary Waters Canoe Area Wilderness. But even here, the TikTok crew had set up banners, logos, portable chargers gleaming under a canopy. Nature had been dressed for television.

Henry stopped for a moment, chest heaving. Sweat ran into his eyes. He adjusted the sleeping bag under his arm, fingers aching from the weight. His body screamed, but his pride screamed louder.

Half a mile already feels like five.

How am I supposed to portage a canoe?

How am I supposed to keep up with Mark? But I will. I have to. Because I won't let them be right. I won't be Grandpa Camper needing rescue.

Mark clapped him on the back. "Almost there. Once we're on the trail, it's just us and the trees. No cameras, no clowns."

Henry managed a weak smile. He took another step forward, into the shadow of the sign, and felt the crowd's laughter thin slightly behind him.

The wilderness was close. He could smell it—pine, damp earth, water waiting somewhere beyond the noise. But between him and that silence lay the weight of his own body, and the eyes of strangers who thought he was already beaten.

Mark shouldered past a last knot of fans, and for a breath the sound fell away—as if someone turned the volume dial down from "carnival" to "earth." A seam opened in the crowd: a lane the width of a canoe, bordered by sneakered feet and the ridiculous shine of ring lights. Beyond that lane: trees, shadows, the dark seam of trail disappearing into green. Henry stared at it the way a parched man stares at a well.

"Through," Mark said. Not loud, not angry. A working voice. He tipped his chin at the gap.

They stepped. A boy in a jersey popped half into their path, phone lifted. "Yo, can we get a quick 'we're surviving' for the feed?"

"Not today," Mark said, not slowing. Henry kept his eyes on the signboard—the weathered wood, the bullet points he already knew by heart. PACK OUT ALL TRASH. NO GLASS. QUIET HOURS. The rules that meant there was still a place on earth ruled by restraint.

"Sir?" A woman with a mic on a telescoping stick matched their pace backward, walking in a practiced crab. "We're doing a segment on multi-generational camping—what would you say to people who worry—"

"Move," Mark said, and there was nothing theatrical in it. Just a door-latch sound. She peeled away.

Someone behind them laughed—high, delighted, oblivious—and then came the line, bright as a thrown coin: "Hope there's a ranger nearby in case Grandpa taps out!"

It landed. The little ring of heads around the speaker bobbed. Henry could have turned; he could have offered a line, an acid reply that would buy him five seconds of face. He didn't. He let the words pass through him like a cold current and placed his boot on the first root of the trail.

The light changed. Heat narrowed. Pine took the air in hand. A hush pooled beneath the canopy—shallow at first, then deepening as they left the gravel. The crowd was still there—of course it was—but the trees braided the sound, combed it thin. Two dozen steps. Fifty. The ring lights fell behind like odd moons.

Henry stopped. Not long. Just a count of four to let the gout's white tooth stop gnawing. He set the sleeping bag down, propped the stove box against his shin, and pressed both palms into the bark of a jack pine. It had the ridged, familiar feel of things that do not perform for cameras. He closed his eyes.

This is the line. The thought arrived in his own voice, low, steady. On one side: spectacle. On the other: usefulness. Carry or don't. Listen or don't. I am not a clip here. I am a man who can move his weight.

"You good?" Mark asked.

"Yeah." He wasn't. He was burning from ankle to hip. He was a heart wearing a man around it. But the trees had placed a cool hand on the back of his neck. He could go.

They walked. The trail pitched slightly, roots like ribs under the dirt. Sun arrived in coins, scattered by needles. A squirrel scolded, then fell silent when it realized the two shapes passing weren't interested in its kingdom. After a minute, Henry heard what he had been listening for without knowing: water, not seen yet, but present—somewhere ahead and to the left—a hollow thrum that made his spine straighten.

The path kinked around a boulder, then widened into a little apron of packed earth. Beyond it: the lake. Dark and close. Not the postcard sweep he had been feeding himself from screens, but a hand-sized oval cut into trees, a place large enough for one canoe to feel small and right.

Mark set the duffel down with a soft grunt. Both men stood a long beat without speaking. The water licked the rock with small sounds. A dragonfly embroidered the air.

"Jesus," Mark said finally, but quietly, as if he didn't want the lake to think he was swearing at it. "There it is."

Henry's throat tightened. He felt suddenly ridiculous for the way tears can come when a thing you have wanted appears in a modest, exact form. No panorama. No hero shot. Just enough blue to hold you.

Behind them, the path coughed up two young men in brand-new boots and shirts the color of sponsorship. One had a camera mounted to his chest like an extra sternum. They looked at Henry and Mark, then at the water, and one said, with automatic cheer, "Content!"

The other nodded with priestly seriousness and lifted his phone.

Mark didn't turn. He unbuckled the straps, pulled the new sleeping bag free, set it aside. "Help me with the canoe," he said, as if there were a canoe, as if it were only a matter of lifting.

There wasn't, not yet. The outfitter's dock and rentals were another quarter mile down, the plan to shuttle a hull back up for this carry. But the word canoe worked anyway. It pinned the next hour to a purpose. Henry breathed into it.

"Give me the stove," Mark said. "I'll take the heavier stuff. You keep your hands for balance."

"I've got it," Henry lied, then handed over the stove. He kept the sleeping bag and a coil of rope, the duffel with clothes that had seemed, in his quiet house, like armor, and here felt like the normal weight of days.

They turned back to the trail for the outfitter spur. The two sponsored boys stepped aside, kindness rehearsed. "You guys heading in deep?" one asked, and the way he said deep made Henry see quotation marks around the word.

"As far as the noise stops," Mark said. That almost made the boys laugh because they thought it was a bit. It wasn't.

The spur tilted down toward the dock. Out on the bigger lake a loon called once—a low joke of a sound, half laugh, half flute. The hairs on Henry's arms stood. The ache in his feet did not go; pain rarely obeys romance. But it was contained now within an arrangement larger than itself.

At the dock, the outfitter stood in his sun-bleached cap tallying clipboards, face turned the color men's faces turn when they spend their lives outside. He looked at Mark and Henry with the exact assessment you grant two men who have carried their share of awkward weight. "You the party for the Kevlar 17?" he asked.

"That's us," Mark said.

He pushed the pad forward. "Sign here. Care for the bow thwart. Wind's turning. Don't let it turn you."

Henry signed. The pen sat right in his hand. For a heartbeat he had the private, foolish feeling that a signature could make a truth again: I am the person who can do the thing I am promising to do.

They shouldered the canoe together. Not the old aluminum thud of youth, but a light, tough arc. Mark took the yoke. Henry lifted the bow, his hands slotting to the grip. The hull rose. The world narrowed to the ribbed light through Kevlar and the sound of boots on dirt.

They walked. Not far, but far enough for breath to become a work, then a pattern. At the first lift of incline, the crowd-noise from the lot rose again in a fringe—

cheers, the syllables of a brand name, the hot click of applause. Under the canoe, Henry could not see faces. This pleased him. His body existed as a function. He did not need to inventory expressions.

"Almost," Mark said, the word puffed back off the hull.

At the put-in, they lowered as if setting a sleeping animal on a bed. The bow kissed water. The little slap sounded like agreement.

"Pack in," Mark said. He had his voice for this, Henry remembered—a coach voice, not of boys, but of men who already know they can be hurt and choose to play anyway.

They slid the duffel under the thwart, clipped the food barrel's straps. The stove nested where it could not bruise a shin. The new sleeping bag, fat and sheepish in its sheen, tucked between hull and pack. Henry palmed it once, acknowledging their truce.

Footsteps scuffed the rock. He looked up. Nature Girl herself had wandered down the fringe of shoreline with two assistants—their gimbal smooth as a hummingbird. She wasn't talking to her phone now. She was looking at the canoe as if seeing a useful object for the first time that day.

"Classic," she said. Not to them. To the air. Then, to her camera, her voice returning to its brightness: "Okay guys, so this is what real portage looks like—some of the OG campers are heading out." She turned that bright kindness on Henry and Mark. "Mind if we grab a quick ten-second clip?"

Mark looked at Henry. The look asked a question without pressure: You or me?

"We're late ," Henry heard himself say. Soft. Not unkind. He put one palm on the gunwale, the other on the rock, and eased himself into the bow. His knees sang in three registers. The canoe rocked, then steadied. The lake took his whole weight without comment.

Nature Girl blinked, then recovered to her smile. "Have an amazing trip!" she chirped, and in fairness, he thought, she almost meant it.

Mark stepped into the stern. The canoe settled with the old intimacy of knowing exactly how two men's gravity wants to sit. He thumbed the push-off, and the bow floated free, pivoting toward the corridor between reeds.

Henry lifted the paddle. His hands remembered the angle better than his mind. Blade bit water. He felt the little catch in his shoulders—the one that used to be a prelude to speed. He drew. Water thickened and moved. The bow slid.

Two strokes. Five. Ten. A breeze slipped across his scalp where a friend had teased him to sunscreen the bald. It felt like the hand of a father he could not remember rightly.

On the shore, the crowd was already bending its noise around a fresh moment—someone hoisting a branded hammock, someone shaking a glittering water filter like a maraca. The van's decals burned in cheerful assertion. But the sound arrived now as what it was: a city two ridgelines away.

"Keep it smooth," Mark said, easy. "Wind at two o'clock. We'll tuck behind that point and let them be their own weather."

Henry nodded. He did not trust his voice. He watched the water under the bow thicken from pewter to black-green, watched the thin moustaches of wave peel off the hull and forget they had been boat at all.

The ache in his feet had not left. The gout gnawed faintly at the hinge of his big toe like a rat too tired to commit. But pain, here, was part of a ledger that balanced. Paddle, pull, breathe, adjust. Not one of those steps required the approval of a stranger.

They cleared the first point. Pine thickened, the bank shouldered up. Sound—actual sound—took over: terns needling, a far knock of wood on wood where someone practiced a new carry, the private vowel the lake makes when wind draws one finger across it.

Mark let them drift. "Look," he said.

A loon rode the skin of the water thirty yards off, head turned, red eye like a bead. It regarded them with the unimpressed calm of something that has survived human eras without ever needing our language for itself. Then it slid under, leaving only rings.

Henry laughed. Helpless and small and entirely his. The laugh startled him; he felt it loosen something that had been cinched for years.

"Still worried about the half mile?" Mark asked, gently. Not teasing.

Henry glanced back. The two o'clock wind kneaded his shirt. He could still pick out the white square of a ring light above the trees if he wanted to. He did not want to.

"I'll worry when we portage," he said, and this time, the first person arrived not as lament but as a contract. I will carry what I can carry. I will set it down when I must. I will pick it up again.

"Good," Mark said. He dipped his paddle once, twice, and the canoe behaved like a dog that knows which way home is.

They did not speak for a while. They didn't have to. The canoe laid a seam between shores—the kind of line even mocking men on corners cannot cross. Sun climbed, then softened. The smell of warmed pitch rose from a deadfall. Somewhere far behind them a cheer went up and died, as all cheers do when there is no game close enough to pin them to.

Henry paddled. The old motion took its place like a tool returned to a hand after a long loan. Each draw paid out a small coin of certainty. Half a mile would hurt. Portages would, too. Sleep would be a negotiation with knees that had their own opinions. He knew all that and found he could hold it.

They rounded another point and the entry lake opened into a throat of water that led toward the chain they'd planned—narrow, shaded, a little darker than his memory liked. Mark leaned forward slightly, as if scenting how the day might go.

"You want the north camps or the east?" he asked.

"North," Henry said, surprising himself. "Sunrise."

"Alright then."

They slid into the throat. A pair of college kids coming out—a girl in a faded ball cap, a boy with a paddle scar on his knuckle—raised their paddles in greeting. No phones lifted. No lines delivered. "How's it in there?" Mark asked.

"Quieter than you'd think," the girl said, grinning. "If you keep going."

"We plan to," Mark said.

They passed. The wakes crossed. For a moment, the canoe rocked gently, as if someone large had laughed under the water.

Henry let the paddle rest on the gunwale and flexed his toes inside his boot, the first mercies of cold sock against warm ache. He eyed the tree line ahead—the way the pines thickened, the occasional birch flashing its ghost-white amid the dark. He thought of the list on his dining table, the rejections stacked like plates for a party no one would attend, the neighbors' porch, the smirk and the round-belly mime, the girl in the hoodie calling him Grandpa. All of it felt, from this angle, like a cartoon left running in another room.

"Tell me when you need to swap," Mark said. "We can break as much as we want. There isn't a camera on earth that can make a fire hurry."

Henry smiled. "I'll tell you," he said. He dipped the paddle again, shallow, then deeper, a man easing back into the grammar of a tongue he had not spoken out loud in years.

Behind them, a last thin cheer rose and fell. Ahead, a loon surfaced with a fish and flicked it down its throat with the simple grace of an animal that has never once apologized for its hunger. The canoe slid on. Pine pressed its scent into the day like a seal.

Henry's feet hurt. His knees would hurt more tonight. He would fumble a knot, curse at a damp match, laugh too loudly and then the right amount. He would carry until he couldn't, then breathe, then carry again. And when he closed his eyes, there would not be a screen in the dark—only the afterimage of water catching light.

He did not say any of this. He paddled. The bow found its seam. The shore receded into a long, listening green.

And the wilderness, indifferent and exacting, received him without commentary, the way a good rink receives the first clean cut of a blade.

Chapter 6

Noise, Noise Everywhere

They chose the northern cove because the wind was with them and because the map, folded and soft with old creases, held a penciled star there from some other trip, some other summer when they'd been men who thought seasons repeated if you wanted them enough. The cove took them in as if nothing in the world had ever been asked of it. No voices. No wakes. The water lay in a dark bowl, the rim tree-thick and the rock warm where the sun had rubbed it all afternoon.

Mark let the canoe coast the last twenty yards. The bow kissed a tongue of granite and stuck there, held by friction and the conspiracy of calm. For a moment neither of them moved. Henry's hands remained on the shaft of the paddle, as if the stillness were an animal they might spook. Even the pain in his feet seemed to lower its voice.

"This one," Mark said, softly. "If it'll have us."

Henry nodded. Please have us. The thought did not feel like begging. It felt like placing two fingers on a pulse: are you here; am I.

They unloaded with the quiet coordination that had once been second nature and now returned, not like youth, but like a tool retrieved from a high shelf— familiar weight, careful use. Mark took the food barrel and the stove and made two trips, each time stepping from canoe to stone to duff to moss with the exactness of a man who has learned what his knees will tolerate. Henry ferried the sleeping bag, the clothing duffel, the coil of rope. He did not examine the crabbed script of his gait. He let function be a kind of modesty.

The site lifted back from the shore into a lamb's-head knoll of jack pine and spruce, the ground floored with needles, the air pitched in resin. A ring of blackened stones stood waiting, the mouth of a small pit where fires had made themselves into memory. Two tent pads were stamped into the living mat: flat, forgiving. A snag leaned at the edge of the clearing like an old linebacker, bleached and faithful.

Mark turned, a boy's grin sneaking over his beard. "You smell that?"

"Pitch," Henry said. "And the lake." He closed his eyes and added, inside, *and something like my own name said back to me without malice.*

They worked. The tent went up with a minimum of cursing—poles threaded, corners squared, fly tugged taut against a sky the color of a good bruise. Mark set the stove on a boulder and clicked the igniter; blue flame took like a quiet decision. Henry staked guy lines, the sleeves of his shirt rolled to the elbow, forearms stippled with sawdust fine as pollen where he'd brushed a dead limb. Sometimes his hands shook. When they did, he paused a breath, looked into the trees until a chickadee revealed itself by movement and made a sound that was both question and answer, then went back to it.

This is what I wanted. A job I can finish. A thing that becomes itself if I simply keep showing up.

By late afternoon, order had begun to replace arrival. The tarp angled a clean wedge of shade over the fire ring. Their packs found their places, a little shy of the tent like dogs that will be called in later. Water boiled, coffee bloomed its holy stink into the needles. Mark raised his mug in a salute too lazy to be ceremonial.

"To quiet," he said.

"To quiet," Henry echoed, and the words didn't feel like defiance so much as a permission.

They sat on the warm rock, boots off, steam breathing upward from tin cups. Out on the lake, wind stitched small furrows, then smoothed them again. A fish dimpled the surface once, twice, nothing dramatic—just proof. Somewhere far off, a woodpecker unstitched bark. The day put its hand on the back of Henry's head and held him the way a barber might, with tenderness hidden inside utility.

"My feet are easing," he said, surprised to hear it aloud.

Mark nodded, not looking over. "They know where they are," he said. "Bodies remember before minds do."

Henry let the line sit. He thought of the moments he'd tried to name in the last months—the lodged humiliation of porches, the embarrassments that bred in kitchens—how naming had sometimes made them worse. Here, the unspeaking did not feel like avoidance. It felt like respect.

They ate simply—ramen mended with sliced summer sausage, a handful of nuts, the last of the crackers that had survived the trip in recognizable squares. Mark talked a little about a lake two days in, long and thin, knotted with islands that would make for a windless day if the weather turned. Henry listened, nodding, the names like rosary beads: Sema, Grub, Pine. He was not the man who could pretend not to hurt. He was, however, still the man who could shape days out of water and distance.

As the light tilted into that late angle that seems to scoop color from the undersides of leaves, they set to wood. Mark took the saw; Henry took the hatchet. They worked an old trunk already down and dry enough to ring. The saw sang on the push and the pull; the hatchet made its old answers. Sweat salty as broth ran from Henry's temples and took with it, if not shame, then a layer of it. For a few minutes, he forgot to inventory himself. Wood split, stacked, fed the neat pyramid in the ring. A first flame lifted, tried the air, and—finding enough—stood on its own.

They didn't talk much around that first fire. They didn't need to. The blaze conducted its tiny orchestra: pop, hiss, the delicate slide of sap finding heat again after years as pitch. The lake found its throat and spoke in syllables of a single vowel, different every time depending on the wind's grammar.

I used to believe I had to be watched to exist, Henry thought, astonished at the thought's simplicity. Out here, I vanish and am more alive than I've been in years.

Twilight came in on long legs. The first star showed up in the only place it could and still surprise him—low, not high—and winked with the bashfulness of something already ancient. A loon's laugh knit itself just far enough away to make them both smile without comment.

Henry lay back on the rock, the ache in his feet now a duller country he could inhabit. The world had edges again. Beneath his shoulder, the warmth of the stone held through the first draft of night. He felt—for the time it takes a single ember to turn and reveal its coal—nearly unburdened.

Four hours later, the night's mouth filled with lights.

It arrived the way storms on lakes do: first a far brightening that does not match the sky's promises, then a sound without a source, then a shape. Voices braided toward them along the water—a cheerful thicket of them, overlapping, amplified. The trees lit in a strange, low daylight that moved and quivered. Mark sat up, elbows on knees. Henry's coffee had gone bitter in its cup on the rock. The loon called again, this time shorter, like a question answered before it was finished.

"Please no," Mark said, not as a protest, but as a reading of the weather.

It was the TikTok van crew—of course it was—and their convoy, lanterns slung from carbon-fiber poles, the beam of a drone's tiny eye skating above like a bug that had learned math. The first canoe scraped into the neighboring campsite's landing like a dinner guest who has mistaken your chair for theirs and is delighted to find you already there.

"Hey guys!" came the bright voice Henry recognized now without having tried. Nature Girl unfurled to her full wattage. "We found the sickest cove! We're setting up for a night shoot—campfire vibes, s'mores, and some gear reviews so you know how to glamp smarter!"

The cove that had been a bowl filled with one candle now glared with a dozen. Headlamps. Lanterns. Phone screens like small moons clutched in confident hands. The timberline took the light and threw it back with an embarrassed glow.

Mark breathed out. "Neighbor etiquette's a lost art."

Henry's mouth filled with a dry taste that wasn't only old coffee. This was ours. We found it without an audience. We asked permission of the ground. He stood up, knees complaining. The party next door multiplied itself: laughter, the smack of coolers, the punctuation of pop-top sighs, the electric zither of a Bluetooth speaker trying to be acoustic guitar.

"Gonna go have a word," Henry said.

Mark glanced at him and then at the party, measuring not just the distance but the man. "Gentle word."

"Gentle," Henry said, though what opened in his chest didn't feel gentle; it felt like the last inch of a dam holding.

He started along the lip of the cove, boots grating the rock, choosing footfalls less for stealth than for not falling—a humble calculus. The party's light walked ahead of its bodies. The air smelled of sugar, aerosol bug dope, the hot electronics smell those battery bricks give off when you ask too much of them. Someone laughed the way people laugh when they know their laugh sounds good on camera.

Then the forest moved in a way it shouldn't.

It was not subtle. It was not metaphor. It was the platform of brush ahead of him parting the way curtains do when someone who has the right to enter does so without apology, and the black, muscle-stitched shape of a bear crossing the trail as if night wore legs.

Henry stopped so suddenly the world kept going for a half-second without him. The bear did not rear, did not huff. It ran. Running, it was closer to a poured shadow than an animal; the sound of it was leaves negotiating with mass.

"Hey—hey—hey," someone at the TikTok site cried, delighted. "Bear content!"

Henry took one step back and his heel found a root. The root didn't move; he did. The backward fold was ridiculous and total. He went down hard, not as he had in the driveway—a man falling under eyes—but as a tree falls: at once, with conviction. The rock lifted up to meet his shoulder. His breath left him like a trick.

Phones pivoted. Light hammered him. For a beat he lay with the stars doing their work and the brand names hovering like day-bugs. The bear had already loped upslope, a black second now, then gone.

"Oh my God," Nature Girl chirped, arriving at a trot, her crew swarming. "Are you okay? We got that—like, we definitely got that. Someone help him up."

Hands took him—gentle, practiced hands that did not know him but knew the choreography of rescue for an audience. He was hauled to sitting in a cradle of competence and attention. Faces hung around him in a wreath, each one bracketed by a rectangle of its own reflection.

"Sir?" a boy said, earnest. "That was insane. You almost died. Can you, like, say something to camera about wilderness risk?"

Henry blinked. His shoulder burned, his hip sang. Anger moved up his throat like heat and became language before he could sand it down.

"Turn that off," he said, and the word off found the depth of a different voice in him, the one that used to end arguments in rooms with windows that didn't open.

A hush—brief, beautiful—fell. Then someone, embarrassed, laughed. Someone else said, "It's just for awareness." Nature Girl tilted her head, receiver tucked to her cheek, and in a coo that had made a million people feel understood, asked, "Are you okay, though? Really?"

"I was," Henry said. "I was very okay. For hours." He gestured back toward where their small camp glowed modestly. "So okay it hurt to notice."

A dozen instinctive replies lit up in their eyes—brand-safe condolences, upbeat pivots. Instead of giving them a target, Henry stood slowly, cradled his shoulder, and swore once—a short, accurate word that any adult will recognize as a release valve, not an attack.

"Hey, man," a kid said, a little wounded. "We were trying to help."

"I know," Henry said. He did. And in knowing it, he also knew that help and showing help are now partners who never go anywhere alone. "Thanks," he added, because being right is cheaper than being decent.

He stepped away. The lights leaned with him, foreign flowers seeking a sun. He lifted a palm—not to bless, not to dismiss, just to indicate a boundary in a world that had been pretending not to believe in them—and the flowers, not quite certain, paused.

"Where are you going?" Mark called softly from the other site, as if they were inside a library that used to teach the town to read.

"For a walk," Henry said. He didn't look back.

The forest accepted him because it had accepted almost everything before him. He threaded between jack pines on a line not drawn by anyone. Light fell away in squares and then in coins and then not at all. The cove's noise compressed into a hummed chord that could be mistaken for insects if you let it. The smell of sugar faded; pitch rose. Somewhere higher up the slope, the bear made the small noises animals make when they have reconvened with themselves on the other side of a fear. Henry did not fear it. He feared the idea of his life being defined in other people's fingers.

Quiet. Just give me whatever quiet is left.

The trail did not exist, not visually. It existed in the way the ground felt when it wanted you to keep your ankle. Roots announced themselves to the feet and the feet answered politely. A spruce showed him its ladder of lower branches, and he turned, because ladders are for going up and he wanted to go in. He did not know how far. He did not know toward what.

He knew only that every step away from the party returned to him a small coin he had been spending without noticing.

The noise of the lake party shrank, then moved sideways, then fell behind a shoulder of land. In its place rose the other noises—the ones that don't perform unless you are still: a moth's dry, foolish thump against a fern; the tiny clack of a vole considering the math of a crossing; the two-syllable punctuation of an owl who can afford to be patient.

Under his palm, bark. Under his boots, duff. Under the bones of his feet, hurt—but reckoned with, not narrating. The throb in his shoulder made a case; the forest did not bother to listen.

He went on like that, not long by a map but long enough by the kind of clock that runs inside, until the cove's last light fell into its own water and the forest closed its own lid. He stopped when the smell shifted—the cool breath of a low place announcing water. A seep, then a trickle, then a slide of black that might be a creek when spring remembers it. He crouched, slow, and touched two fingers to the damp. He made the sign he used to make without thinking before meals, a gesture he no longer believed meant something to anyone else and that now, in the dark, came back fluent.

I am still here. I am not for their film. I am not for anyone's film.

He sat with his back to a tree and let the dark settle not just around him but into him, the way a good silence does. He did not count the minutes. He did not practice a speech for the campers; he did not practice a speech for himself. He listened until listening made itself into a room he could walk around inside without bumping his shins.

After a time—the kind of time that ends in a body deciding to stand because the hips insisted—he got up. He turned so that his better knee did the work first. He set his palm on bark and felt the grooves the way a blind man reads a headline that won't matter tomorrow. Then he walked back toward the lake by feel and by the dull shine the night gives to water when it is sure you are not going to pretend you discovered it.

Behind him, somewhere in a cove that would be cleaned and left by sun, a cheer went up because a camera had been turned off successfully to prove how little cameras matter. Ahead of him, at a small fire that had learned his name without asking, a man waited who would ask only if he wanted a sip of whiskey Between those two points, in trees that had watched all our noises without commentary, Henry learned the trick of a right-sized step again: lift, place, test, shift, carry on.

He did not know, exactly, what to do tomorrow about any of it. He knew only that for tonight, the forest did not require a conclusion.

He walked until the pines opened their dark hands and gave him back the lake, and in the middle of it sat the loon, black as a sentence that ends at the right place, watching him with a red eye that never had a use for applause.

He found the trail by the smell of their fire before he saw its light—the low, animal breath of heat warming pine pitch. The cove lay down there like a cupped hand; the party's glitter had thinned, though it still pulsed in the neighboring site in restless waves, a tide that refused slack. Mark sat on the rock with his hands around a mug, the fire coaxed low. He didn't stand; he didn't ask. He looked over and made room in the silence he'd been keeping for both of them.

Henry nodded, a short tilt that said he was back. He went to the tent, slid a hand under the vestibule, and drew out the rod tube. The simple ritual steadied him: uncap, sections into fingers, ferrules meeting with that soft, satisfying kiss; line threaded through guides that caught a little in the damp air; a small black jig from an Altoids tin bitten onto the leader with teeth that still remembered the pressure required. He could feel the weight of the lake now like a word he hadn't said aloud in years.

"I'm going to take the canoe," he said.

Mark looked up. "You want company?"

"I want the water quiet for fifteen minutes." Henry said.

Mark understood. "Watch the sky," he said, nodding toward the western tree line. "She's building."

Henry glanced. The west had indeed gathered itself: not flashy, not theatrical—just a deepening. The evening breeze had turned catlike, rubbing once against the cheek, then gone. He chose to take the counsel as caution, not prevention.

The canoe slid off the granite with the remembered scrape that speaks both apology and promise. He steadied a knee in the bow, swung the other over, and settled with an old man's groan he didn't argue with. Paddle tucked under one knee, rod in hand, he pushed off with the flat of the blade and let the first yard be drift. The water accepted him in small syllables. Behind, Mark's fire ticked. Beyond, the neighbor site flared and dimmed, flared and dimmed, a party learning its own limits.

Out on the mouth of the cove the lake widened just enough to feel like a permission slip. He let the canoe nose along the shadow line where shore gave way to open. He cast—the quiet sound of string leaving the reel, the little gulp of line through guides—and watched the jig find the black under the black. He counted down with his mouth closed, as if numbers were scent an animal might spook at.

The first tap was so delicate it felt imagined. Then another—honest, modest life saying here. He lifted the tip. The rod bowed, not a cartoon, not a brag, just a curve that brought his wrist into a conversation it hadn't had since before the porch talk and the laughter and the new sleeping bag's insult. He smiled, alone. The fish came quick, small and silver and exactly enough. He thumbed the hook free and let it slide away with the least splash it could manage.

A loon called, nearer now, the note trembling along the water like a wire pulled–taut. He let the canoe drift. He could have stayed like that for hours.

But the wind nosed again—this time with a smell under it: metal and clay and far-off electricity. The western trees became one shade darker in a way that rearranged the whole lake. He looked up at the sky and saw the kind of cloud that doesn't boast, only arrives.

"Alright," he said, not to the lake so much as to the old logic that lives between weather and bone.

He took two hurried casts he didn't need, as if to bank some proof of having been there, then laid the rod along the thwarts and took the paddle clean in both hands. The first drops came as a rumor—cold on his scalp, a pinprick on the back of the neck. Then the rumor committed. Rain drew its net. It was not dramatic, not yet, but it was thorough, a steady threading of the space between sky and water.

The canoe changed its mind under him, light to the wind now, wanting to weathercock. He corrected by feel, bow nosing toward the cove. The shore slipped nearer, then seemed to retract, then admitted him. By the time he reached the rock, his shirt clung and the small of his back carried a cool river.

Mark was up, tarp angled, hands ready to catch the bow. "There she is," he said, voice pitched to practical.

Together they slid the canoe onto the rock until it stopped wanting to leave.

"Good?" Mark asked.

"Wet," Henry said, smiling despite himself. The rain sharpened the pitch-smell; the rock made its own low music as drops fretted at old lichen.

Mark reached for a dry towel. "I'll make you tea," he said, already moving. "Get out of those."

Henry nodded and ducked under the tarp's edge toward the tent. The fire was half-sheltered, a thrifty flame keeping its powder dry. He stripped his shirt, the wet fabric dragging a fraction of a second longer over his shoulders than dignity would prefer. He toed off boots, peeled socks that were suddenly all lake, wrestled his belt with fingers that wanted, unhelpfully, to hurry.

Pants and shoes off, getting ready to dry with a towel, when the noise and light appeared.

The light—the wrong kind: white, hard-edged, purposeful. It lanced through the tarp seam and found him in the melancholy privacy of his waist.

"Hey guys!" a voice sang, far too close. "We're doing a rain segment—wilderness realities!"

Henry's hands froze. He turned just enough to see the camera crew at the edge of their site, nature-proof ponchos crisp, gimbals steady, eyes hungry with the good-natured avarice of people who believe in sharing. Another light blinked on, doubling the humiliation, bleaching the small human act of changing into performance.

"Whoa," someone in the crew said, half-laughing. "Careful there—PG-13." A second voice, delighted with its own cleverness, added, "It's fine—some men like bears!" The laughter that followed was quick and warm and thoughtless, a bonfire tossed on with a handful of straw.

Heat climbed Henry's neck that had nothing to do with the rain. For a split second a reply rose to his tongue—a strike that would feel good for the length of the utterance and poison him for an hour. He swallowed it. He took the towel, turned his back fully, and finished what he was doing like a man finishing any honest task, not a contestant in someone else's show.

Mark stepped between them without ceremony, a wall made of a man. "Not cool," he said to the nearest lens, voice flat. "New rule: if you can read a tent zipper from where you stand, you're too close."

"Oh, c'mon," an assistant said, palms up, grinning as if the grin had enough absolution in it for everyone. "We're just having fun. It's a vibe—authenticity."

"Your fun is in our house," Mark said. He did not raise his voice. It was the way he said our that did the work.

A brief pocket of silence opened—a rain-silence, loud with drops on leaves, the lake's skin talking to itself. One of the crew had the decency to look at his shoes. Another said, softer, "We're sorry, man." Nature Girl herself, visible just behind them like a lighthouse someone had wheeled over, gave a tiny, apologetic smile that could have sold a thousand apologies to anyone not tired.

Henry pulled on a dry shirt. The cotton clung differently, heavier with promise than the last with water. He didn't look at them. He didn't look at Mark. He reached for the tent zipper and, with a long, patient draw, closed the door on the rain and the lamps and the neighborly shrug.

Inside, the tent held the smell of new fabric and old trips. The patter on the fly came clean—no commentary, no captions. He lay back on the pad and felt his shoulder's complaint, his feet's slow thunder, the heat left by the canoe in his forearms. Those belonged to him, and they spoke a language he had earned.

Outside, he heard Mark move the stove under the tarp, heard the low susurrus of men in ponchos conferring about angles and optics, heard the rain put the final period on the evening's sentences. Someone laughed again, but now the sound was thinner, the kind of laugh people deploy when they've been told the party is over and are pretending not to understand.

Henry turned on his side, the pad sighing with him. He pulled the sleeping bag up to his chest and let its warmth find the places the lake had stolen. He closed his eyes.

Tomorrow, we go farther in. Past them. Past the noise. Past whatever in me wants to answer back. The thought landed and didn't need to defend itself.

The rain worked the tent like fingers on a drum turned low. He let it play him to the dim edge of sleep, where the lake's voice became a thing under the boat again and his hands, in dream, found the paddle at exactly the right angle. He did not hear the last apology offered outside, or whether it was words or a simple stepping back. He didn't need it. He was already gone, shoulders slack, jaw unclenched, drifting at last in the only content that mattered—the kind that asks nothing to be seen.

Chapter 7

Quiet Rocks

They broke camp at first light, the cove still holding last night's rain in small polished pockets along the rock. Mark moved like a man who had practiced this sequence more than once: bag the fly, shake the tent, fold and roll in three steady breaths. Henry matched him—not fast, not pretty, but competent. He packed the new sleeping bag with an annoyed tenderness, as if it were a dog that had misbehaved but meant well. The fire ring gave back its last heat, a cat's breath on his palm when he cupped it above the stones; he scattered the ash and brushed the black from his hands onto the knees of his pants, a streak that looked like something he might have earned.

The lake was a different animal this morning—brighter along the ribs, but quieter, too, as if rain had combed it straight. They slid the canoe into that scalp-slick sheen and pushed off without a word. The neighboring site— yesterday's carnival—was a mess of half-sleeping shapes and tarps, a few stubborn ring lights still burning like planets that had forgotten to set. No one filmed their departure. No one called out.

A loon rode the seam where shadow became water and swiveled its red eye toward them, then turned away, uninterested.

They shaped a line across the lake toward a scatter of low islands, knotted with spruce and jack pine. The map had promised emptiness there; their eyes confirmed it—a run of narrow shores without the bright scatter of nylon, the kind of empty that is not absence but permission. Mark held the stern steady while Henry called small corrections with his paddle, a quiet code. They had not spoken about last night's lights or the joke made under the tarp. They didn't need to. Men sometimes carry their angers like pots off a heat: set them aside, let them cool, decide in daylight if they are worth eating.

The nearest of the islands proved itself with a granite shelf that made a landing, a rise of duff generous enough for a tent, a ring of old stones where someone careful had once burned careful fires. No footprints. No wrappers. No sound but water and the particular hush pines keep when they approve.

"This one," Mark said.

"This one," Henry agreed, and felt the small lift inside that accompanies a decision made without audience.

The island was not far from their last camp, site, which they could still see, but far enough away from the TikTok team that was all they needed. In-between was a rocky island, baren of trees, but Henry imaged it as a castle surrounded by a moat. The castle that would protect them from the abnormal TikTok team.

Stopping, they began to unload.

Henry stepped carefully, his big toe flexing its complaint at each shift from rock to needles. He breathed through it and didn't narrate. The tent went up faster than yesterday—body memory resuming its post—and the fly took the breeze like a sail trimmed right. Mark strung a line between two trees and slung socks that had never seen a dryer into honest air. Coffee hissed, bloomed, was handed over in a battered tin mug. They sat on the warm rock and watched their breath not show, the day already past the place where mornings insist on proof.

The first conversation arrived later, the way good ones do: not staged at the water's edge, not announced, but while doing something plain—sorting the food barrel on the flat stone, deciding which dinners were patience and which were speed.

"You going back?" Mark asked, not looking up. He meant the old job. He meant the kind of office that smells like carpet and ambition.

Henry set a pouch of rice beside a coil of rope. "Back where?" he said, and meant it.

"Work like you did," Mark said. "That life."

Henry smiled without humor. "If it's waiting, it's got a damn good poker face."

Mark started to say something—comfort probably, or a joke to turn the ground—then didn't. He snapped the lid on the coffee tin and wiped a ring of brown from the rock with his sleeve. "You keep sending the stuff out?"

"Every day," Henry said.

"And?"

"Mostly silence. Sometimes 'no.' Sometimes 'we loved you but.'" He shrugged. "They want more recent versions of me. They want the man I was when their interns weren't born."

Mark nodded slowly. A crow heckled them from the far spruce and flew off when it saw there was nothing to steal. "Look," he said, "nobody wants to tell a friend his foot's on the wrong pedal. But I'll say it gentle: the market's not the one you learned. It turned while you were carrying a canoe in the other direction."

Henry's jaw tightened, then released. "I know."

"Do you?" Mark asked. There was no edge in it. More like a hand placed on a shoulder.

Henry ran a finger along the seam of the food barrel, feeling the bite of the plastic edge. "I had a client," he said. "Last year. Big one. Wanted to overhaul their stack—security, storage, the whole cathedral. I told them sure. Then they said they wanted to center it on AI." He said the last two letters like he was saying the name of a dog that had bitten him. "I told them AI was a fad. That we'd be cleaning up the mess in five years." He laughed, short and wrong. "I said it in a room with people who were twenty-five and had grown up with a phone as a first language."

Mark whistled, almost soundless. "You say it like that?"

"Cleaner," Henry said. "More clever. But yes."

"And your boss?"

"Smiled the smile that means we'll talk later," Henry said. He looked past Mark to the line of water, the dull shine that fills a man's eyes when he stares even if he's pretending not to. "We talked later. He called it refreshing to have someone skeptical. Then he took me off the account because he needed someone 'aligned with the client's long-term vision.'" The phrase came out intact, a souvenir after a car accident. "I told myself I'd been principled. I told myself I'd saved the company money by not chasing a balloon." He rubbed his face. "Truth is I didn't want to learn it. I didn't want to be clumsy at the place I'd been slick."

Mark didn't fill the quiet. Wind leaned through the pines and said nothing.

"I keep asking for the world that made me," Henry said finally. "But it's not coming back. There's a new language out there and I'm mad at it because I don't speak it without an accent."

Mark nodded. "Accent's alright," he said. "It's the refusal that kills a man." He looked up then, meeting Henry's eyes. "You going to learn it?"

Henry inhaled to say yes. Exhaled. "I don't know."

"That's an answer," Mark said, no judgment in it. He set a hand flat on the rock and leaned, stretching a back that had been carrying men since college. "You'll hate me for this next one."

"Try me."

"Your wife," Mark said. "How's it going to go?"

Henry's mouth flattened. He folded a packet of instant potatoes until air left it with a soft sigh. "She's already gone," he said, and the sentence, spoken without flourish, made a small true shape in the air. "Not legally. Not on paper. But the part that believed me—believed in me—it's gone." He touched the rim of the mug to his front teeth and felt the faint click. "She'll ask for a divorce when it doesn't feel like a crisis. She'll do it kindly. She's good at kindness when she wants nothing from it."

"I'm sorry," Mark said.

"So am I," Henry said. He meant for everything.

They didn't go into it more. The island wouldn't have minded, but the men did. There are things you leave whole by not taking them apart on the first try. They tied off the line. They stowed the barrel in the shade. They walked the perimeter without comment, a patrol that was half habit, half gratitude. A chipmunk told them they were too large; a gull told them they were not interesting at all.

By noon, the island felt like theirs the way a rental that fits does: unsure of permanence, comfortable in function. Mark shook the last of the rain out of the life vests and hung them to dry. Henry did a small inventory with his shoulders and decided they would hold a paddle again without filing a complaint.

"Fish?" Mark asked.

"Fish," Henry said.

They carried the canoe over the small spill of rock and slid it into that easy, honest water. The air lay warm on their forearms. The island's trees stood behind them like a jury that had already agreed not to convict.

They paddled out to a saddle where the map promised depth. Mark set them in a slow drift, and Henry took the first cast, the jig slicing the skin of the lake, the line paying out in that sound that always means possibility. He counted without counting. The jig wandered down to where fish dream of darker fish. He lifted, felt nothing, lifted again and felt the small tick a hand makes when it decides to touch yours. He set the hook. The rod bowed.

He grinned—this time boyish, unashamed—and brought the fish up through the inches like a remembered word. It came quick—a walleye slick as wet bronze. He admired it and let it go, the fins flicking his thumb in what felt like appreciation.

They traded casts, fell into a language. A few more fish—small, bright, sufficient—made a handful of moments that didn't require anyone's approval. The lake wrinkled under a fresh whisper of wind; cloud moved across the sun like a thoughtful hand shading a book.

Then the big one hit.

Not the cartoon tug or the sudden cartwheel you tell stories about too big. It was heavier than the others by just enough to bring Henry's core into the motion— hips, back, shoulder working a line like a single verb. The rod bent. The canoe shifted. Mark took a corrective stroke, and Henry felt the creature below take what it wanted and then give back just enough for dignity.

"Oh," Henry said, quietly, reverently. "Hello."

"Easy," Mark murmured. "Let it run if it needs."

It needed. The drag coughed out line in reluctant syllables. The fish arced under the canoe. Henry dipped the tip to spare it breaking and saw, in that instant, how easily things you care about find the only rock within a hundred yards.

"Careful," Mark said, already adjusting, already there.

Henry breathed. He gave line. He took line. The fish rose once in his mind, silver and thick as a forearm, and he felt again—not in bravado but in gratitude—the live conversation between a man, a tool, and a thing that does not know him and does not need to.

The rod creaked.

It was a sound he recognized before his ear did: old graphite stressed past its boast. He eased pressure and the fish chose that second to surge. The rod made a soft, shocked sound—a hinge giving—and then a more final one. It snapped clean eight inches above the handle. The tip took its own small journey toward the bow; the broken midsection sprang and slapped Henry's forearm with the indignation of a thing betrayed.

"Dammit," Mark hissed—not angry at Henry, angry at physics.

For a second Henry sat there with the handle in his hand, line sliding through his fingers like a small, uncatchable river. Then habit told him to hand-line, and he pinched. The fish pulled—once, twice—with the plain authority that lives in muscle shaped by cold water. The line bit his fingers. He held anyway.

"Don't lose a thumb for it," Mark said, voice low, real.

"I've lost worse," Henry said, not meaning body parts. He felt the fish surge again and then felt what all men feel when weight leaves the system—an emptiness that is not absence but the knowledge that something has returned to where it belongs.

The line went slack. The broken tip bobbed along the surface like a little white flag surrendering to nobody. Henry blinked at it. One corner of his mouth lifted, not toward a smile exactly, but toward some acknowledgment that you can't keep everything, and maybe that is the point.

"Well," Mark said after a beat. "He won."

"He did," Henry said. He laughed then, short and helpless. "I don't even think I'm mad."

"You're soaked in humility," Mark said. "That's close."

Henry reeled what was left. The rod handle looked obscene—just a cork grip and a stub, like a sentence that ends before it admits its subject. He lay it across the thwarts, palmed the bruised spot where the midsection had bit him, and let his eyes go soft over the water.

"Call it?" Mark asked, gentle.

"Yeah," Henry said. "Before the lake decides to take my pants."

They turned the bow toward the island. The paddle home was quiet, not sullen. The kind of quiet that follows a good story ending where it should. The canoe's bow etched a thin line across the surface that the wind erased as soon as it could. That seemed fair.

Back on the granite, they hauled the hull far enough onto the rock to keep it from deciding to leave. Mark set the stove under the tarp and laid two cups on the stone like a ritual. "Whiskey or coffee first?" he asked.

"Yes," Henry said, and the word had company. He dug in the food barrel until his fingers found the flask—old stainless, dented where a younger man had fallen on ice doing something he'd tell nobody. He handed it to Mark, who took a disciplined swallow and passed it back. Henry drank. The heat wasn't fire exactly—more like the old radiators in a city apartment turning on in October and announcing that the body has seasons it gets to keep.

They built a small, honest fire. Not the party kind. The cook kind. The talk kind. It took the match without stipulation and climbed to its proper size. Mark sat on his heels and fed it a narrow run of split wood, each piece accepted with a quick, grateful flare.

They spoke, not in speeches, but in the half-sentences and long seams men use when they are not trying to perform wisdom at each other.

"You know," Mark said, "that fish—if you'd landed it, you'd have had a new story about skill. Now you've got a truer one about luck and timing and how things go when they don't go."

"I liked him better not seeing him," Henry said, surprising himself. "It kept him honest."

Mark smiled into the fire. "You going to buy a new rod?"

"I am," Henry said. "And I'm going to learn the thing I said was a fad. Not because it will save me. Because I am tired of refusing the future and calling it principle."

Mark turned that over, nodding. "That'll be good for you. For whatever comes."

"And if she asks for the divorce," Henry added, voice steady, "I won't beg. I'll say yes kindly and ask if she wants the good plates." He looked up. "I can't be the man she married. I can be a decent man she used to know."

Wind moved through the topmost pines and the fire answered with its smallest language—tick, lick, sigh. The whiskey made a warm ring in their bellies that married well to the day's work. Above the treeline, first stars took their stations, unconcerned with men's missteps or victories.

Mark lifted the flask again and made a face that was not grimace, not grin. "To losing fish we didn't deserve to keep," he said.

"To learning late," Henry added.

They drank. The lake nearby adjusted the weight of one wave against another. Somewhere far across, a branch snapped as a deer changed its mind. The island held them without comment, which was all either man had wanted from anyone for months.

They let the fire fall a little and then fed it modestly, a conversation continued without insisting on itself. Henry stretched his legs toward the heat and watched steam draw out of his damp cuffs. The sting in his toe had retreated to a dull pulse—still there, still his—no longer the author of the paragraph.

I can learn a new thing, he thought, and the first person did not apologize for being hopeful.

He looked at the stub of the rod, propped against a rock like a reminder without cruelty, and he did not feel ruined. He felt, just then, like a man on an island with a friend and a modest fire, in possession of enough night to think and not so much that the thinking would drown him. He felt like a man who might, tomorrow, paddle farther in than he had planned, and if the wind came wrong, could still read it.

"Another?" Mark asked, offering the flask.

"Just a little," Henry said. "I want to remember that I said all this."

They drank. The fire learned their names a second time and spoke them back as warmth. When the whiskey was capped and the cups were turned upside down to keep the dew honest, they sat in the kind of silence that feels earned, and the night—glad of men behaving—looked after them as if they were, for an hour, exactly the size they ought to be.

Chapter 8

Scouting Out Noise

The morning broke with a crispness that settled over the lake like a clean sheet. Mist curled off the water, drifting into the trees, softening the rugged outline of the island where Henry and Mark had made camp. The night had been long, filled with restless turning in the tents, the low pop of embers in the fire pit, and the distant cry of a loon echoing through the darkness.

Henry emerged stiffly from his tent, running a hand through his thinning hair. His knees cracked as he stood upright, and he squinted against the morning light. Mark was already up, crouched by the fire, coaxing life out of the coals with practiced ease.

"Coffee's nearly ready," Mark said without looking up. His voice carried the calm authority of someone who had spent enough years outdoors to make fire-building as natural as tying his shoes.

Henry grunted in acknowledgment, easing himself onto a camp chair. The smell of instant coffee stirred something close to comfort inside him. He cradled the mug when Mark handed it over, letting the warmth seep into his fingers.

"You gonna try again today?" Mark asked.

"With what?" Henry gestured at his broken rod leaning against a log. The memory of yesterday's failed fishing attempt still stung. He'd hooked something big, something worth bragging about, but the line had snapped and the pole had splashed into the lake.

Another loss. Another reminder of what he couldn't hold on to.

Mark reached into the canoe and pulled out a second rod. It was older but sturdy, the cork handle worn smooth by years of use. "I brought a spare," he said simply, holding it out. "Take it."

Henry stared at it, suspicious of the gesture. He hated feeling pitied. But Mark's face was open, patient. No mockery, no judgment—just an offer.

"You sure?" Henry asked finally.

"Sure. Besides, two poles mean twice the fish. And I'm not cooking beans again tonight if I can help it."

That cracked the edge of Henry's gloom. He took the rod, running his fingers over the handle. It felt good in his hands—balanced, alive with possibility. For the first time in days, maybe weeks, he felt a glimmer of anticipation instead of dread.

They loaded the canoe with minimal fuss. Mark at the stern, Henry at the bow. The water was calm, a pane of glass reflecting the sky, broken only by the occasional ripple of a fish rising. They paddled out toward deeper water, their strokes steady and in rhythm, the silence between them companionable.

Mark handed Henry a lure box. "Pick something shiny. Pike love flash."

Henry rummaged through the battered tin, finally choosing a silver spoon lure that caught the morning light like a shard of mirror. He clipped it onto the line with clumsy fingers, tongue caught between his teeth.

"Not bad," Mark said, watching him. "Let it sink a bit before you reel in. Slow and steady."

Henry cast out, the line arcing gracefully before splashing into the lake. He let it sink, then began reeling, his movements stiff but deliberate. His breath caught every time the lure bumped the weeds. Nothing. He cast again. And again.

Minutes stretched into half an hour. Doubt crept back in. He imagined his wife's voice: You're always chasing things you can't catch.

Then it happened. A sharp tug. The line went taut, vibrating with life. Henry froze.

"Set the hook!" Mark barked.

Henry jerked the rod upward, heart pounding. The line pulled back hard, the rod bowing, the reel screaming as line tore off. Something big. Something powerful.

"Easy," Mark coached. "Let him run, then reel when he slows."

Henry's arms shook with the strain, but adrenaline surged through him. He gave line, reeled, gave more. The fish fought, thrashing beneath the surface, sending up sprays of silver water. Henry gritted his teeth, muscles burning.

"Keep the tip up!" Mark shouted.

For what felt like forever, it was man versus fish. Henry's world narrowed to the taut line, the pull in his hands, the raw determination not to lose again. Finally, the fish broke the surface, flashing green and gold in the sunlight—a northern pike, easily three feet long.

Mark leaned over with the net, scooping it up in one clean motion. The fish writhed, powerful even out of water, but it was caught.

Henry stared, chest heaving. "I did it," he whispered, almost not believing it. "I actually did it."

"You sure as hell did," Mark said with a grin. "That's a beauty."

Henry laughed then, a raw, unpolished sound he hadn't heard from himself in years. It bubbled up, surprising and pure. For once, he wasn't thinking about failure or regret. He was just a man who'd caught a fish.

They headed back to shore, Henry cradling the net like a trophy. On land, Mark made quick work of cleaning the pike, his knife flashing in the sun. The smell of fresh fish soon mingled with the smoke of the fire.

Henry watched, still dazed by the win. "Haven't felt this good in a long time," he admitted.

Mark glanced up. "That's the point, Henry. Sometimes it's not about big life changes. Sometimes it's just about catching one damn fish."

When the meat hit the pan, sizzling in butter, the aroma was intoxicating. They sat by the fire, plates in hand, eating hungrily. The flesh was firm, flaky, and rich with lake flavor. For Henry, each bite was more than food—it was proof that he could still succeed, that joy wasn't completely out of reach.

"This is the best meal I've had in years," Henry said through a mouthful, smiling genuinely.

Mark chuckled. "Told you. Nothing beats fish you catch yourself."

They ate in comfortable silence, the lake stretching out before them, the sun warm on their backs. For a moment, it felt like things might be okay.

The sound of voices broke the calm.

At first faint, carried on the breeze—shouts and laughter. Then clearer: boys, a group of them, moving toward the shore, to the spot where they were camped the day before.

Henry sighed heavily, setting down his plate. The peace dissolved like mist. "What now?"

Mark listened. "Sounds like Scouts. Probably on a canoe trip."

Henry's first instinct was irritation. The area had felt like theirs, private and quiet. Now it would be invaded by noise, by chatter, by reminders of a world he wasn't sure he belonged in anymore. He rubbed his temples, bracing himself.

The first figures appeared between the trees—boys in khaki shirts and neckerchiefs, lugging gear, their voices rising in cheerful banter. Behind them, one leader, that's odd, just one chaperone, one middle-aged men with broad shoulders and a weathered face.

One of the boys spotted Henry and Mark by the fire. "Hey! There are people here!" he called, excitement in his tone.

The troop spilled onto the clearing, a dozen strong, eyes wide at the sight of the campfire and the fish cooking over it.

Henry stood, forcing a smile. "Afternoon, gentlemen," he said, his voice carrying a friendliness he had to manufacture.

The scoutmaster stepped forward, offering a hand. "Didn't expect anyone else out here. Hope we're not intruding."

Henry shook his hand firmly. "Not at all. Plenty of island to share."

"When I was walking it this morning, there is a camp just inside the trees, and beyond is a ravine that splits the island, might be fun for the kids to explore." Stated Henry.

But the boys were more interested in the fish. The boys crowded around, fascinated and full of questions.

Questions tumbled out: "How big was it?" "What lure did you use?" "Can we see the rod?"

For once, Henry didn't feel like the butt of a joke.

He felt like the expert, the man with the story, the one who had done something worth admiring.

He straightened, answering their questions with a confidence he hadn't felt in years.

Mark watched quietly, a small smile on his face, as Henry basked in the unexpected role.

Walking over the Scout leader, Mark spoke "Big troop for one man."

"Yea, the two other chaperones are coming, but they both got food poisoning a few nights ago in town. I have our toys, with us, so they can come in tomorrow and find us. We got a lot of older boys, that have done this repeatedly, so we should be fine." Answered the Scout leader.

"Well if you need any help, with anything reach out." Said Mark.

_____

The afternoon shifted. The island was no longer silent, but the noise wasn't unwelcome.

The scouts pitched tents, gathered firewood, and filled the clearing with energy. Henry, instead of retreating, found himself leaning in—helping one boy tie a line, showing another how to handle a reel.

For the first time in a long while, he wasn't thinking about failure, about his wife, about lost jobs and fading relevance. He was simply there, present, part of something.

And as the sun dipped low over the water, Henry realized that maybe this was what he'd needed all along: not to escape the world, but to rejoin it, even in small, unexpected ways.

Chapter 9

Seriously Not Again

The morning came slow, as if reluctant to rise. A gray wash of light seeped through the thin nylon walls of the tent, carrying with it the damp smell of pine needles and lake water. Henry groaned as he shifted, his hips stiff from the foam pad that seemed to grow thinner every night. He rolled over and squinted at the zipper door, listening to the muffled calls of birds beyond, and the faint gurgle in his gut that told him nature's call wasn't going to wait for politeness or comfort.

He sat up, bones cracking like distant twigs. "Christ," he muttered, rubbing his knee. The air was cool but not biting, the kind that carried dew on its breath. Mark was still asleep in the other tent, or maybe just lying still with that infuriating patience of his. Henry envied it — the way Mark could let the world roll past without rising in protest. For Henry, everything seemed to demand a protest these days.

He dug into the pack, retrieved the roll of toilet paper wrapped neatly in a plastic bag — one of Mark's little preparedness habits — and set off into the woods. The ground was springy, the soil damp, ferns brushing against his shins as he went deeper. Privacy was a relative thing in the Boundary Waters, but he figured fifty yards in was enough. He found a little hollow between two red pines, the ground mossy and soft, dappled sunlight dripping through the canopy overhead.

"God's porcelain throne," he muttered, lowering himself with a grunt. Pants bunched around his ankles, he let himself breathe out. A loon wailed far off on the lake.

The air smelled like wet bark and sap. For a moment, Henry almost felt at peace — if peace could be found with bare ass in the dirt, staring at the roots of a tree.

Then it came. The sound.

Not birdsong, not water. Voices. The kind he'd learned to recognize — too quick, too loud, laced with laughter that wasn't for the moment but for the recording of it.

TikTok.

Henry's stomach froze faster than his bowels. He stiffened, listening. The chatter grew closer, a chorus of youthful energy, layered with the unmistakable buzz of a phone capturing video. "Yo, keep rolling, bro!" "This light is insane." "No, no, angle it up, you're missing the shot."

Henry's eyes went wide. You've got to be kidding me.

Frantic, he clawed for his pants, yanking at the denim like a man trying to pull himself out of quicksand. His boot heel caught on a root. He wobbled. For half a second he thought he had it — dignity just barely salvaged — and then he pitched forward.

Face first.

The moss and dirt rushed up at him, smearing across his cheek and nose, his pants still tangled mid-thigh. His arms flailed, toilet paper flying into a bush.

The voices stopped. Then erupted.

"Oh my God!" one of them howled. "Dude, are you getting this?!"

"I'm already live, man! This is gold!"

A girl's voice, high and horrified but laughing all the same: "Oh nooo, Grandpa just ate dirt!"

Henry spat out a clump of pine needles, rage boiling hotter than embarrassment. He twisted on the ground, trying to pull his pants up with as much dignity as one could when mooning the under-30 demographic of America.

Three figures stood on the path a few yards away. Two young men with shaggy hair and branded hoodies, phones held aloft like torches. A woman with a ring light clipped to her phone, biting her lip to keep from laughing. All three looked half-embarrassed, half-thrilled at their find — a wilderness blooper reel delivered by fate.

"Sir, you okay?" one of them asked between chuckles. "Need a hand?"

"Get the hell away from me!" Henry barked, swatting at them as though they were mosquitoes. "Don't you dare film me!"

But he could see the red light glowing on their screens, the faint tremor in their shoulders as they tried not to laugh too loudly. His shame was already preserved, floating somewhere in the cloud, waiting to be clipped, captioned, and tagged.

"Respect, respect," one of them said, lowering his phone but not stopping the recording. "No cap though, that was a gnarly fall."

Henry yanked his pants up, his hands shaking. His face burned with equal parts dirt and fury. "I said get the hell out of here!"

The girl winced sympathetically, though the corner of her mouth betrayed amusement. "We didn't mean to— um—interrupt. Sorry, sir."

Henry didn't dignify her with a response. He stormed past them, head low, muttering curses. The laughter followed him, thinly veiled but undeniable.

Back at camp, Mark was crouched by the fire pit, blowing on embers. He looked up as Henry stomped into the clearing, twigs stuck in his hair, face streaked brown, expression thunderous.

"Jesus," Mark said calmly. "Fall in?"

Henry jabbed a finger toward the woods. "Them. Goddamn TikTokers. No peace, Mark. Not even in the middle of the Boundary Waters. Can't even take a shit without being recorded for the whole damn world!"

Mark blinked, then smothered a grin. "They saw you?"

"They filmed me!" Henry roared. "Me, on my knees, pants down, face in the dirt — filmed! Like some goddamn blooper reel!"

Mark stood, brushing his hands off on his pants. "That's unfortunate."

"Unfortunate?!" Henry threw his arms up. "It's humiliating! What the hell happened to privacy? To decency? I came out here to get away from the world and it follows me like a disease with Wi-Fi!"

Mark held his gaze, his calmness like a stone against Henry's crashing waves. "You want coffee?"

"I want peace!" Henry snapped. "But apparently that doesn't exist anymore." He kicked at the dirt, sending a puff of dust into the air. "Even out here, they come swarming in with their cameras and hashtags. Apparently, they wanted to talk to the Scouts. It's enough to make a man lose his mind."

Mark let him rant, nodding occasionally. When Henry finally paused, chest heaving, Mark said evenly, "We can always move again. There's plenty of islands."

Henry froze. "Move? Again? We just got settled!"

"Better than you blowing a gasket every time someone drifts near," Mark said. "Besides, it's the Boundary Waters. Moving's half the point."

Henry scowled, but deep down he knew Mark was right. His anger was a fire with nowhere to go, and the longer they stayed, the more fuel TikTok would throw on it.

The decision was made for them a short while later, when the voices carried across the water. The TikTok crew had found the Boy Scouts.

Henry stood at the edge of the clearing, arms crossed, watching as the kids gathered around the influencers like disciples. Phones out, questions flying, Scouts grinning awkwardly while the TikTokers narrated their wilderness adventure for an invisible audience.

"Here we are, deep in the Boundary Waters, finding actual Boy Scouts in their natural habitat!" one of the young men said dramatically. "Tell us, little dudes, what's it like to rough it without Wi-Fi?"

"Probably satellites, but I understand your point." Said Mark.

Then from across the fields into the tree line, came laughter, and lots of it.

Henry could see the TikTok team talking with the scouts.

The Scouts laughed, some shy, some eager. The scoutmaster looked uneasy but tolerated it, sensing perhaps that resistance would only make things worse.

Henry's blood boiled. "They're interviewing the Scouts now. Like it's some goddamn reality show. Christ almighty."

Mark sighed, shouldering a pack. "Then we move."

Reluctantly, Henry helped break camp. The canoe rocked under the weight of their gear, the water slapping against its sides like applause for his humiliation. They paddled across a narrow channel, the voices of TikTok fading behind them, until they reached a small rocky island not much more than a spine of granite and a scatter of stunted pines.

The landing was rough, the ground uneven. But it was quiet. Blessedly, undeniably quiet.

Henry dragged the packs onto shore and dropped onto a boulder, staring out at the lake. His reflection wavered in the water, distorted and strange. For the first time since the fall, he let himself exhale.

But even in the silence, he couldn't shake the image — himself sprawled in the dirt, pants down, laughter echoing. A moment that would live longer online than in memory.

He closed his eyes, jaw tight. Peace was here, for now. But he wondered how long it would last.

Chapter 9

Storming Nights

The day began with a kind of deceptive peace that Henry no longer trusted. The lake lay flat and untroubled, a mirrored sheet of glass reflecting the pale September sky. No wind ruffled the pines that lined the shore, no boats cut the surface. Even the loons seemed reluctant to call, as if they too had decided to leave the air undisturbed.

Henry unzipped the tent flap with stiff fingers, blinking at the light that rushed in. He sat on the rock ledge outside, stretching his sore back, listening to the sounds—or the lack of them. Mark was already crouched by the stove, measuring out oatmeal into the dented pot, his movements efficient, as steady as they'd been since the first day of this trip.

"Morning," Mark said without looking up.

Henry grunted. He took the mug Mark handed him, black coffee that scalded his tongue but revived his chest. "Better than yesterday," he admitted. "Slept without dreaming about cameras."

Mark smiled faintly. "That's an improvement."

Across the water came faint voices—laughter carried on the still air. Henry's shoulders tensed until he realized it wasn't near. Just distant echoes from the Scouts' camp on the larger island across the bay. The laughter rose, fell, then broke into scattered shouts. He shook his head, muttering, "Kids never shut up."

Mark stirred the pot, unbothered. "That's what kids do."

"They don't just laugh anymore," Henry grumbled. "They broadcast it. Package it. Sell it to each other in little slices." He slurped his coffee, scowling at the memory of yesterday's humiliation. His fall, his ass, immortalized on some stranger's feed.

Mark didn't bite. He just handed Henry a bowl of oatmeal, sprinkled with a few raisins. They ate in silence, listening to the faint background of cheer from across the water.

By midmorning, Henry found himself loosening. They cast their lines from the rocky shore, letting the lures sink into the clear depths. Nothing bit, but the rhythm was soothing—cast, reel, reset. Mark caught a small perch and tossed it back with a casual flick. Henry didn't catch anything, but he didn't curse this time.

When the sun rose higher, they returned to camp. Henry busied himself patching a strap on his pack, muttering about cheap stitching. Mark cleaned out the cooking gear, humming tunelessly. For a stretch, it felt almost like what Henry had come out here for: quiet labor, steady time, the kind that filled hours without demanding anything in return.

But then Mark pulled out the radio.

The little device was old, battered, duct-taped on one corner. Mark twisted the dial, static scratching before a voice crackled through. The reception was thin, warped by distance, but clear enough.

"… storm system moving east across Minnesota… expected impact Boundary Waters region late afternoon into evening… gusts up to forty… possible hail, heavy rainfall… campers advised to secure equipment and move away from open water…"

Mark turned the dial down, listening intently until the voice dissolved back into static. He clicked it off.

Henry looked up from the strap he was threading. "What's that mean?"

"Storm's coming," Mark said flatly. "Big one."

Henry felt the weight settle in his gut. "Of course it is."

Mark stood, brushing dirt from his knees. "We'll need to secure everything. Canoe up, tents staked tighter. Could get ugly out here if the wind comes hard."

Henry muttered, "Nothing stays good for long.""

"We might want to head back to a larger island and move inland." – Mark responded.

"Fuck no, I am done moving just to have peace." – Said Henry.

Mark didn't reply. He moved with quiet efficiency, checking ropes, testing knots, securing food packs. Henry followed, dragging the canoe higher up the rocks until his back screamed, then wedging it against a boulder. They tied the tents down with spare line, added heavy stones to the corners. Every loose item was tucked or strapped.

The air was shifting too. The stillness that had dominated the morning began to break. A breeze stirred the treetops, bringing with it the faint smell of rain. The horizon thickened with a gray bruise of cloud.

Henry wiped sweat from his forehead. "Feels like it's already here."

"Not yet," Mark said. "But it's coming."

Across the bay, movement caught Henry's eye. He pulled out the binoculars. . The Scouts were breaking camp. A neat little parade of khaki shirts and neon rain covers moved inland, packs on their shoulders, following the scoutmaster deeper into the woods. Henry leaned forward, tracking them carefully.

They weren't wandering aimlessly. They were filing into the same ravine he had spotted the day before, a natural cut through the middle of the island, sheltered by high ridges and thick trees. He had noticed it then, thinking it looked like the kind of place animals bedded down in storms. Now the Scouts were using it with the same instinct.

"Smart," Mark said quietly. "They'll be safer deeper in the woods, near the ravine."

Henry nodded, though unease prickled at him. He remembered seeing it yesterday, the way the ravine cut deep like a scar. It wasn't comfortable land—full of roots, rocks, fallen timber—but it was hidden, and safe from the wind that would whip across open water. The

Scouts disappeared one by one into its shadow until only the shoreline remained.

Something stirred in Henry's chest as he watched them. A pang of envy, almost. They had a leader, a purpose, a plan. They moved like a unit, purposeful and protected. He and Mark—just two aging men on a bald, rocky island—felt suddenly fragile in comparison.

He shook it off by throwing himself into the work. There was gear to lash, rope to double-check, tarps to adjust. Henry felt his arms ache as he tugged the lines tighter, his knees protest as he crouched to wedge stones around the tent pegs. But there was something else too, something he hadn't felt in months.

He felt alive.

Every knot pulled tight was proof that he could still do something that mattered. Every boulder he rolled against the tarp edge gave him a rush of worth, as if he was holding the storm itself at bay. His chest heaved with exertion, sweat running down his back, but it wasn't the sweat of futility—it was work with purpose.

He paused once, straightening, hands on hips, and looked out over the lake. The clouds were stacking higher now, turning the horizon the color of lead. The breeze had teeth. The Scouts were gone, safe in their ravine, and here he was—standing solid, rope burn on his palms, watching nature gather its fury.

For the first time in a long time, Henry felt useful. Worthwhile.

Mark noticed it too. He watched Henry hauling the canoe higher with a kind of stubborn fire in his eyes, watched him wipe his brow with the back of his hand like a man half his age. Mark smiled to himself but said nothing. He knew better than to break the spell.

But when Henry caught him watching, his pride faltered into embarrassment. He muttered, "Don't look at me like that."

"Like what?" Mark asked gently.

"Like you're humoring me. I know I'm slow, I know I'm clumsy. Just... don't."

Mark shook his head. "Wasn't humoring you. I was respecting you. Big difference."

Henry looked away, throat tight. He bent to retie a rope, hiding the flush in his cheeks.

Still, when the wind rose again and rattled the tent poles, his bravado cracked. The rocky island felt suddenly too exposed, too bare. The Scouts were sheltered in their ravine, the influencers had vanished, and he and Mark were standing in the open like lightning rods.

Henry's chest clenched. "Feels like we're naked out here," he muttered.

Mark didn't dismiss it. He just nodded, his voice calm. "It is exposed. But we've done what we can. Sometimes that's all you can do."

Henry swallowed hard. The air carried the metallic tang of rain now, and the first low rumble of thunder rolled across the distance. He crossed his arms, trying to hide the tremor in his hands.

"Well," he said, half to himself, "here we go."

Chapter 10

Lighting The Storm

The storm hit its zenith with the fury of something personal, as if the sky had finally noticed the two men clinging to their rock and decided to punish them specifically.

The wind no longer came in gusts. It was constant now, a wall pressing against them, howling so loud Henry could barely hear his own thoughts. The rain lashed sideways, needles stabbing his face and hands, soaking him deeper than he thought possible. Water streamed down the granite, pooling in every crevice, turning their island into a slick, gleaming anvil in the center of a boiling sea.

Lightning split the world every minute, sometimes every thirty seconds. Each flash turned Mark into a pale statue, turned the tents into fragile skeletons trembling in the gale, turned Henry into a quivering shadow clinging to stone. The thunder followed immediately, cracking so hard Henry swore he could feel it in his bones.

"This is it!" Henry shouted, half-mad laughter bubbling out of him. "This is how we go! Two middle-aged morons, roasted like hotdogs on God's barbecue!"

Mark ducked lower, checking the canoe's lines again. "Keep your head down!" he barked.

Henry dropped flat, pressing his chest to the rock, but the laughter didn't stop. The fear was too much, spilling over, twisting into something manic. Every boom of thunder felt like a punchline. Every bolt of lightning lit up the absurdity of their situation — two damp fools thinking they could outlast nature with a few ropes and tarps.

"Bet the TikTok crew's crying now!" he bellowed. "Bet their ring lights shorted out the second the rain hit! Imagine them, clutching their dead phones like rosaries! 'Oh no, bro, the cloud's gone, the cloud's gone!'"

He pounded his palm against the wet granite, choking on laughter and rainwater both. "No hashtags for you, you little bastards! No trending page for 'Old Man Falls in the Dirt Part Two'! You'll be lucky if you can post 'Help, We're Drowning' before your batteries die!"

Lightning tore across the sky, the thunder so close it sounded like the earth splitting open. Henry flinched, then howled with laughter again, his voice cracked and ragged. "Oh, if only I could see it! Their $300 sneakers full of water, their fancy wireless mics sizzling in the mud, the look on their faces when they realize their precious followers can't see them now. All alone, just like us, except dumber!"

Mark actually smirked at that, though he shook his head. He braced his body against the wind, his hand steady on Henry's back to keep him grounded. "Easy," he said, voice still calm despite the madness around them. "Laugh if it helps. But don't let go."

Henry clung tighter to the stone, knuckles white, rain pouring into his mouth as he wheezed through hysterics. "Christ, Mark, this is comedy! We should've sold tickets! 'Two Old Men Get Their Asses Kicked by God, Live in the Boundary Waters!' Would've gone viral if the cell service worked!"

Another bolt hit so close the sky turned white, and for an instant Henry swore he saw the surface of the lake explode, steam hissing upward. He shrieked, then broke into more laughter, almost sobbing now.

Mark's hand squeezed his shoulder, firm. "It's just the storm, Henry. It'll pass. They always do."

Henry spat rainwater, shaking his head violently. "Not for me! Never passes for me! Always more storms, more screwups, more people laughing at me. At least this time the whole damn world's too wet to record it!"

The wind screamed, bending the trees across the bay into ragged silhouettes. Their tents shuddered violently, poles bowing. One corner ripped free, the tarp flapping like a wounded bird. Henry scrambled to grab it, nearly sliding on the slick granite, cackling as he fought.

"Ha! Take that, you son of a bitch!" he yelled at the sky, jamming a rock down on the loose edge. "You won't take my tent without a fight! This isn't some Amazon return I'm sending back to you!"

The thunder swallowed his words, but he shouted them anyway, drenched, terrified, delirious with laughter.

Mark knelt beside him, retying the guy line with hands that moved like machines. He didn't laugh, didn't scold.

He just worked. Henry stared at him, the smirk still twitching on his lips, and marveled at the absurdity.

"You're insane," Henry panted. "You're calm in a storm like this, and I'm—" He broke off, wheezing another laugh. "I'm a sitcom character. That's what I am. Some punchline for the internet. Except tonight, the internet's gone! Dead! And I'm the only one laughing!"

The storm howled, the lake heaved, the lightning stitched the sky into blinding webs. Henry pressed himself down against the rock, his chest aching from laughter and fear both. His eyes burned with salt and rain, but he kept grinning.

For the first time in years, he wasn't thinking about his job, his wife, his failures. He wasn't thinking about anything except surviving the next blast of wind, the next bolt of fire from the sky, and the thought of those smug little TikTokers discovering that nature didn't care about their followers.

And in that twisted, awful, perfect moment, Henry laughed like he meant it.

The storm did not plateau. It climbed. Every gust was stronger than the one before, every wave taller, every rumble of thunder deeper and closer. What had begun as a wild squall now felt like the wrath of some ancient thing finally remembering it was alive.

Henry crouched low beside the tent, his jacket plastered to him like a second skin, the rain so relentless it blurred the world into smears of gray. He could barely see ten yards through the downpour, and what he saw was chaos — ropes straining, stakes trembling in the ground, spray exploding up from the rocks as waves pummeled the island.

The air was thick with ozone, metallic and sharp. Lightning ripped across the sky again, so close he felt the hairs on his arms lift. The thunder was immediate, violent, a whipcrack that sent him sprawling flat to the ground. His chest heaved. His ears rang. He wanted to bury himself under the stone, to crawl inside it like an animal, away from the sky's fury.

"This island was a mistake!" he shouted, not sure if Mark could hear him over the storm. His words were snatched away by the wind before they even left his lips.

Mark was twenty feet away, bent over the canoe. Even lashed and hauled into the shallow hollow, it had begun to shift under the force of the gale. The rope snapped taut, straining against the boulder. Mark threw his weight on it, arms braced, trying to keep it from jerking loose.

Henry stumbled toward him, slipping on the slick granite. His boots skidded, and he dropped to his knees, crawling the last few feet. The canoe bucked like a living thing, its fiberglass hull shuddering as the wind shoved at it.

"Help me!" Mark barked.

Henry grabbed at the rope, his hands burning as it slid against his palms. Together they pulled, yanking it tighter, trying to wedge it deeper into the rock's crevice. The wind shrieked in their ears, the rain stung like needles, and all the while the canoe fought them.

For a moment Henry thought they'd lose it — that it would tear free, tumble back into the lake, and be swallowed by the waves. Panic clawed at him. Without the canoe, they were stranded. No way back. Just two men on a bald rock, marooned by their own bad choices.

With a guttural roar, he heaved backward, putting every ounce of his weight into the rope. Mark mirrored him, and together they dragged the canoe another foot higher onto the granite. Mark jammed the rope around the boulder again, tying a knot so tight Henry thought his fingers might snap.

Finally, it held. The canoe shuddered but stayed put, the line humming like a live wire under the strain.

Henry collapsed onto the rock, chest heaving, rain pouring into his mouth. He spat and laughed bitterly, the sound half-drowned by the wind. "We're idiots," he gasped. "Old idiots trying to play at being explorers. Should've gone to that ravine with the Scouts."

Mark sat beside him, equally soaked, his hair plastered to his forehead. "Maybe," he said. His voice was calm, maddeningly calm, as if agreeing with Henry would cost him nothing. "But we didn't. So now we hold."

Lightning lit the world again, and in its flash Henry saw Mark's face — lined, steady, eyes clear despite the chaos around them. It steadied him, too, if only for a second.

But the fear gnawed back in. Henry's heart thudded so hard he thought it might burst. He pressed his palms into the wet rock, staring at the heaving lake. Waves taller than he'd ever seen smashed against the shore, exploding into white plumes. The spray drenched him over and over, each burst a slap of cold.

"This is how it ends," Henry muttered, words slipping out before he could catch them. "On a damn rock, in the middle of nowhere, washed away like driftwood."

Mark didn't argue. He just sat, breathing, as though his stillness alone could anchor them both.

Henry laughed again, sharp and wild. "Bet the TikTok brats aren't laughing now! Bet their phones are swimming in mud puddles! All their power banks fried! No hashtags, no filters — just wet, shivering kids wishing they had a real damn compass."

The image bloomed in his mind, vivid against the storm: the smug little crew, huddled under some flimsy tarp, phones dead, ring lights sputtering out with a sad fizz. He could almost hear their whining, "Bro, the Wi-Fi's gone!" "Dude, my camera's fried!" The thought filled him with savage glee.

Lightning tore overhead, followed instantly by a crack so loud it split the air in two. The sound rattled Henry's teeth, left his ears buzzing. He ducked, pressing his forehead to the wet rock, laughing through the fear. "No livestream for that one, huh?"

The storm raged on. The tents strained, their guy lines jerking. One pole bent under the pressure, threatening to snap. Henry scrambled toward it, rain blinding him, fingers numb. He braced it with his shoulder, shoving it upright as Mark retied the line. His body shook with effort, every muscle screaming, but he held.

For a moment, for one mad moment, Henry felt something like triumph. He was fighting, actually fighting, not sitting at home staring at rejection emails, not hiding from his wife's cold silences, not wallowing in humiliation. He was here, alive, braced against the storm.

The lightning flashed again, close enough that the air sizzled. Henry flinched, terror surging, but he held the pole. He shouted into the roar, voice breaking, "Come on, you bastard! Give me what you've got!"

Thunder swallowed his words whole.

Mark's hand clapped his shoulder, grounding him, steadying him. "That's enough," he said, voice raised but calm. "Let the rope do the work now."

Henry stepped back, chest heaving, soaked to the marrow. He met Mark's eyes, saw the steadiness there, and nodded.

The wind howled on. The rain hammered. But the tent stood, the canoe held, and the two men braced themselves on their little rock while the storm tested every knot, every nerve, every ounce of resolve they had left.

The storm hit its zenith with the fury of something personal, as if the sky had finally noticed the two men clinging to their rock and decided to punish them specifically.

The wind no longer came in gusts. It was constant now, a wall pressing against them, howling so loud Henry could barely hear his own thoughts. The rain lashed sideways, needles stabbing his face and hands, soaking him deeper than he thought possible. Water streamed down the granite, pooling in every crevice, turning their island into a slick, gleaming anvil in the center of a boiling sea.

Lightning split the world every minute, sometimes every thirty seconds. Each flash turned Mark into a pale statue, turned the tents into fragile skeletons trembling in the gale, turned Henry into a quivering shadow clinging to stone. The thunder followed immediately, cracking so hard Henry swore he could feel it in his bones.

"This is it!" Henry shouted, half-mad laughter bubbling out of him. "This is how we go! Two middle-aged morons, roasted like hotdogs on God's barbecue!"

Mark ducked lower, checking the canoe's lines again. "Keep your head down!" he barked.

Henry dropped flat, pressing his chest to the rock, but the laughter didn't stop. The fear was too much, spilling over, twisting into something manic. Every boom of thunder felt like a punchline. Every bolt of lightning lit up the absurdity of their situation — two damp fools thinking they could outlast nature with a few ropes and tarps.

"Bet the TikTok crew's crying now!" he bellowed. "Bet their ring lights shorted out the second the rain hit! Imagine them, clutching their dead phones like rosaries! 'Oh no, bro, the cloud's gone, the cloud's gone!'"

He pounded his palm against the wet granite, choking on laughter and rainwater both. "No hashtags for you, you little bastards! No trending page for 'Old Man Falls in the Dirt Part Two'! You'll be lucky if you can post 'Help, We're Drowning' before your batteries die!"

Lightning tore across the sky, the thunder so close it sounded like the earth splitting open. Henry flinched, then howled with laughter again, his voice cracked and ragged. "Oh, if only I could see it! Their $300 sneakers full of water, their fancy wireless mics sizzling in the mud, the look on their faces when they realize their precious followers can't see them now. All alone, just like us, except dumber!"

Mark actually smirked at that, though he shook his head. He braced his body against the wind, his hand steady on Henry's back to keep him grounded. "Easy," he said, voice still calm despite the madness around them. "Laugh if it helps. But don't let go."

Henry clung tighter to the stone, knuckles white, rain pouring into his mouth as he wheezed through hysterics. "Christ, Mark, this is comedy! We should've sold tickets! 'Two Old Men Get Their Asses Kicked by God, Live in the Boundary Waters!' Would've gone viral if the Wi-Fi worked!"

Another bolt hit so close the sky turned white, and for an instant Henry swore he saw the surface of the lake explode, steam hissing upward. He shrieked, then broke into more laughter, almost sobbing now.

Mark's hand squeezed his shoulder, firm. "It's just the storm, Henry. It'll pass. They always do."

Henry spat rainwater, shaking his head violently. "Not for me! Never passes for me! Always more storms, more screwups, more people laughing at me. At least this time the whole damn world's too wet to record it!"

The wind screamed, bending the trees across the bay into ragged silhouettes. Their tents shuddered violently, poles bowing. One corner ripped free, the tarp flapping like a wounded bird. Henry scrambled to grab it, nearly sliding on the slick granite, cackling as he fought.

"Ha! Take that, you son of a bitch!" he yelled at the sky, jamming a rock down on the loose edge. "You won't take my tent without a fight! This isn't some Amazon return I'm sending back to you!"

The thunder swallowed his words, but he shouted them anyway, drenched, terrified, delirious with laughter.

Mark knelt beside him, retying the guy line with hands that moved like machines. He didn't laugh, didn't scold. He just worked. Henry stared at him, the smirk still twitching on his lips, and marveled at the absurdity.

"You're insane," Henry panted. "You're calm in a storm like this, and I'm—" He broke off, wheezing another laugh. "I'm a sitcom character. That's what I am. Some punchline for the internet. Except tonight, the internet's gone! Dead! And I'm the only one laughing!"

The storm howled, the lake heaved, the lightning stitched the sky into blinding webs. Henry pressed himself down against the rock, his chest aching from laughter and fear both. His eyes burned with salt and rain, but he kept grinning.

For the first time in years, he wasn't thinking about his job, his wife, his failures. He wasn't thinking about anything except surviving the next blast of wind, the next bolt of fire from the sky, and the thought of those smug little TikTokers discovering that nature didn't care about their followers.

And in that twisted, awful, perfect moment, Henry laughed like he meant it.

Chapter 11

No Peace For The Failure

The lightning changed the storm from noise to threat.

Wind and rain had been brutal, yes—pummeling, battering, a test of knots and nerves—but lightning gave the night teeth. Every few heartbeats the sky split open, raw white searing the undersides of clouds and turning the lake a sheet of fleeting glass. The flashes time-stamped the chaos: wind howled, rain knifed sideways, then—flash—the world appeared in surgical clarity for a single breath before darkness slammed back in.

Henry counted in the gaps because there was nothing else to do: one Mississippi, two Mississippi, three—crack. Too close, again. He pressed his chest against the slick rock and felt it vibrate as thunder rolled through the stone and up his ribs. Water coursed around his forearms in thin rivers. The guy lines hummed at a pitch that made his teeth itch.

"Down!" Mark shouted, and Henry ducked, though he was already prone, already as low as a man could get without tunneling into granite. He turned his head toward the bay, blinking rain from his lashes. Another white vein stitched the cloud belly from west to east. Flash. The far island leapt out of shadow: a wall of trees, a slash of pale granite beach, the dark mouth of the ravine where the Scouts had vanished hours ago.

He held the image—trees, beach, ravine—as the darkness rushed back. A second flash snapped over the same place—closer, lower, hunting. Thunder arrived like an iron door slamming.

"Mark," Henry yelled, "it's focusing over there!"

Mark didn't answer immediately; he was cinching the second line on the canoe, his body braced, shoulders squared against the push of the wind. When he lifted his head he followed Henry's gaze across the water. In the strobing light the forest looked like a field of bayonets.

"Yep," Mark said. "Same cell pivoting. It's anchoring on the ridge."

"Why?"

"Topography," Mark said, and then, because there was no good reason lightning did anything but because, he added, "Bad luck."

The third flash didn't look like the others. It came straight down—no sideways scribble, no half-heart writing of light. A spear. Henry saw it in the stuttered instant: a white lance punching into a jack pine that grew at the shoulder of the ravine's entrance, a tree he'd noticed earlier for its stubborn angle, the way it leaned like an old man defying the wind. The strike hit the crown. For a fraction of a fraction of a second there was only light. Then the light became flame.

"Oh God," Henry said, barely sound at all.

The pine didn't so much ignite as become fire. It bloomed, orange rushing out from needles as if the tree exhaled a century's worth of summer in one violent breath. Resin turned to napalm. The crown went from green to furnace in the same heartbeat the thunder cracked across their backs.

"Mark!" Henry's voice pitched high. He clawed at the rock to rise and slid back on knees too wet to grip.

"I see it," Mark said, voice clipped. He did not turn away. He did not pretend it was rain-trick light. Flames ran, bright lines down the trunk where the strike had ripped bark away, and as they ran down they threw sparks sideways into the understory at the ravine's mouth— tufts of dead grass, a lace of last year's bracken, the papery skirts of birch. It had been dry for a week. Henry remembered the dust that puffed up when they'd dragged the canoe, the way pine duff sighed like talc beneath his boot. Dry. We joked about the dust. We joked.

"Holy—" Henry swallowed the last word because the sky answered with another spear.

Flash.

Crack.

Ten yards downslope from the first tree, a red pine took it like a tuning fork, and in the white-hot afterimage Henry couldn't see anything but the vertical pillar of brightness, clean and merciless. When darkness fell again, that red pine wore a skirt of embers. Then it, too, went to flame.

The wind that had been their enemy now became the fire's accomplice. It barreled across the channel and seized the new flames like a bellows, bent them sideways, poured them along the very path the Scouts had taken into the ravine. In another flash Henry saw the geometry: the narrow throat of the ravine, the slight uphill grade, the chute of understory that would behave like a wick. He saw it as clearly as a diagram labeled Run.

"They're in there," Henry said. "Mark, the boys. That's the entrance. That's the path."

"Damn it, I know," Mark said.

"Mark." It wasn't a question anymore; it was a plea twisted tight by lightning-lit images. A column of boys, backpacks bobbing, the scoutmaster counting heads as they vanished into safety. Safety. He tasted the word now and found it tinny. He could see the orange push, like a hand through the brush, reaching where kids had walked not three hours ago.

The next strike of lightning shook the earth they stood on.

It was too dangerous to paddle across to help the scouts, but what choice did they have.

One scoutmaster alone, with 13 kids, fire running towards them.

Running towards the ravine.

But the rain whipped so hard, in Henry's face, that it hurt to look.

Yet, Henry had to look, had to think.

Rain hammered their island. The contradiction of it—water everywhere, and still fire—felt like a trick. But Henry knew enough. He knew lightning split trees open, boiled the sap, turned needles into candles. He knew wet didn't erase flame if resin decided to carry it.

"Wind shift," Mark said. "We get an east bend, that line lays right into the ravine."

"How long do we have?"

Mark didn't answer. Henry turned, and in the next flash he saw why: Mark wasn't calculating minutes; he was calculating ifs. If the gusts kept at this angle, if the fuel load in the ravine throat was thick, if the rain slackened under the downdraft, if another strike lit something deeper in the canopy. The kind of math that had no numbers, only weights in a man's jaw.

The lake between them and the far island boiled with whitened caps. The distance—what was it? Two hundred yards? Three? In daylight and calm it had felt like a shrug. Now it read as moat.

A fresh peel of thunder insisted on its primacy. Henry flinched, and in the duck of his head, a mean thought flashed: Let the TikTok crew try to film that. He saw them for half a second in a comic panel—ring light hissing out, battery packs drowning in pockets, captions dying on thumbs as another slash of light turned them from narrators into witnesses. He did not smile. The humor was ash-dry in his mouth, and all it did was underline the sick drop of his stomach.

He pushed to his hands and knees and crawled to the island's western lip for a cleaner angle. The rain had cut visibility to a rag curtain, but the fire didn't care about curtains. It announced itself in color: a deep, soaked night everywhere, and in one place, a hot animal orange. The first pine's crown was a torch. The second tree wore flame like a coat. Beneath them, the brush at the ravine yawed with embers that leapt and sank with each gust, a swarm of sparks trying to become a line.

"Mark, that's their way in," Henry said again, as if repetition could convince the two burning trees to hear him and lean back out of the path. "They're behind that."

"Or deeper," Mark countered. "The ravine runs a long way. If the scoutmaster's worth anything he put them on the lee side of the bend. They'll feel the heat before they see flame."

"Heat before flame," Henry echoed, a useless prayer. The sky carved itself again and thunder pressed his teeth together. He had the sudden, childish urge to call out across the water—Hey! Hey in there!—as if shouting could outrun wind and rain and the geometry of slope and fuel.

Another strike landed somewhere to the north, unseen behind the bulk of the island. The flash threw the two current fires into negative; for a blink they seemed to suck the light rather than give it. Then the rain between islands thickened again, and all Henry could do was track the pulse of orange at the ravine mouth, a heartbeat he couldn't touch.

Mark slid alongside him on his elbows, keeping himself as low as the surface of the rock would allow. Close, Henry saw the water flatten Mark's hair into dark lines against his scalp, saw rain run off his nose in a steady thread. Mark's eyes were the same as they'd been when the tent pole bent, when the canoe tried to go—focused, steady, taking in what could be taken in.

"What do we do?" Henry said.

"Watch," Mark said first, and Henry nearly swung at him for it. But then Mark added, "And be ready. If the wind eases enough to make the crossing survivable, we move. Not before."

"We can't just sit here."

"We also can't out swim the lightning."

Henry bit his lip until he tasted copper. He wanted a plan big enough to beat weather, wanted the kind of certainty he could put his whole body into and not have it shatter beneath him. But the lake had its own laws and the sky enforced them. Their canoe, even double-lashed, juddered with each new shove of air. The channel looked like a mouth full of broken teeth.

"What about signaling?" Henry said, grasping. "Whistle? Light?"

Mark tapped his chest pocket where the whistle curled on a length of paracord. "If we get a lull. Sound carries oddly in this. Could just call fire to them. Or panic. Remember: they know what to do in wind—down, clear a patch, wet bandanas. The scoutmaster will be counting."

"I don't know that," Henry said, and hated the tremor in his throat. "I don't know him."

Mark's jaw flexed. "You're right. We don't."

Lightning flogged the ridge again, not a spear this time but a sideways scrawl that lit a strip of canopy a hundred yards beyond the ravine. The thunder chased it, and the wind—vindictive, tireless—changed note, an octave lower, as if it had dragged something larger into its throat.

The burning trees answered by leaning. It was an illusion—Henry knew that, he did—but the flame made the trunks feel like bodies, and the gust made the bodies feel as if they bent toward the path in the way that people lean in to listen. The fire took a step, then another: an understory bush, then a collapsed snag, both surrendering their shape to orange in a blink. The ground between two trees ran with little comets as bark sloughed off and tumbled, burning, into the duff. Sparks scattered, failed, scattered, found purchase, tried again. The ravine mouth pulsed brighter. The wind took a long breath and blew harder.

"Jesus," Henry whispered. He was not a praying man, but he understood, in his bones, the grammar of please. "They're in there."

Mark's hand found his forearm and closed. "I know."

"This is my fault," Henry said, not because logic supported it but because shame was a lens he lived behind. "I wanted to move. I wanted away from them. If we'd stayed, if we'd—"

"Henry." Mark's voice rode a lull with precision, soft but cut clean. "Lightning doesn't take requests."

Henry swallowed and stared. The rain beaded in his eyelashes until the island across the water was a smear and the fire was two glow-balls doubling and tripling as his vision jittered. He shook his head hard, clearing it, and the shapes resolved: the first pine's crown breaking, a shower of embers like a meteor dump; the second tree's trunk split, a wound of light down its center where the strike had torn it.

He felt the strangeness of the moment, too—the way fear sharpened him. Earlier, hauling the canoe, he'd felt alive because his muscles had something to do. Now he felt alive because his senses had been stripped of everything but what mattered: sight locked on orange, ears tuned to wind and the drum of rain, skin waiting for the next electric shiver that meant a strike had come too close. Alive the way prey is alive in the breath before the predator chooses.

Another flash. Another thunder-hammer. The sheet of rain thinned for three seconds, and in those three seconds Henry saw motion in the ravine that was not fire: a darker ripple against the deeper dark, as if a shadow detached itself and ran. He jolted upright, then flattened again, heart stuttering.

"Mark—I saw—someone—"

Mark's head snapped to the gap. His silence was a tensioned line. The rain thickened again, and the hole in the green closed with gray.

"Could've been flame shift," Mark said.

"It moved against the wind," Henry said. He wanted Mark to fight him so Henry could insist harder, could make the shape into a boy with a neon pack cover, into the scoutmaster's hat, into certainty. But the rain took the moment back and chewed it into noise.

They waited. The fire worked on. The lake beat its fists against their rock. Lightning sewed the sky and ripped its seams in the same stitch.

"Okay," Mark said finally, flinty now in a way that meant the calculus had clicked. "We stage. If it lays down, we go. If it doesn't, we're no use to anyone dead."

"How do we stage?" Henry said, the question a relief. A plan, even a conditional one, was a rope across a drop.

"Dry bag with the big first-aid," Mark said, counting with his hand. "Two headlamps, whistle, ponchos—it's dumb, but it's better than nothing. Lifejackets. We run light, with basics. Headlights whistles, rope, first aid kit, water, life jackets. If the wind eases enough to get out and the lightning gives us ten seconds of kindness, we push to the lee side below their landing and haul up from there. We don't go into the trees unless we have to. You hear me? Open water is safer than a crown fire."

"I hear you," Henry said. He didn't know if he believed any version of safer, but the specifics steadied him: headlamps, whistle, ponchos. Do this, then this. His hands wanted tasks the way a shaken dog wants a hand on its ribs.

"Get the kit," Mark said. "I'll keep eyes."

Henry crabbed backward over the rock, keeping himself scuffed and low. In the tent vestibule the world narrowed to nylon and his own breath. He shoved aside the stove bag and the food sack and dug for the bright yellow dry bag, fingers dumb with rain and adrenaline. The zipper fought him; he forced it, then pulled out the big first-aid roll, the space blanket packets, the triangular bandage, the headlamps. He looped whistles over his own neck and Mark's. The familiar weight of plastic at his sternum made him feel like a kid in swimming lessons, ridiculous and somehow safe.

He shrugged into the lifejacket, cinched it until it bit his ribs, and crawled back into the storm. Wind shouldered him. Rain tried to push him back inside. He pushed anyway.

Mark didn't look at him, eyes glued to the entrance where the scouts went in.

Henry lay parallel, shoved the dry bag under his belly so the wind wouldn't take it, and followed Mark's gaze.

For a handful of breaths the rain softened and the lightning slowed. Not much. Just enough that the fire's edges sharpened. The two torch-trees were now anchors, their radiance steady. The ground fire at their feet pulsed and crept, a low animal crawling toward the cut where the Scouts had gone. The wind's long-breath cadence—the inhale that gathered, the exhale that bullied—meant the creep wasn't smooth. In the inhale, flame lifted. In the exhale, it slithered.

The lull gave them a sound Henry hadn't known he wanted: a voice. Faint. Shredded by water and distance. Not words; pitch. A call. Another. A whistle trilled twice, then again. Mark's eyes cut to Henry. Henry's eyes were already on Mark.

"They're there," Henry said. He could feel the sentence in his bones the way he'd felt thunder: true before proof.

"Or they were," Mark said. But his hand dropped to the dry bag, and his body shifted in the way a sprinter coils before the gun.

Lightning cracked, close and savage. They both curled, heels to hamstrings, covering the back of their necks like schoolkids drilled for a storm. The thunder pounded over them, through them, shook the island so hard Henry's teeth met with a click. When he lifted his head, the lull had closed, the rain back to a wall.

"So we wait," Henry said, because saying it out loud made the waiting a thing, not a void.

"So we wait," Mark echoed.

Henry lay there, cheek to stone, breath sawing, eyes burning under rain. He let the wrongness of the moment press through him: that water could not defeat fire because wind had decided to choose sides; that two burning trees could become a gate across a path he'd watched children take; that he could feel simultaneously useless and necessary, terrified and—damn it—alive. Alive not like a victor, not like a man who knew what to do, but like a wire humming between two storms.

Another flash. Another roll. Another breath. The orange at the ravine brightened, dimmed, crawled.

"Batteries are wet," Henry said suddenly, voice flat, not laughing now, just stating a fact to the sky. "If they're out there—the TikTok kids—their batteries are wet."

Mark didn't answer. It wasn't the weather for jokes. But Henry realized he hadn't been joking. He had meant: No one is filming this. It's just us. It's just this. No audience. No script. For once, humiliation had no platform. Fear had no comment section. Only the wind got to weigh in.

"Ready," Mark said.

Henry nodded, and both men pressed flatter to the rock, bodies aligned toward the ravine like compass needles, waiting for the next small mercy the storm might give.

The canoe rocked like it had been waiting for Henry.

The first push from shore shoved them straight into a wall of chop. The bow lifted, slapped down, lifted again. Spray stung Henry's face, cold needles biting his skin. His poncho clung wetly to his shoulders, the hood already sliding back. He jammed it forward, gripped the paddle, and tried to steady his breathing.

"Short strokes!" the scoutmaster barked from the bow. "Keep time with me!"

Henry nodded, though he wasn't sure if the man could even see it. He jabbed his paddle into the water, yanked, then reset, yanked again. But his rhythm was off. For every clean stroke the scoutmaster dug in, Henry fumbled one — catching too much water, smacking the side of the hull, or plunging too deep and jerking the canoe sideways.

Just 300 yards Henry kept telling himself.

300 yards.

But with every stoke the pain, took over, his arms splitting, his face soaked with sweat and rain.

50 yards.

Sideways the canoe pushed against the water, the water pushed by the wind.

Each stroke, was a fight against Mother Nature, who had an axe to grind with Henry.

At 100 yards the canoe now sideways, started to tip, luckily, Mark was able to find a shallow rock, and push his paddle against the rock, stabilizing the canoe.

Henry now angry.

Not angry, pissed off.

All his fear gone, only raw emotion pushed him.

Mark continuing to steering, saw the shift in Henry.

Henry was no longer a man, but a man filled with rage.

Rage against the wind.

Rage against mother nature.

A man who knew he needed to help, and no amount of wind was stopping him.

The last 200 yards, seemed to disappear in an instant.

No words were needed as they landed on the island.

All around them, the island was on fire, here at the opening where they setup camp just a few days before, was brighter than daylight as the fire burned everything in its path.

Chapter 12

Fighting Against Time

The moment they left the lake behind, the world closed in.

Smoke thickened until Henry's headlamp barely pierced more than an arm's length. The beam caught particles that swirled like ghosts, each one glowing ember-orange before vanishing into the haze. The air was no longer something to breathe — it was something to swallow, something that clawed back at his throat and left his chest aching. Every step was a decision. Forward into blindness.

The forest was unrecognizable. Landmarks he thought would anchor them — the slope of a hill, the curve of shoreline — had vanished in the fire's transformation. Trees had turned to skeletal torches, their bark cracking and weeping resin. Roots glowed red beneath the soil like veins under skin. Henry tried to orient himself, to picture the map in his head: the ravine had been marked east of the landing, tucked behind a granite ridge. If they kept their heading, if they kept walking straight, they'd find it.

But the fire didn't allow straight lines.

Ash fell in sheets, slicking the ground until his boots slipped like on ice. Heat pressed at his skin in invisible waves. And worst of all, sound betrayed him. The forest roared, snapped, groaned — so loud he couldn't tell if a tree was collapsing ten feet away or a hundred. His ears rang with it, the way artillery must echo in war.

Mark coughed into his damp shirt, his headlamp jerking side to side. "Can't see a damn thing," he muttered. His voice was small against the fire's bellow.

Henry pressed on. His legs already burned, his thighs thick with lactic acid. He was not built for this anymore, not at forty-eight with a belly that had grown heavier in years of office chairs and late-night stress eating. Each step reminded him — the jiggle at his waist, the wheeze in his chest. He had once been lighter, faster, someone the younger men at work called reliable. That version of him seemed like another man now, one who had died quietly under fluorescent lights.

But tonight, if he failed, children would die.

He whispered under his breath, lips moving against wet cotton. It wasn't a prayer he'd learned in church — he hadn't been there in years. It was raw, improvised.

"Don't let me fail them. Don't let me fail again. Please. Please, God, or whoever's left in this fire, guide me through this smoke. "

His hand brushed the duffel strap at his shoulder like a talisman. Inside, spare shirts for the boys. Proof they weren't walking blind. Proof someone had thought of them.

The ground shifted upward. They scrambled over a slope of stone slick with ash. Halfway up, Henry's boot slipped, his knee slamming down hard enough to make stars burst behind his eyes. Pain flared — sharp, electric — and for a moment he froze, gasping. His headlamp beam jittered, illuminating the gouge where his knee had struck. Mark's hand was there in an instant, pulling him up.

"You good?" Mark barked.

Henry wanted to say yes, but the truth stuck. His chest was heaving too hard, his body shaking like a furnace about to give out. He felt heavy, useless. Not now. Don't break now.

"I'm fine," he lied, forcing his leg forward.

At the ridge's top, the fire showed them its face. Ahead, the forest was a wall of orange. Whole pines lit from root to crown, flames spiraling skyward in twisted columns. Heat slapped them in waves, like opening an oven door a thousand times over. Henry raised an arm to shield his eyes, but the fire was everywhere. There was no shielding from it.

"We need to find the ravine," Mark shouted over the roar. "If it's sheltered, the kids will have stayed put!"

Henry nodded, but doubt knifed through him. If they stayed put, they're already choking to death. He shoved the thought down. One foot in front of the other.

They angled left, trying to skirt the worst of the flames. For a time the smoke seemed to ease, the headlamps catching glimpses of ground that wasn't yet ablaze. They moved faster, stumbling over roots, ducking under branches. The duffel bounced against Henry's hip. His shirt-mask had gone hot, almost scalding, each breath a struggle.

Then the forest screamed.

It was the sound of a tree giving way — a drawn-out moan followed by a splintering crack. Henry froze, instincts ancient, before he could even think. His lamp swept upward. A pine, its base burning white-hot, tilted in slow, awful surrender.

"Move!" Henry shouted, shoving Mark sideways.

The tree came down with a sound like thunder, crashing across their path, spraying embers in every direction. The shockwave of air knocked Henry back a step, his knees nearly giving. Heat blasted them, sparks stinging his arms. The trunk lay before them, massive, impassable, flames licking along its length.

Mark swore, dragging his damp shirt tighter across his mouth. "We can't get through that!"

Henry's heart sank. The path he'd imagined, the straight line east, was gone. Blocked. And with the smoke closing in, the chance of circling wide without getting hopelessly lost shrank to nothing. His stomach twisted. The weight of every failure, every wrong turn in his life, seemed to crash with that tree.

He pressed a hand to the burning ground, steadying himself. His prayer rose again,

Not noble this time, but desperate. *"Don't let this be where it ends. Not here. Not like this. Don't let me be the man who couldn't find them."*

The smoke pressed closer, thicker. And somewhere beyond it, faint but real, Henry thought he heard something different. Not fire. Not trees. A sound softer, human. Crying.

The sound came first as a whimper. High-pitched, wavering, fragile against the constant bellow of fire. Henry froze mid-step, one hand out to stop Mark. His lamp beam swung wildly through the smoke, seeking shapes.

"There!" Henry rasped, his voice shredded. "Did you hear—"

Mark raised a hand, straining to listen. Another note rose, a low moan twisting into something almost human. For one desperate second, Henry believed it — believed the boys were there, huddled, weeping. His heart lurched in his chest, ready to run.

He did it, he had found the children.

But then the truth revealed itself.

A tree groaned as its core split, water in the trunk boiling to steam. The sound cracked like sobbing, drawn out, hollow. Another nearby pine keened the same way, bending against its death throes. The chorus rose around them — not children crying, but the forest itself, mourning.

Henry's breath faltered. He stumbled to a knee, clutching the wet shirt against his mouth as if that alone could block the sound. The hope that had carried him forward snapped.

"Not them," Mark muttered. His lamp caught the tortured bark of a collapsing tree, its glowing wounds alive with sparks. "Jesus, Henry. It's just the wood."

Just the wood. The phrase twisted like a knife. Henry wanted to scream, to tear at the smoke, to demand the voices give back what he thought he'd heard. His throat clenched, and his chest heaved not just from the smoke but from rage.

"Damn it!" he roared, his voice breaking. He slammed his fist into the ashen ground. Sparks leapt. "Damn it, damn it!"

The words were raw, torn from years of anger he'd swallowed — anger at himself, at missed chances, at jobs lost and promises broken. All of it erupted here, in the middle of the burning woods, where failure wasn't just his burden anymore. If he didn't find them, children would die.

Mark crouched beside him, a hand firm on his shoulder. "Breathe, man. We keep going. That's all there is."

Henry dragged air through the hot fabric, each breath rasping like sandpaper. His mind reeled with images: scouts with faces covered in soot, waiting, waiting, their small bodies curled against stone, trusting that someone would come. And if I don't... The thought was unbearable.

The smell hit next.

It was sharp, acrid — different from burning pine. More metallic. Sweet, cloying, rotten. Henry gagged before he could stop himself, yanking his shirt tighter to his face. His stomach twisted, bile rising.

Mark swore softly. "Animals."

Henry agreed, the other option was unthinkable.

It was not the kids, it just was not.

God would not allow that to happen.

Henry simply agreed.

The truth was it was not the kids. But animals.

Somewhere in the underbrush, rabbits, foxes, raccoons — anything without wings — had been trapped. The fire had taken them first, and now the wind carried the stench of their burning. Fat sizzling. Fur gone to ash. Bones cracking in the heat.

Henry's head spun. He forced himself not to picture it — but the images came anyway. A fawn curled under a log, a nest of squirrels in a hollow. The scouts are not animals, he told himself. They're not gone. Not yet.

A sudden crash snapped them both upright.

From the wall of smoke to their left, a shape burst forth — massive, violent, alive. A deer barreled across their path, its body half-scorched, patches of fur blackened, skin raw and glistening. Its eyes were wild, white-ringed, rolling with terror. Steam rose from its heaving flanks as it leapt, staggering but unstoppable.

Henry flinched back, almost dropping the duffel. The animal's hooves struck ash and sparks flew. For a heartbeat, its silhouette glowed against the fire — a ghost of the wilderness fleeing extinction. Then it was gone, swallowed back into the smoke.

Silence fell in its wake, broken only by the fire's roar. Henry's pulse hammered in his temples.

"That's what we're running from," Mark said hoarsely.

Henry shook his head. "No. That's what we're running with."

Mark gave him a sharp look, confused.

"The deer didn't stop," Henry said, forcing strength into his voice. His fists clenched until his nails cut skin. "It didn't lay down and die. It kept moving. That's what we do. That's what the kids are doing. They're waiting for us to lead."

His anger shifted, coiling into resolve. Every failure in his life — every moment of weakness — became fuel now. He could hate himself later, drown in regret later. But now, he would not stop. Not until he had the scouts in his hands.

He adjusted the duffel strap, set his jaw, and pushed forward into the flames.

Mark did not want to say it out loud.

But it was time to turn back, time to think about giving up.

The flames are too thick, too hot, too much smoke.

Mark could not see feet ahead.

The image felt obscene in its simplicity and the ease of it made his stomach twist. How could they turn their backs on smoke and heat and the possibility of children trapped in a ravine while the world burned behind them?

The thought became a small, burning thing of its own — one step easier than continuing.

Henry began to go dark with the same thoughts, he pictured grunting as he shoved the canoe free, water slapping the hull, the engine thrumming, and then the two of them sitting there in the dark, watching the orange wall of the island recede. He thought of his own house, of his kids asleep under patched quilts, of the refrigerator light left on for late-night bread raids, of the small mundane comforts that had once defined his life.

There was relief in it — real, near-soporific relief — the kind that comes when a man imagines he can hand himself back his life, put the weight of the world down for an hour and maybe forever.

His mind began a litany of plausible excuses, rationales like flares thrown up into the dark: the fire was too unpredictable, they'd be trapped themselves, the risk wasn't worth it. He could return to the shore and sip cool water and watch the emergency crews — if they arrived — do better-trained things. He could let professionals handle it. He could, and the sentence sat heavy and sweet on his tongue like a forbidden dessert.

He thought then of all the people in his life who had once shrugged at him in disappointment. He'd absorbed those shrugs for years — the job losses, the missed PTA meetings, the times he promised and then missed. A pattern. A rusted hinge on a door he was always too tired to oil. He had convinced himself that most of those losses had meaning only for him. But now his choices had scale.

Failure here did not close a door; it end-stopped a story for children who had trusted adults to lead. If he left, he imagined the faces that would confront him later — the Scoutmaster's, perhaps the parents' — and the small, accusing tilt to their heads that would be worse than any raised voice.

He thought about the weight of the duffel on his shoulder: wet shirts, headlamps, rope, bandages. It was not a metaphoric weight. It bruised his collarbone, shifted with every step. It was tangible proof: they had come prepared. They had thought enough to bring spare shirts to dampen the smoke from a child's face. That practical kindness sat like lead in the bag, and it was also a promise. If they turned back, the bag would be a box of lies. He could not live with that kind of lie. Not anymore.

Mark's breath came a rasp off to his left. Henry felt the man's presence more than he heard it; the smoke warped the world into a tactile blur, and the outline of his partner — broad-shouldered, steady-eyed — was a kind of anchor. Henry wanted, as he had since childhood, to be the anchor for someone else. The idea had become a small ferocity in him: the stubborn refusal to be the man who would always leave things halfway done.

He drew in a breath and tasted wood and something closer to iron. For a flash he imagined the boys: a neat line of neckerchiefs, flapping in a night wind that felt suddenly colder in his chest than it did on his face. A gaggle of voices humming camp songs, suddenly still. He could see their little backs, and the way he wanted to reach them made his chest ache.

They stood where the path forked into nothing. The map in his head had dissolved, and the forest, lit from within, had become an endless wall of orange and black. Henry swallowed. The water in his shirt had long warmed; the fabric had been scalded in places, glued to his neck. Sparks had caught on stray fibers and had been averted with clumsy hands. Pain had a way of making a man more honest: there were no illusions left, only the immediate, palpable tasks.

"Fuck it, fuck it all." Henry breathed, making the decision with the flat, pragmatic air of a man signing a contract he could not read. "We press on."

"Henry, we need to think about getting out alive ourselves." Shouted Mark.

"Fuck it." Shouted Henry back.

Herny's face was a mix of every emotion, every feeling. Anger, sadnesses, weakness, strength. It was a face of turmoil, like his life had become.

Mark's hand squeezed his shoulder. For the first time that night Henry allowed himself to register the sensation: something like gratitude, something like forgiveness. They pushed deeper.

The world narrowed to the tasks of moving: step, lift, duck low under the hanging arms of burning branches, twist to avoid a shower of cinders. The ash was slick and treacherous. Every footfall had to be deliberate. One misstep and the earth itself might give beneath them: charred roots could collapse into a smoke-filled hole, a decades-old log could be a kiln of heat. They learned to trust the sound they made on the ground, the hollow thud indicating air underneath, the dull thump meaning solid enough to trust.

The trees wavered in the orange light like an audience in motion. Wings of sparks rolled off trunks and rose to join the conflagration above. The underbrush had been reduced to a thin layer of crunchy detritus. The air tasted of ash and old fires and a metallic tang that Henry could not identify and did not want to name.

They moved like men in a trance, pulled by duty more than by hope. Henry's thoughts were a constant thin wire of worry: the Scouts, the ravine, the Scoutmaster, his own family at home. He thought of every time he had chosen the safer option in life, the times he had let fear of embarrassment — of looking foolish — sink his courage. Tonight humiliation didn't exist. Only consequence did.

"Henry, you see lights?" Mark hissed at one point, voice barely audible over the roar.

Henry froze, throat working. For a second he thought the smoke had given them a break: a pinprick in the world, a cold white in the orange sea. He swung his lamp, slow, careful. The beam cut through the smoke and picked up — there! — a pale glint pinned low to the earth. It might have been a rock catching reflected fire, or the sheen off a wet surface. He stepped closer.

"Probably just resin," Mark said, close to a whisper. His breath smelled like burned sugar and something ironlike. "Don't let it fool you."

A low creak made them both jerk. Behind them, another tree leaned, its cambium glistening with the sheen of boiling sap. The air shuddered with the prelude to collapse. Henry grabbed Mark's arm and they scrambled, the world becoming a narrow corridor between falling giants. A pine the size of a small house parted from its roots and toppled, missing them by a breath. The sound was a physical thing, a thunderous strike that left ringing in their ears.

"Enough of that," Mark panted. "I'm done watching trees try to kill us."

They laughed then, two disconnected sounds that were more of a pressure release than anything else. The laughter dissolved quickly, absorbed by the roar. Henry's lungs felt like bellows forced to move with flames clawing at the edges.

At one moment, forced to stop by a fallen limb that bisected the path, Henry doubled over and placed both hands on his knees. The heat was a pain in his skull; his masked mouth tasted like something metallic. He closed his eyes and the world inverted — not the physical, but the psychological: everything he had ever not done rose up like an inventory in his mind. The faces of his ex-colleagues, the vacations canceled, the times he had promised to be home earlier and then stayed late to stack paper for someone else. The list was a chain around his neck, clinking with small, ugly coins.

But something vaulted in Henry's chest like a trapped animal. He took one step, then another, and the prints grew deeper as they descended. The ravine might be near. The tracks led downhill, toward a dark trench that swallowed their lamp beams. Henry's legs, worried and heavy, forgot to protest for a moment. The duffel hammered against his hip like a warning bell.

They followed the line of dirt, the dirt that grew more wet and it lead them to a narrowing valley. The air grew damper, the steam from the lake drifting through the smoke like an afterthought. The ravine presented itself as an absence rather than a place: a carved-out throat in the earth where older water had once run, its sides slicked with moss that now steamed as if someone had poured a kettle over it.

The bottom of the ravine was shadowed and cool — a fragile mercy. The path banked down between rock faces that glowed at their edges. Henry's lamp threw their beams into a narrow slot where the fire's appetite found less to consume. The noise of the world above was a duller roar here, muffled by stone.

For a moment Henry allowed himself to think of the boys, huddled and cold perhaps, and he imagined he could hear soft murmurings. His heart soared; he dared to believe. Then he realized the sound was the venting of steam as hot air met cool stone, and the swing of his hope crashed into tired reality.

He moved forward regardless, each step as much a confession as an act: I will not be the man who leaves them waiting. The duffel dug a line across his shoulder; sweat stung his eyes and turned streaks of dirt into rivulets on his skin. The forest above kept sighing as it burned, but within the ravine, the sound of the trees was complex and layered with other noises: a far whimper that may have been pact with the wind; the clink of a tin cup caught on a rock; a small, repeated shuffle like the movement of many tiny feet.

Henry tasted the air, trying not to be led by what he wanted to hear. He focused on evidence — the tracks, the tin cup, the soggy imprint of a coat sleeve left on a rock. They were signs that someone had been through here not long ago. Maybe the Scoutmaster had led them. Maybe they had taken shelter deeper. Maybe — and Henry would not let himself finish that last may.

They crept forward, the ravine walls pressing in, the path narrowing to a single line of ash. A falling ember landed on the duffel and hissed, tray of small sparks showering their boots. Henry brushed it away. He felt clumsy and too old for this life and precisely equipped for it all at once.

At the bottom of the ravine, the air cooled enough to sting. Henry's thoughts were a tight, tuneless drum that beat a mantra: find them, find them, find them. Failure was not a philosophical option anymore; it was a category that applied to living bodies. He could not file it and forget it.

They rounded a bend and the world opened some small way.

There, huddled in a shallow hollow at the ravine's edge, were the remains of a small camp: a tangle of neckerchiefs, a half-burnt sleeping bag, a small folding chair collapsed against a rock. Henry's breath hitched so hard it felt like the world might end there. He swore softly, the word a prayer and a curse both. The camp looked abandoned in a way that made his bones ache with dread.

Then, a small sound — not a cry but a stifled hiccup — made his whole body move. He heard a whisper of nylon, the sniff of someone trying to hold back a sob. Henry swallowed a sound that wasn't quite a sob himself and lifted his lamp higher.

Two small faces peered out between the roots of a tree, rimmed in soot, eyes wide as the moon and luminous with terror. The boys were small enough that the ravine hid most of them; only their heads and shoulders showed, lined up like beads. Behind them, the Scoutmaster sat rigid with a coat wrapped around his knees, his jaw set in a way that betrayed both fear and relief.

Alive.

Alive is all Henry thought of.

Chapter 13

Scouting A Way Out

The ravine was quieter than Henry had expected.

He'd braced himself for the sound of crying children, for the panicked buzz of questions or pleas, for something loud and messy. What he found instead was silence. The kind of silence that wrapped around his ears and made the fire above sound like it belonged to another planet. The kind of silence that felt like it had weight.

The children were there, huddled into uneven clusters — four here, five there, three tucked tight into a pocket under a leaning pine. Their faces were pale, streaked with soot. Eyes wide but glassy, mouths slack. They looked less like boys and more like abandoned dolls, fragile things propped together for warmth. Their scout uniforms — khaki shirts, neckerchiefs, merit-badge sashes — were smudged nearly black. Some of them had their arms wrapped around their knees, others clutched each other's hands, but none moved when Henry and Mark stumbled into the clearing.

For a sick second, Henry thought they were dead. The stillness, the blank eyes, the way not even a whimper rose — it was the stillness of prey animals who had given up struggling. His stomach dropped and bile burned his throat.

Then a boy blinked. A slow, heavy blink. And the silence broke into tiny sounds: a shallow inhale, the scrape of shoes shifting against rock, a ragged cough.

"Jesus," Mark muttered, his voice muffled by the wet shirt around his mouth. His lamp beam danced across the group. "They're alive."

Alive, yes. But frozen.

Henry could understand why they were frozen, the noise of trees popping like firecrackers, flames, as high as you could see. Smoke, soot and smells of wood and burning animals, made it apocalyptic.

So fear from children was to be expected.

But what Henry did not see shocked him, he do no see an adult.

Henry scanned the ravine for an adult.

It took longer than it should have to find him. The Scoutmaster sat off to the side, pressed against the ravine wall as though trying to meld into stone. His hat was gone, his shirt black with soot. His arms wrapped his knees, his eyes stared forward, but there was no recognition when Henry's light landed on him. His jaw hung slightly open, breath shallow. A man unmoored.

"Sir?" Mark tried, stepping closer. "Scoutmaster?"

No reaction.

Henry felt anger rise, hot as the fire itself. He pushed it down — there wasn't time to waste it here. He dropped the duffel, unzipped it with shaking fingers, and pulled out the extra shirts. He crouched in front of the nearest cluster of boys. They shrank back at first, eyes darting as if he were another nightmare conjured by the fire.

"Hey," Henry said softly, forcing gentleness into his smoke-shredded voice. "It's okay. We're here to get you out. You hear me? Out."

No response. Just the same blank, exhausted faces.

Mark knelt beside him, pulled a water bottle from the duffel, and unscrewed it. "Sip," he said, pressing it into the hand of the nearest boy. The child flinched, then raised the bottle to his cracked lips. The sound of swallowing was small but electric. A few of the other scouts stirred, eyes flicking toward the water.

"We need to get them together," Henry muttered. "All of them. If they're scattered like this, they'll panic."

Mark nodded and moved toward the Scoutmaster, crouching low. "Sir, we need you to help. Your boys need—"

But the man's eyes didn't even track.

"Lost," Mark said grimly, returning to Henry. "He's just... gone."

Henry clenched his fists. He wanted to shake the man, to drag him back into the world. But the fire didn't care about intentions, and time was burning as quickly as the trees.

One of the boys finally spoke. His voice was thin, papery. "Tommy..."

Henry leaned close. "What about Tommy?"

The boy licked soot-cracked lips. "He went to... find a way out. Scoutmaster... he wouldn't... he didn't..." The words trailed, eyes filling with tears that didn't fall.

Henry's pulse hammered. A missing boy. Out there in the woods alone.

"When?" he demanded, harsher than he meant. "When did he go?"

The boy flinched. Henry softened his tone. "Hey, hey, it's alright. Just tell me. When?"

"Before... before you came," another boy whispered. "He went... up there." A trembling hand pointed toward the ravine's lip, where smoke rolled down like a river.

Henry swore under his breath. A child — alone — in that inferno.

He turned to Mark, urgency flooding his veins. "Get them together. All of them. Give them water. Wet their shirts. Whatever you have to do to get them ready to move. I'll get Tommy."

Mark's eyes widened. "You can't go alone—"

"I have to," Henry cut him off. "He's out there. Fifty yards, a hundred, whatever it is, I'll find him. If we wait, he's gone."

Mark hesitated, then nodded sharply. "Fine. But I'll hold this group together. Don't you get lost, Henry."

Henry turned to the Scoutmaster, who still hadn't moved. His fury boiled over. "Listen to me," he snapped. "If we stay here, you all die. The ravine will choke with smoke. The fire is closing in from every side. There is no safety here."

The man blinked slowly, lips parting. But no words came.

Henry swore again, grabbed the duffel, and swung it onto his shoulder. He looked once more at the clusters of children — some sipping water now, some just staring at him with hollow eyes.

"I'll be back," he told them. He meant it like a promise, like an oath.

Then he turned, scrambled up the ravine wall, and plunged back into the fire to find the boy.

The fire had a voice.

Not a single sound but a thousand layered, competing voices — roaring, hissing, shrieking as if the entire forest had decided to speak at once. It wasn't like the crackle of a campfire or the clean snap of pine in a hearth. This voice was jagged, animal, alive. It filled every corner of Henry's head, so loud it seemed to come from inside his chest as much as from the burning trees.

He had to force himself to move forward.

The first step into the inferno felt like stepping off a cliff into heat itself. The air rolled at him in waves, hot enough to prickle the skin of his face, to sting the edges of his eyes. He pulled his shirt collar up over his mouth and nose, but the smoke found its way through instantly. Acrid, suffocating. He coughed until he bent double, hands on his knees, lungs convulsing. Ash coated his tongue like bitter sand, and when he spat, the saliva was gray.

"Tommy!" he tried to shout.

The name cracked and vanished into the roar. It was like shouting into the ocean — the fire ate the sound whole. No echo, no return. He could have been alone in another universe.

The ground was treacherous beneath him. Each step sank into soil that had been baked to brittle dust. He put his hand against a trunk for balance and screamed, yanking it back. The bark was blistering hot, splitting open with glowing orange seams. The smell of pitch oozed from the cracks, sharp and chemical, as if the tree itself were bleeding fire. His palm throbbed, skin already bubbling into blisters. He pressed it against his jeans, teeth gritted, but there was no real relief.

The forest was becoming unrecognizable. Shapes warped in the smoke — trees stretched tall and skeletal, their crowns dissolving into flames. Branches snapped overhead and rained down sparks and blackened needles. Each fall was a small explosion. Somewhere nearby, something massive collapsed. The sound began as a groan, then became a shattering crash that made the ground tremble. Henry ducked, heart hammering, ash stinging his scalp.

He stumbled forward, eyes watering. A root caught his boot, sending him crashing down hard on one knee. Pain rattled up through his thigh and into his spine. His breath came ragged. It wasn't breathing anymore — just dragging smoke into lungs that screamed against it. He couldn't tell if there was any oxygen left in this corner of the world.

"Tommy!" he tried again. It came out raw, shredded, almost inaudible.

He thought of the boy's face. Small, freckled, the kind of face that still believed rules mattered because adults said they did. He remembered how Tommy had sat the night before, clutching his scout manual like it was scripture, eyes wide at campfire stories, shivering in the night air but refusing to admit it. Henry had promised himself — had promised Mark — that none of these kids would come to harm under his watch.

Now the boy was gone, somewhere inside this burning labyrinth.

Henry pushed forward again. His throat burned with each breath. His knees shook from the effort of staying upright.

And then he saw it.

At first it was only a shape on the ground. His brain tried to make sense of it, and for a single, hopeful instant he thought it was Tommy. But no — it was a deer. Or what had been a deer. Its body lay twisted against the base of a cedar, legs locked stiff in death. Patches of fur had burned away, skin blackened and cracked. The eyes were open, glassy, reflecting flame.

The smell hit a second later.

It was meat — cooked, but not clean. The scent of rot tangled with the sweetness of charred flesh. His stomach revolted, bile burning the back of his throat. He staggered sideways, one hand to his mouth, gagging. He forced himself to keep moving, eyes fixed ahead, but the image stamped itself inside his skull.

The forest shifted again. A gust of wind funneled the fire sideways, sending a river of smoke pouring down into the ravine. It rolled over Henry like water, blinding him. The world shrank to gray. His eyes burned until tears cut lines through the soot on his cheeks. His head spun. He stumbled, arms out like a blind man, boots dragging through ash.

The dizziness grew. His knees buckled. He went down to one hand — the blistered one — and cried out at the pain. He tried to pull himself back up, but his lungs refused. The smoke pressed down, pressed in. He thought of how quickly a man could die from suffocation. Minutes. Maybe less, in this place.

For one wild instant, he saw his daughters. The younger one in her soccer uniform, hair plastered to her forehead with sweat, grinning as she waved at him from the field. The older one on her bike, wobbling at the end of the driveway, shouting for him to let go of the seat. He thought of the promise he had made to his wife — that this trip would be safe, a week of woods and canoes, no danger greater than a mosquito bite. He thought of failing her.

Then — a sound.

Small. Fragile. Not the voice of fire but something else. A hitching breath. A whimper.

Henry froze, straining to hear.

"Tommy?" he rasped. His throat was raw, the name almost lost.

There was no answer at first. Only the shifting roar. He feared he had imagined it. That the smoke was tricking him.

Then it came again. A cough. Weak. Childlike.

Henry forced himself forward, half-crawling now. His palms sank into ash, his blisters screaming. He coughed, spat, dragged himself another step, then another. The world blurred — shapes, shadows, glowing embers.

And then — there.

A figure. Small, crouched against the length of a fallen log. Arms locked around knees, head buried low. His scout uniform was unrecognizable, khaki smeared black, merit badges hidden under soot. His hair was gray with ash, his face streaked with it. He trembled but didn't move when Henry collapsed to his knees beside him.

"Tommy!" Henry grabbed his shoulder, shaking gently.

The boy lifted his head. His eyes were wide, glassy, lips cracked and bleeding from heat. He looked at Henry as if unsure whether he was real.

"I—I left," Tommy stammered. His voice was shredded, raw. "The Scoutmaster... he froze. He didn't move. I didn't know what to do. I just ran."

Henry's chest clenched. He wanted to tell the boy that it wasn't cowardice. That panic was natural, that he had done the only thing he could. But the fire was too close, too loud, the heat pressing harder every second. This wasn't the time for comfort.

"You're alive," Henry said, voice rough but steady. "That's what matters. Now we go back. Together."

Tommy's hands shot out, clutching Henry's arm with desperate strength. The grip was so fierce it startled Henry — the strength of terror.

The fire cracked nearby, a tree splitting in half. The flames roared as if they had noticed the two of them, dared them to move.

Henry pulled Tommy to his feet. The boy swayed, knees trembling, and Henry caught him, pulling his arm over his own shoulders. The path back was somewhere behind the smoke, hidden, waiting.

The fight to return would be harder than anything they had faced so far.

The fire pressed closer.

Henry braced Tommy against his side, one arm hooked tight around the boy's waist. Tommy's legs were rubber, stumbling with each step, his boots dragging through ash. The boy's weight wasn't much, but in Henry's weakened state it felt like carrying stone.

They couldn't walk upright. The smoke clawed at them, a suffocating wall that thickened with every yard. Henry dropped to one knee, pulling Tommy down with him. "Crawl," he rasped. His voice was shredded, but Tommy nodded, eyes wide with obedience.

They went forward on hands and knees.

The earth was hot beneath Henry's palms. Each press into the ash sent fresh pain searing through his blistered skin. He gritted his teeth and pushed on, dragging Tommy when the boy faltered. The smoke was lower to the ground but not absent; it seeped into their throats, pressed into their nostrils. Henry could feel it clogging his chest, turning every breath into a fight.

A crack split the air. Instinct made him throw himself sideways, pulling Tommy down with him. A tree toppled where they'd just been crawling, its trunk exploding in sparks, flames licking up into the air. The heat was a furnace blast. Henry shielded Tommy with his body until the worst of it passed.

The boy trembled beneath him. "We're gonna die," Tommy whispered, voice small, broken.

Henry forced his eyes to meet his. "Not today," he said. The words scraped his throat raw, but he meant them. "Not while I've got you."

Tommy blinked, ash streaking down his cheeks like tears. He nodded, barely.

They pushed on.

The fire was everywhere now. It had personalities — one moment snarling, the next whispering as it crept along a fallen log. Henry swore it was following them, hunting them like prey. Sparks rained around them, stinging when they landed on skin. His shirt collar had burned through; the fabric scratched his neck, exposing raw flesh to the heat.

He coughed again, harder this time, his whole body shuddering. Black spots burst in his vision. For one terrifying moment he saw his kitchen back home, sunlight across the table, his wife pouring coffee. The hallucination vanished with the next breath, leaving him disoriented.

"Stay with me," Henry muttered to himself, though Tommy heard it too and clung tighter to his arm.

They found a small break — a ditch carved by water long ago. Henry dropped them into it, the cooler air a momentary blessing. He let Tommy lean against the dirt wall. The boy's chest heaved, eyes glassy, but he was alive.

Henry risked a glance upward. The sky was gone. Only smoke and fire and falling ash. The world had narrowed to survival.

A sound cut through: voices.

At first Henry thought it was the fire again, playing tricks. But then he caught it clearly — human shouts, faint but real. He pushed up, clutching Tommy's shoulder. "Hear that?"

Tommy's eyes widened. He nodded frantically.

"That's them. The others."

He hauled Tommy up again. Together they crawled out of the ditch and pressed forward, angling toward the sound. Each yard felt longer than the last. Henry's legs shook, his lungs burned. Tommy stumbled twice, nearly falling, but Henry dragged him back up.

A shape emerged through the haze — a figure waving. Then another. The silhouettes of boys, clustered together. And there, tall and steady, Mark's voice cutting across the roar: "This way! Hurry!"

Relief slammed into Henry so hard his knees buckled. They had made it back. Not safe yet — not out of the fire — but back to the group, back to the living.

He shoved Tommy ahead of him, every last scrap of strength bent on pushing the boy toward safety.

Behind them, a tree snapped, flames surging high as if furious at their escape.

Chapter 14

The Escape

For a long moment, the ravine held its breath.

Tommy stood in the circle of boys like a figure returned from the dead. His small chest heaved, soot streaked his cheeks, his eyes were wild but alive. The other scouts reached for him hesitantly, as if afraid he might vanish again into smoke. One boy touched his sleeve, another brushed his shoulder, and then suddenly the circle collapsed inward. They wrapped him up in their arms, clumsy and desperate, half-hugging, half-grabbing as if to anchor him to the earth.

The sound that rose was the first real sound Henry had heard from them all night — the broken, stuttering chorus of children crying. Not the eerie mimicry of trees, not the creak of trunks splitting, but real tears. Relief and fear mingled, sobs hiccupped through soot-choked throats.

Henry sagged onto his knees. His lamp tilted downward, beam spilling across blackened rock. His lungs burned as if he'd inhaled fire itself. Sweat poured down his face, soaking the shirt tied across his mouth until it clung like glue. He tried to swallow but his throat was too raw.

A hand gripped his shoulder, grounding him. Mark crouched beside him, his own face streaked and grim but steady. "You did it," he said softly, voice barely audible over the fire's roar. "You found him."

Henry closed his eyes. He wanted to answer, but words failed. His body was trembling, not from fear but from the sheer drain of it all — the climb, the search, the crushing relief of success. He thought of his kids, their small hands in his, and the image blurred with Tommy's soot-streaked face. A child saved. A child brought back.

He let out a sound that was half-sob, half-laugh. It scared him, the rawness of it, but he didn't stop. For once in his life, he hadn't failed.

Mark squeezed his shoulder. "Don't fall apart yet. We're not out."

Henry nodded, forcing himself upright. His legs felt like wet rope. He dragged in another breath, the smoke stabbing his chest like knives, and blinked his eyes clear.

The boys were calmer now, though tears still streaked through their soot masks. They clung to Tommy as if he were a talisman. One of the younger ones whispered, "I thought he was gone." Another answered, "We're all gone if we stay."

Henry heard it. He let it fuel him.

He turned to the Scoutmaster. The man hadn't moved from his place against the wall. His eyes flicked once toward Tommy, then back to the ground. No relief, no command, nothing. Just emptiness.

"Sir," Henry said, voice hoarse but sharp. "You see? They can't stay here. None of us can."

The Scoutmaster's lips parted, a dry crackle of sound emerging. "It's... safer here. The fire will pass."

Henry's anger flared. "It won't pass. It's closing in. You can feel it, can't you? The heat's worse every minute. This ravine will fill with smoke, and then it's a coffin."

The man's eyes slid away, unfocused.

Henry wanted to scream, but Mark's hand tightened on his arm. "Forget him," Mark muttered. "We've got the kids. He'll follow when he sees we mean it."

Henry swallowed hard, forced his fury into focus. He turned back to the boys. They were watching him now — not the Scoutmaster. Him. Their eyes were wide and searching, looking for a signal, for direction, for the thing the adult who had sworn to protect them could no longer give.

He dropped the duffel and pulled it open. "Listen up," he rasped, loud enough for the whole ravine to hear. His voice cracked, but it carried. "We're getting out. One by one, all of you. No one stays. You hear me?"

Some of the boys nodded hesitantly. Others just stared.

Henry pulled out the spare shirts, dunked them into a pool of water that had collected in the ravine's base, and wrung them out. He pressed one into Tommy's hands. "Hold it over your mouth. Like this. Breathe through it. It'll help."

The boy obeyed instantly. Seeing him, a few others stirred and reached for cloth too. Henry passed them out, dipping and wringing, shoving them gently into trembling hands. The boys pressed them to their faces, tentative at first, then firmer as they realized they could breathe easier.

Mark worked alongside him, uncapping water bottles, pouring small sips into waiting mouths. "Not too much at once," he said, voice firm but kind. "Sip, then pass. Everyone gets some."

Slowly, something shifted in the ravine. The paralyzed stillness cracked. The boys straightened, some wiping their eyes, others clutching their damp cloths like shields. Hope was fragile, but it was here, alive among them now.

Henry felt it, like oxygen rushing back into a suffocated lung.

He crouched low so his lamp beam caught their eyes. "You're scouts," he said. "You've trained for hard things. This is the hardest you'll ever face. But you're not alone. We're with you. And together, we walk out. Step by step. Understand?"

A few nodded. One boy whispered, "Together."

Henry nodded back, throat tightening. Together.

He sat back on his heels, breath shuddering. Saving Tommy had done more than bring one boy home — it had broken the spell of fear that had frozen them all. It had reminded them that escape was possible, that survival was worth trying for.

For Henry, it was more than that. He thought of every time in his life he had let someone down, every time he'd chosen retreat over fight. Tonight, he had gone out into hell itself and returned with a boy alive. That truth burned brighter than the fire.

He looked at Mark. His friend's eyes were weary, rimmed red from smoke, but steady. Mark gave a small nod, as if to say: We've got them now. We can do this.

Henry squared his shoulders, the duffel heavy against his side. "Alright," he said, louder now. "Drink. Rest. But just for a minute. Then we move. The fire's coming, and we won't wait for it."

The boys clutched their cloths and bottles, glancing at each other, at Henry, at Tommy. Fear still lingered, but it was different now — not paralyzing, but sharpened into readiness.

Henry saw it and allowed himself one small, fierce thought: We're going to make it.

For a minute that seemed stretched taut as wire, the ravine held two plans at once: the Scoutmaster's stillness and Henry's movement. The boys hovered between them the way sparks hover before they either catch or die.

Henry refused to let the moment drift back to paralysis. He knelt so his lamp made a small moon in the soot and spoke to the boys, not to the man against the wall.

"Count off," he rasped. "Left to right. Loud enough for me and Mark to hear."

A beat, then a squeaky "One," from a boy with a red neckerchief gone black. "Two," from a taller kid with freckles masked beneath ash. "Three... four..." The numbers tumbled forward, each one a small flag planted. Counting gave them a task. Counting made them visible.

"Thirteen," the last boy finished, voice a thread.

"Fourteen," Tommy added, lifting his hand. He glanced at Henry, as if asking permission to exist. Henry nodded and pressed his palm to the boy's shoulder for one brief second.

"Fourteen," Henry repeated. "Fourteen boys, one Scoutmaster, two of us. Seventeen souls out. Nobody stays."

The man against the wall lifted his head, as if waking. "The protocol," he said thickly. "If trapped—find shelter, wait for the fire to pass." He gestured vaguely to the ravine. "This shelter."

Henry kept his eyes on the boys. "Protocols assume oxygen and time. We don't have either."

The Scoutmaster's jaw set. "Panic kills more than flame. We wait."

"Waiting's a choice too," Henry said, the anger in him honed to something surgical. "It's choosing to die slow instead of trying to live hard."

He didn't shout. He didn't need to. The boys were listening with the focus of prey that has decided it wants to be something else.

Mark stepped between Henry and the Scoutmaster, voice even, palms up. "Sir, we respect you. We do. But let us take them. Come with us. If we're wrong, you can tell us so on the other side. If you're wrong, you'll never say anything to anyone again."

Something in that practical cruelty landed. The Scoutmaster's eyes slid toward Tommy, then down to the hands of the smallest boy, hands that were shaking hard enough to rattle his water bottle. He didn't answer, but he didn't argue again either. That was enough.

Henry tore open the duffel wider. "Here's the plan," he said. "Buddy system. Choose a partner and stick like glue. Bigger kid with smaller kid. If your buddy falls, you don't drag him—you yell for me or Mark. Everyone gets a wet cloth. Everyone sips water now, not later. You'll want to gulp. Don't. Sips."

"We also tie each group with a rope, and each group to each other. We walk in a line two by two. Mark, the scoutmaster and myself, will walk in between and around as needed."

They moved, and the ravine moved with them. Boys paired off, some naturally—friends that slid together without looking—others guided by Mark's palm on a shoulder, a gentle push. Henry dipped shirts in the shallow pool that glistened like a miracle, wrung them out with hands that trembled and pressed them into small hands. He showed them how to hold the cloth tight to nose and mouth. He looked each boy in the eyes, one by one, and told him a simple truth that could double as a command. "You can do this." Then he said it again: "You can do this."

He found the smallest boy—nine, maybe ten, the kind of ten that still believed pocket knives were magic—and slung the duffel across his chest to free his arms. "You're with me," Henry said. "Hold on to my belt. If I stop, you stop; if I walk, you walk."

"Okay," the boy whispered. "My name is Eli."

"Good. I'm Henry." He felt absurdly grateful to hear a name that wasn't a number.

Mark did a headcount, finger moving as if ticking beads. "Fourteen boys," he said, and then, looking at the man against the wall, "and one very needed Scoutmaster."

The Scoutmaster's lips twitched. A nod, almost imperceptible. His hands flexed as if they'd been asleep and were remembering their job. He rose. It wasn't graceful. It didn't need to be.

Henry turned his lamp toward the ravine lip. Smoke rolled down it in waves like a sluggish river reversing course. The fire above sounded closer than it had ten minutes ago, closer than breath. He mapped the way in his head, the way back to the canoe that was blocked, the way around the blowdown that had sealed the direct route.

"Not up there," he said, pointing to the lip where they'd entered. "Too hot now. We take the right fork, follow the floor of the ravine as it curves. There's a place where the walls drop to scrub. We punch through there. It adds distance, buys air."

"You sure?" Mark asked.

"No," Henry said, blunt. "But it's the best bad route we've got."

He put Eli's hand on his belt and tightened his own grip on the boy's wrist until they both felt it as a promise. "Line up," he told the others. "Two by two behind us. Mark, you're rear guard. Scoutmaster, you're midline. You hold the middle you were supposed to hold all along."

The man absorbed the sentence, a wince crossing his face. "Yes," he said. A single word, soft as ash.

Henry set them moving.

The first steps seemed ceremonial, too quiet for the world they stepped toward. The ravine's sandy floor muffled their footfalls, cloth-masked breaths a hiss that synchronized into a ragged rhythm. Henry counted without meaning to—five steps, ten, fifteen—small numbers that kept bigger ones at bay. He made the boys count, too, in pairs, a low murmur under the roar.

"One... two... three..." Not for tallying distance but for replacing panic with pattern.

They climbed the first slope as a creature with many legs. Henry went palm to stone, pulling himself up and hauling Eli behind. Hands reached down from above—Tommy's among them—to grab Eli's forearms and boost. "Good," Henry said. "Yes." He didn't save praise for the end; he spent it like water, small sips that wet dry mouths.

At the lip the heat hit them like a wall. The air wavered in fronts, invisible waves that pressed and then released, pressed and released. Henry felt the old, humiliating awareness of his own weight flare and nearly choke him. His thighs were slabs of pain. But his body was a tool tonight, not a verdict. Tools get used. Tools serve.

A tree to their left moaned—a living thing breaking—then fell somewhere beyond sight, sending a rush of hot wind that pushed their line sideways. The boys swayed; somebody squeaked; someone else said "it's okay, it's okay," too fast. Henry shot his hand back, caught the slack in the line, pulled them all metaphorically straight. "Eyes on my back," he barked, then modified his tone. "Eyes here. That's it."

They threaded between two blackened trunks into a corridor of less fire. Henry chose it not because it looked safe but because it looked less immediately fatal. He had, over the years, become adept at that choice: not good vs. bad, but less-bad vs. worst. It had never felt noble. Tonight it did.

The smell changed again, and Henry's stomach rolled. The rank sweetness of burned fur, the iron tang of blood, the faint ammonia of fear. The boys inhaled through their wet cloths and made small animal sounds that made Henry want to put his hands over their ears. He talked instead. "Through," he said. "Through, through." He didn't tell them what they were smelling. You don't name every thing a child doesn't need to carry.

They met fire. Not a wall, not a towering column—the kind that makes the pictures on the news—but a litter of low flame chewing the ground. It licked at punky wood and curled the edges of ferns to black fists. The path went right through it, the way a city sidewalk sometimes runs straight through a puddle too wide to step around.

Henry turned to Mark and lifted a brow. Mark's answer was a tight grin that said, we're idiots, and go. Henry stamped a toe into the edge of flame. It guttered, reared up again. He grabbed a branch with his free hand and used it like a broom, sweeping embers sideways into a moist patch where the fire sulked and died. The boys didn't gasp; they watched, intent, as if the lesson were about sweeping rather than survival.

They stepped quick. Flames licked at pants cuffs and found nothing to love; the damp cloths made them stubbornly unappetizing. Henry judged each boy's jump, ready to snag a collar if a foot slowed. Eli cleared it barely. Henry hauled him the last inch and murmured praise that was for both of them.

The ravine forked again. Left was bright as a forge. Right was dimmer, a sullen orange with honest darkness beyond it. Henry took right and felt his body unclench one notch. He let himself think, just briefly, of cold things: of ice on the garage floor, of the metallic chill of a winter morning. The thought steadied his legs more than any prayer.

A cry cut across the line—not terror, pain. "Ow—my ankle!" The word ankle turned the line in a ripple. Henry pivoted. A boy midline—Caleb, he thought, the freckled one—was down on one knee, face contorted. The Scoutmaster stood over him, hands hovering uselessly, as if afraid to touch.

"Weight off it," Henry said, getting there moment-fast. He pressed two fingers along the boy's shin, feeling for wrong shapes. Nothing grotesque. Swollen already. A sprain, not a break, if luck was finally rationing them its crumbs. He stripped a shirt from the duffel, tore it into a long strip, and bound the ankle hard enough to make Caleb hiss.

"You're gonna ride," Henry told him. He looked up. "Dylan," he said to a broad-shouldered teen who'd been steady as a fencepost all night, "can you piggyback him forty yards at a time?"

Dylan's eyes flashed—fear, then pride. "Yes, sir."

"Good. You tell me when you need a swap. Mark, back him if he wobbles."

The Scoutmaster coughed. "I can—" he began.

Henry cut him a small piece of dignity. "Take rear of pair three. Keep their spacing clean."

The man nodded, grateful for the assignment. Lines of command were reweaving in ways that mattered.

They moved again. The line had rhythm now. When Dylan grunted, another boy stepped in under Caleb's weight for a stretch, the way teamwork is supposed to work when it's not ceremonial but oxygen. The boys began to murmur to each other, little practical phrases—"your cloth slipped," "hold my sleeve," "step there"—and those phrases were a choir Henry hadn't realized he needed.

They reached the place Henry had gambled on: the ravine's right wall slumped into a tangle of scrub and half-burnt saplings. Beyond it, in the smoke, the terrain sagged toward the lake—a faint gradient the body could feel even when the eye couldn't. He put his shoulder to a sapling and shoved until it snapped. Mark took the next. The boys passed the pieces back, building a narrow, stomped corridor through the snagged brush. It scratched hands, snagged on belts, tried to pull them backward. They went forward anyway.

"Left foot, right foot," Henry said. "Again." He didn't know if he was talking to himself or to Eli or to the entire line. It didn't matter.

Heat rose in a long sigh—the fire behind them inhaling for a harder push. The sound made Henry's skin try to climb off his muscles. He did not speed up. Panic is the friend of poor footing. He set a pace a child could manage and kept it steady. If the fire wanted them, it would have to do more than roar.

They broke through the scrub into a stand of birch whose paper bark peeled in long, curling tongues. The light changed. It was still orange, still wrong, but there was more of it and, under it, a suggestion of blue-gray darkness—the lake's promise. The air tasted wetter. Henry's whole chest loosened.

A deer trail stitched the birches together, a narrow seam where hooves had made choices. Henry took it. The ground here was ash on loam rather than ash on rock; it gave and held them, forgiving clumsy feet. Twice a boy slipped and twice hands shot out and made a net.

Above, a new sound wrote itself over the roar: the slap of small waves on charred reeds. Henry almost cried. He swallowed hard instead and lifted his arm. "Hear it?" he called, risking volume. "That's your prize. That's your way."

The boys listened and then, astonishingly, some of them smiled. Even behind cloths, the smiles changed their eyes. Tommy reached for another boy's hand and squeezed. Eli tugged Henry's belt, as if to say, there, you did hear it, right?

A final obstacle waited: another fallen trunk lay canted across the deer trail, its root ball a black disc taller than Henry. This one he couldn't sweep aside like embers. He put his hands on the bark. It flaked and burned his palms. He didn't pull away. He walked his fingers along it, found a notch where the trunk had split. He planted his foot on a knob of wood and heaved himself up. It was graceless. It worked.

"Sit on top," he told each boy. "Slide down the back. Don't jump. It's ash over holes—you jump, you vanish." He posted himself at the far side, one arm under each set of armpits as they slid, turning their momentum into controlled descent. Mark did the same on the near side, boosting them to the top, low-voiced, patient. The Scoutmaster steadied the midline like a man remembering the shape of purpose.

Dylan came last with Caleb clamped to his back. For a second Dylan's foot slipped and the line collectively inhaled. Mark's hand shot to Dylan's belt; Henry's forearms locked under Caleb's thighs; for a weird suspended heartbeat they existed as an awkward, smoking sculpture of trust. Then gravity found sense and they were down together. Dylan laughed once, too loud, then clamped his jaw shut. "Sorry," he whispered to Caleb, who shook his head and said, "Do it again," and they both grinned behind their cloths like the children they were.

Past the trunk, the birches thinned. The air cooled further, carried over the water. The world began to smell like lake—mud and fish and something green—shoving out the worst of the burned-sweet stench. Henry felt that scent in his spine. It meant a boat. It meant the pontoon they'd shoved up onto the bank and the canoe they'd dragged high like a talisman. It meant leaving.

The shoreline appeared first as negative space—a band of darkness where flame had nothing to grip. Then as a scatter of shapes: the aluminum gleam of the pontoon's rail, pitted with heat; the canoe's blue hull streaked with soot; the reeds now just lines of wet wire. The lake itself lay beyond, flexing and breathing, oblivious to fire except where wind pressed light upon it.

Henry stopped the line ten paces shy of open ground. "Listen," he said, making eye contact down the chain until he felt the attention return like current. "We're not safe yet. We've got one canoe and seventeen of us. We don't overload. We don't panic. We ferry."

Henry divided by weight and size. It felt obscene to make the choice—this one now, that one wait—but needs had to be sorted.

Now the hard part, get off the island.

Chapter 15

Ferry Time

Mark, Henry and the now fully awake Scoutmaster stood by the canoe, near the water's edge, looking at the rocky outcrop island, where Mark and Henry made camp.

The good news was it was only 300 yards, a short 300 yards, and no real trees for the fire to jump to.

"I will take the first load of two boys across with the scout master," said Mark. "You stay here and keep them calm. Don't worry, we will both get our chance to move them, but for now save your strength and let's get them across."

Seventeen people in all needed to get off the island; at two kids per load, it seemed an impossible task—but if worse comes to worst they swim for it.

Seven trips back and forth, but at 15 times 300 yards in the wind and rain.. and the whitecaps It seemed an impossible task.

Behind them Henry heard the fire still consuming everything in its path. The kids, nervous but resolute, looked like windmills as they rotated between looking at the water and the fire fully encircling the island, coming closer by the minute.

The shoreline hissed like a cast-iron pan. Heat came at them in pulses, invisible waves that turned breath into work. The canoe's blue hull, streaked with soot, looked almost absurdly delicate—like a toy set in front of a blast furnace. But it floated, and it obeyed physics, and physics still worked even when the world felt like it was coming apart.

Henry crouched and ran a hand along the canoe, wiping off a drift of ash. His fingers came up black. He rubbed them against his pants, then met the Scoutmaster's eyes.

"You with us?" Henry asked.

The man nodded once. Something had come back into his face in the last ten minutes—a grim awareness, a willingness to do the next right thing. His voice, when it returned, was low. "I'll go with the first pair. Help keep them down. Keep them calm."

Henry scanned the boys. Fourteen faces—no, not just faces, names—watched him from the dim mouth of the ravine: Tommy, Eli, Caleb with the bound ankle, Dylan who'd carried him; a cluster of smaller ones who hadn't yet learned how to hide fear behind a joke. Cloths were pressed to mouths, damp and blessed. Behind them, the ravine walls funneled smoke up and away for the moment. That moment was a gift with a mean expiration date.

"We're going to do this like a drill," Henry said, pitching his voice so it carried but didn't carry panic. "Two at a time in the canoe with Mark and the Scoutmaster. When they shove off, nobody follows, nobody leans, nobody waves. You keep low and you listen. When they get to the rock, they'll unload and come back for the next two. We'll rotate. Sip water now, not later. If your throat feels raw, you're doing it right."

The boys nodded—more a tremor than a gesture, but it was assent.

Mark knelt at the bow and patted the thwart. "First two," he said. "You and you. Knees on the pad, hands on the gunwale, heads down when I say."

Two boys moved, legs stiff with fear and smoke. The Scoutmaster climbed in last, setting himself midships with his arms ready, old habit settling on him like a jacket he'd finally shrugged back into. Henry steadied the canoe as Mark pushed off.

The lake took the weight. Water lapped soot from the hull, tucking the boat into its own clean logic. Mark's first strokes were deep and deliberate; the canoe translated those strokes into forward motion as if relieved to be doing the one thing that made sense. The Scoutmaster kept a palm on each boy's shoulder, eyes on Henry until distance turned his gaze to a dark bead in the glow.

Henry exhaled. He turned back to the line of boys and forced his hands not to shake as he uncapped a bottle. "Sip," he said, passing it to Eli. "Then pass. Small sips." Eli obeyed, eyes never leaving the canoe's white wake.

Behind them, the island breathed smoke. It sounded like a furnace door left open, like someone larger than the night was taking long, hot breaths. Sparks skittered over the shallows and died.

Henry spoke without thinking, letting the cadence of logistics steady him. "Second pair, be ready—but not ready like rushing. Ready like waiting right here until I tell you to move."

Tommy, who had already won and lost the night and found himself returned to it, stood at the front of the line, damp cloth in place, eyes glittering in the light of their headlamps. "Three hundred yards?" he asked, as if measuring a sprint he might one day brag about.

"On a calm day, five minutes," Henry said. "Tonight? As long as it takes."

"How many trips?" another boy asked.

"Fifteen, if we count back and forth" Henry answered. "Two by two until it's done."

"That's a lot," the boy said.

"Better than zero," Henry replied, and the joke—if it was one—landed as a small, honest comfort. Someone snorted. Someone else unclenched their hands.

Henry listened for the first docking. He'd camped on that rock for two nights—he knew its sounds: the hollow clonk of aluminum against stone, the rasp of a hull sliding up. But tonight with the wind, rain and fire. Henry could not hear anything.

Seeing them come in towards shore, Henry looked at his watch 20 minutes.

Henry was shocked, what he calculated at 10 minute trip was more than double.

The fire closing in, the ash pouring down, Henry was not sure they had time.

"Next two," Henry said.

He steadied the canoe when it nosed the soot-slick stones again. Mark's face was a mask: black with ash, striped where sweat had carved channels. They said nothing; there was nothing to say that would add oxygen to the air. Mark reset two fresh bodies into the canoe like fragile cargo, the Scoutmaster boarded, and they slid out again.

The rhythm took hold. Water, rock, signal, water. Henry kept the waiting small—a cluster of boys beneath the ravine lip, bowed under the press of heat, quiet with focused fear. He moved among them, checking cloths, handing out the last of their water in half-mouthfuls, touching a shoulder here, a sleeve there. He was not a man who touched people much; tonight his hands had learned a new language.

On the third return, Mark's arms looked heavier. He was fast and good in a boat—had been since high school, when he'd tried out for everything and stuck with nothing except the feel of a paddle—but the fire stole air in a way that made even excellence inefficient. He slid up, reset, launched. Henry began counting not in trips but in children removed from the problem. Four safe.

Six. Eight. Each number hung weightless for a second, then sank into his chest and warmed him.

By the time the third pair reached the rock, the fire on the main island's windward side had brightened to a harsh, living white. Heat licked their ankles from twenty feet away. The damp cloths grew hot to the touch. The boys didn't complain. They pressed them harder to their faces and watched the canoe like it was a spell someone had to get exactly right for it to keep working.

The Scoutmaster, in the canoe on every run, found his footing in the job. He hunched low, murmuring instructions to small ears, planting wide hands gently on shaking backs when cross-chop shivered through the hull. He looked older each time the canoe came back—older and steadier. The shame in his eyes had found an outlet called work.

Henry rotated the next two into place and, as he did, lifted his eyes past their heads to the far left of the water. There, the rocky outcrop rose stubborn and bald, its pines stunted, its back cove shallow but protected. Their little camp—two bedrolls, a coffee pot they'd meant to use again at dawn—waited there like the memory of a normal day he could not entirely remember how to access. He pictured the boys huddled on that rock now, the Scoutmaster counting, his own bedroll empty. He pictured the next trips, and the next.

When Mark beached on the third return and bent for breath, Henry pressed a bottle into his hand. "Sip," he said, smiling weakly at the inversion.

Mark drank, swilled, spat black. "Fourth run," he said. "You keep them ready. I'm not stopping. The wind's going to turn and I don't want to be here when it does."

He pushed off before Henry could answer, a man against a clock only he could hear ticking.

The fourth run started clean and stayed clean for fifty yards. Then Mark's head turned—not the flick of a wary paddler checking his course, but a full-bodied twist like he'd heard his name. He didn't stop paddling. He didn't even slow. He shouted across water in a voice like gravel.

"HEY! BACK COVE! WE NEED HANDS! GUIDES! HELP!"

Henry peered through heat ripples and smoke. Beyond the outcrop's shoulder, a second set of lights jittered low to the water—phone torches bobbing like will-o'-the-wisps. Multiple canoes into the lee, outboards sputtering, and six shadows scrambled over rock. Someone held a camera high above his head as if it were a fragile heirloom that must be kept dry. Another shouldered a coil of rope like a stagehand arriving late to a show.

Upon return, Mark told Henry, he thought he saw guides dropping people off at the rocky island.

Henry prayed they would return and head towards them to get the children.

But Henry could see Mark was done. His arms shook, uncontrollably. Mark's eyes still had determination, but his body none.

Henry shouted to Mark, to get out. Mark at first refused, but he knew he was spent. Reluctantly he climbed out of the canoe, and Henry took his place as the next two kids climbed in.

"Next two," he said, and the phrase was a prayer.

Between Henry's fresh strength, they made to the rocky outcrop in record time.

Eight kids safe, now, eight kids, just three more trips and it was over.

Henry was feeling good.

On the back side of the rocky outcrop, Henry saw the guides dropping off the tik-tok crew and heading towards the engulfed island.

"Thank God." Henry said quietly.

Henry now invigorated, push his paddle deep into the water, but the wind and waves made it turn.

The canoe now fully sideways against the waves, began to tip.

Henry's chest tightened. Don't panic. He tried to match the scoutmaster's tempo — dip, pull, lift, reset. But the lake fought back with its own rhythm, and Henry was a beat behind, always behind.

A swell lifted the bow high, then slammed it down with a crash that sent water splashing into the hull.

"Hold steady!" the scoutmaster shouted. His own paddle dug deep, keeping the bow pointed forward. "Breathe, Henry! Stay with me!"

Henry jammed his paddle back into the water, but his arms felt like lead. His shoulders screamed. His lungs burned from smoke and effort. Panic prickled hot in his chest.

Another swell rose, higher this time. The canoe tilted, teetered, then righted itself. Henry gasped, but his paddle caught only air. He overcorrected, plunged too hard, and the canoe lurched.

The next wave hit broadside.

The canoe bucked. Henry felt his stomach drop, the world tilting under him. His paddle skidded out of his grip, clattering into the bottom of the canoe. He lunged for it — and that was the mistake.

The boat tipped. His balance went.

Then the lake swallowed him.

The cold was an electric shock, slamming his chest, stealing his breath. The world became bubbles and darkness, the roar of water in his ears. Panic exploded. He flailed, arms thrashing, legs kicking blindly. The lifejacket hauled him up, but his poncho tangled, dragging, twisting around his arms like a net.

He surfaced choking, eyes wild, gulping water with each gasp. The canoe loomed a few feet away.

"Henry! Float!"

Henry coughed, sputtered, kicked uselessly. The poncho clung like seaweed, dragging him sideways. Every breath came laced with water. His mind shrieked: I'm drowning. I'm drowning.

Then a shape above him. the scoutmaster, cutting clean, his strokes purposeful. He reached Henry in seconds, grabbed him by the straps of his lifejacket. "Stop fighting!" he barked. "I've got you!"

Henry clawed at the man's arm anyway, desperate, terrified. The scoutmaster shook him hard, eyes blazing even through the spray. "Henry! Stop! Let me do it!"

Something in the command broke through. Henry sagged, gasping, coughing, barely able to keep his head above water. The scoutmaster rolled onto his back, hauling Henry against him, kicking powerfully toward the rocky outcrop.

The boys on the island stared at him, terrified and silent.

Through the his haze, he thought he heard voices — faint, jeering. He lifted his head weakly, blinking water from his eyes.

Phones held high.

Filming.

Henry collapsed onto the wet granite like a rag doll tossed ashore. His limbs trembled uncontrollably, his breath came in hacking coughs, and his poncho clung to him like seaweed. Each exhale sounded ragged, wheezy, as though his chest had forgotten how to work.

Henry laid there for who knows how long, heart racing, water spitting up his face flush.

He felt himself shut off, no real reason, exhaustion and relief knowing the guides will get the rest of them off the burning island.

He laid long enough for Mark to crouched beside him, steady hands on Henry's shoulders. "Easy," he murmured, pulling the hood back from Henry's face. "Breathe slow. You're alright."

Henry wanted to argue, to spit out that he wasn't alright, that nothing about choking on lake water and being dragged like deadweight was alright. But his lungs rebelled, convulsing in another coughing fit that left him gasping.

Looking up, he clearly saw them now.

They were filming.

Filming him.

Henry's gut turned. He pushed himself up on one elbow, chest aching. "They're—" His voice cracked, useless. He coughed, tried again. "They're filming us."

Mark's eyes flicked across the water. His jaw tightened, but his voice remained calm. "Ignore them. Doesn't matter right now."

"It matters," Henry rasped, humiliation boiling in his chest. "They saw—saw me—" Another cough wracked him, cutting the words to pieces.

Mark pressed him gently back down. "You're out for now. Save your strength. Everyone is recused now, we are all safe here."

The shoreline was chaos: coughing boys huddled under wet ponchos, smoke curling above the tree line, the lake's endless chop battering the rocks. And through it all, Henry sat useless, his breath ragged, his body shivering with both cold and humiliation.

Relief rippled through the group like a tide. A few boys began to cry — quiet, shuddering sobs released now that the danger was behind them. Others clung to each other in silence.

Henry lay back on the stone, rain tapping his face, and felt his own chest loosen. Alive. They were alive. The fire could have swallowed them all, but it hadn't. Not today.

Yet the relief was sour. The TikTok crew still filmed, their laughter faint but relentless. Henry pictured tomorrow: his flailing body looped on strangers' screens, his humiliation captioned with hashtags. The world wouldn't see the rescue, the courage of the scoutmaster or the grit of Mark. They'd see him. Drowning. Again.

Mark dropped beside him, sweat and rain streaming down his face. He clapped Henry's shoulder once, solid and grounding. "They're safe. That's what matters."

Henry shut his eyes, shame and gratitude warring inside him.

Safe. Yes.

But at what cost?

His pride?

His dignity?

The boys gathered close under ponchos, the scoutmaster checking each for burns, cuts, smoke inhalation. He moved like a man running on fumes, but he never wavered. His whistle still hung around his neck, bright against the soot on his shirt.

Another gust carried the smell of resin and ash. Henry turned his head. Across the channel, the island was gone, consumed. The two torch-pines had collapsed into glowing skeletons, sparks still leaping skyward. The fire had claimed the path completely, turning it into a ribbon of flame.

Henry shivered. If they'd waited another twenty minutes, the boys would have been trapped.

Burned alive.

He closed his eyes again, the image of the TikTok crew burned into the dark behind his eyelids. Their phones raised, their laughter cutting. He wondered how many people would watch. How many would laugh. How many would scroll past without ever knowing the whole story.

When he opened his eyes, Mark was still beside him, calm as ever. The scoutmaster was still moving down the line of boys.

The fire was still roaring, but the boys were safe.

Henry drew a shaky breath. Maybe that's enough.

But in the pit of his gut, he knew it wasn't.

Chapter 16

No Storm No Peace

When the storm finally passed, it didn't leave triumph in its wake. It left silence.

The rain tapered to a mist, thin and uneven, dripping from branches in tired rivulets. The sky cracked open just enough to show streaks of bruised purple and fading gray, the clouds rolling east. Wind, once a scream, had dwindled into ragged breaths. The lake heaved with long, rolling swells, but even they seemed exhausted, each wave slapping the rock with a sound that was more weary than violent.

Henry sat on the granite outcrop with the Scouts clustered around him. Wet ponchos clung to narrow shoulders, bandanas still tied over mouths though the smoke made them cough anyway. Their neon pack covers, so bright hours earlier, now hung limp, streaked with soot, ash stuck to them in black flecks. The boys huddled together for warmth, knees pulled tight to chests, whispering only in small spurts before silence reclaimed them.

Mark crouched by the canoe, looping the last of the ropes around a jagged spur of rock. His movements were methodical, steady as always. The scoutmaster moved along the line of boys, checking one by one, his voice hoarse but firm: "You alright? You breathing okay? Any burns? Stay low, stay calm." Each boy nodded, though some eyes welled with tears, others stared blankly into the distance. Trauma had different faces, Henry realized.

Across the channel, their former island was gone. Not literally — the shape was still there, the slope, the ravine — but the forest itself had been consumed. From the shoreline to the ridge, the entire expanse was fire. Trees stood like black candles, crowns aflame, trunks glowing with fissures of orange heat. Where the ravine mouth had been, a rolling furnace now howled, fire leaping upward in curtains. Sparks rose in swirling columns, joining the thinning clouds.

Around them other islands were starting to burn, to catch from the dry season, and trees were on fire.

The sight hit Henry harder than the storm had. He stared, his throat tight, his chest hollow. That was where the boys had been — minutes, maybe half an hour ago. If they'd waited, even just a little longer... He shook the thought off before it finished.

One of the Scouts, the smallest, whimpered and buried his face in his buddy's arm. The buddy patted him stiffly, eyes locked on the inferno. "It's like the whole forest turned to gasoline," he whispered.

Henry swallowed hard. He wanted to say something, anything comforting. Instead he rasped, "You're safe here." The words sounded fragile, paper-thin against the roar of fire.

The scoutmaster straightened, his face streaked with soot, his whistle dangling like a badge of survival. He glanced at Mark, then at Henry. His eyes lingered on Henry a second too long — not accusing, not grateful, just measuring. Henry looked away, heat burning his cheeks that had nothing to do with the fire across the water.

Mark walked over, crouched beside him. "How's your chest?"

Henry coughed once, winced, and waved him off. "Still breathing."

"Good enough," Mark said. He didn't press, didn't coddle. Just clapped Henry's shoulder once, solid.

Henry appreciated that — and hated it. He didn't want steady reassurance. He wanted to erase the memory of flailing in the lake, of the scoutmaster's arms hauling him up like a child. He wanted to be invisible. But here he was, surrounded by boys who had seen every humiliating second.

The fire cracked across the bay. Another tree collapsed with a roar, sparks shooting skyward. The smallest boy whimpered again. Henry looked at him, felt an ache twist through his gut.

"You kept together," Henry said hoarsely. The words tumbled out before he thought them through. "Back there. In the ravine. That wasn't easy."

The boy peeked at him, eyes watery. "I thought we were gonna die."

Henry's throat closed. "So did I," he admitted quietly. "But you didn't. That's what matters."

The boy blinked, then leaned harder into his buddy.

Henry stared at the fire again. The air tasted like smoke and resin, sharp enough to sting his tongue. His lungs ached. His arms still trembled. But beneath the shame, a strange sensation gnawed at him. He felt... alive. Wrecked, useless, humiliated — but alive in a way his years at home, hunched at a desk or scrolling rejection emails, had never given him.

He hated that realization. Hated it because it meant the wilderness had given him something he couldn't deny, even while it stripped him of pride.

Mark stood, scanning the lake's horizon. "Storm's cleared enough, and the guides called in a rescue. They will be here in no time."

As if in answer, a faint hum floated through the thinning air. Low at first, then growing. The boys looked up, startled. One pointed skyward. "Plane?"

Henry listened. The hum deepened, pulsing, steady. A chopper, maybe two. He squinted into the fading clouds. Nothing yet, but the sound was unmistakable. Help was on its way.

The boys stirred, whispering, some relief cracking through the silence.

Henry's gut twisted. Rescue meant safety, yes. But it also meant witnesses. More eyes. More stories. And with the TikTok crew still across the water, their phones glowing like hungry eyes, he knew what version of the story would spread first. Not the fire. Not the rescue. Him. Falling.

Mark seemed to read his thoughts. He crouched again, voice low. "Don't stew on it. You kept moving. That's enough."

Henry shook his head bitterly. "They'll remember me drowning."

"Better drowning and hauled out than burned alive," Mark said simply.

Henry barked a harsh laugh that ended in a cough. He wanted to argue, but couldn't. Not with the fire still howling across the bay, proof of what could have been.

The scoutmaster blew two sharp blasts on his whistle, rallying the boys' attention. "Eyes here! We hold steady. Help's coming."

The boys snapped their gazes to him, their fear momentarily replaced with focus. Henry watched, envy gnawing at him. That whistle, that voice — it carried authority. His own voice had cracked like a teenager's when he'd tried.

He leaned back on the cold rock, the sound of the approaching choppers growing louder, the fire across the bay eating the last of the ravine. The storm had passed, but Henry's shame clung like a second skin.

Alive. Humiliated. Waiting.

Henry's fists clenched, as the TikTok crew approached.

Their leader — Bleach Hair — beamed at the boys. "Heyyyy, survivors! You guys are legends."

The Scouts blinked, some shrinking back, others perking up with nervous smiles. One boy whispered, "They have, like, a million followers."

Another elbowed him, whispering, "Five million."

Henry groaned. "Jesus Christ."

Bleach Hair turned his phone on the group, camera sweeping across their soot-streaked faces. "Everyone give it up for these heroes, man. Stuck in the fire, made it out. How's it feel, boys?"

The scoutmaster stepped forward, blocking the camera with his body. His voice was shredded but sharp. "Put the phones down. These kids need water and rest, not interviews."

Bleach Hair blinked, then grinned wider. "Don't worry, chief, we're already trending. Hashtag ScoutsSurvive. Help's on the way 'cause of us. You're welcome."

Henry lurched to his feet before he realized he was moving. Rage spiked, hot enough to push past his exhaustion. "You didn't save them," he snarled. His voice cracked, but it carried. "You called. That's it. The scoutmaster saved them. Mark saved them. You—" He jabbed a finger toward the phones. "You were too busy laughing."

The crew exchanged looks, their grins faltering for a moment. Then one of them, shorter, wearing a backwards cap, raised his phone higher. "Dude's mad. Yo, check this out, he's heated. #WildernessKaren."

Laughter erupted from the group, the sound high and grating.

Henry's vision tunneled. He wanted to snatch the phone, hurl it into the lake, watch it sink. His fists curled, his body trembling.

Mark's hand landed heavy on his shoulder. "Not worth it," he said quietly, steady as a rock.

Henry shook, but the grip anchored him. He sank back down onto the granite, his chest heaving.

The scoutmaster's jaw tightened. "You're in the way. Step back."

For a moment, Henry thought Bleach Hair might argue. But the man must've read something in the scoutmaster's eyes, because he grinned, held up his hands, and backed off a step. "No worries, chief. We're just here to document. People need to know what happened."

One of the boys muttered, "People need to stop shoving cameras in our faces."

Henry almost smiled at that. Almost.

The crew retreated a few paces, but their phones never lowered. They angled for shots of the burning island, of the exhausted Scouts, of themselves framed nobly against smoke and fire. They narrated every moment in stage whispers that weren't whispers at all.

"Scouts huddled here, look at 'em, tough kids. True wilderness vibes. And across the water, total devastation."

Henry shut his eyes. The sound of their voices, the fake gravitas, scraped across his nerves worse than the storm had.

One boy crawled closer to him, whispering. "Did they really call the cops?"

Henry opened his eyes, met the boy's soot-streaked face. He hesitated, then sighed. "Yeah. They did."

The boy nodded slowly, then frowned. "But they didn't help us out of the fire."

Henry swallowed hard. "No. They didn't."

Mark crouched beside them both, voice low so only Henry heard. "Let it go. They'll spin their story. Doesn't change the truth."

Henry wanted to believe that. He really did. But across the lake, the fire still raged, and across the rock, phones still gleamed like predatory eyes. And he knew — truth didn't matter once it was packaged into thirty-second clips.

He leaned back against the cold stone, coughing, trying to steady himself. The boys were alive. That was the fact that mattered. He repeated it in his head like a mantra. Alive. Alive. Alive.

But the laughter of the TikTok crew carried on the wind, mocking the silence between his breaths.

Time stretched strangely after the TikTok crew settled in.

The storm was gone now, leaving a pale, washed-out sky. The fire across the channel still raged, though the worst of the crown flare seemed to be settling into a steady burn. Smoke rose in thick ribbons, drifting east with the retreating clouds. Every few minutes, a tree collapsed, cracking like a gunshot before disappearing in a shower of sparks.

On the rocky outcrop, life contracted into small, weary tasks. Mark coaxed a pocket stove to life, heating water in a battered pot. The scoutmaster parceled out the last of the trail mix from a crushed plastic bag, making sure each boy got a handful. The Scouts ate quietly, some chewing methodically, others just holding the nuts and raisins in their palms like they weren't sure food was still meant for them.

The TikTok crew sat a short distance away, but not far enough. Their phones never left their hands. They spoke in low tones but always just loud enough to be overheard. "Look at this shot," one said, angling toward the burning ridge. "Straight cinematic." Another replied, "Gotta get the kids in frame though — real human angle." Laughter followed, tinny and grating.

Henry sat on the edge of the rock, arms wrapped around his knees, trying to keep his breathing even. His body still shook in occasional spasms, muscles clenching at random as though his fall into the lake were still happening. Every cough raked his chest.

The boys whispered behind him. He didn't want to listen, but the words slipped through anyway.

"He fell in."

"Yeah, the scoutmaster had to pull him out."

"Thought he was dead for a second."

"Why was he even paddling if he couldn't—"

Henry pressed his palms over his ears. It didn't help. The voices weren't cruel, exactly. Just matter-of-fact, the way kids reported weather. But each syllable landed like a blow.

He rocked forward, staring at the water. The surface still heaved with the storm's leftovers, long swells rolling past the island. He imagined himself sinking under them again, poncho dragging him down, his arms flailing. Somewhere, right now, that loop was probably being uploaded. Millions of strangers would see it, stripped of context, played for laughs. Drowning Man Meme, some text would read.

Mark eased down beside him, steam rising from two cups in his hands. He offered one. "Drink."

Henry took it reluctantly. The bitter warmth of instant coffee spread through his chest, cutting some of the chill. For a moment, he almost thanked him. Then one of the TikTokers laughed sharply, and the moment shattered.

"I'm a joke," Henry muttered.

Mark sipped calmly. "You're alive."

Henry turned to glare. "Alive and pathetic. Great combo."

Mark didn't rise to it. He never did. Just sipped, eyes on the fire across the channel. "Pathetic men don't carry canoes uphill. Pathetic men don't walk into smoke to pull kids out of a ravine."

Henry snorted, bitter. "I didn't pull anyone out. I barely pulled myself."

Mark's gaze flicked toward him, steady, unreadable. "Doesn't change the fact you went in."

Henry shook his head. The coffee tasted like ash now.

The scoutmaster's whistle cut through the murmurs. "Alright, eyes up." The boys straightened reflexively, their weariness momentarily forgotten. The man's voice was rough, but his tone carried authority. "You all did good today. You listened, you stayed with your buddies, and you followed through. That's why you're sitting here now instead of…" He gestured vaguely toward the burning island. None of them needed him to finish.

The boys nodded solemnly.

Then the scoutmaster did something Henry didn't expect. He turned, pointed toward him. "And you're alive because of him."

Henry froze.

The boys turned too, eyes widening.

The scoutmaster continued. "He didn't quit when things got bad. He went into that ravine with us. He kept you moving. He made sure you didn't freeze up." His gaze swept the group. "You all heard him. Whistle, voice, pushing you forward. Don't forget that."

Henry's throat tightened. He wanted to protest, to say No, that was you, you saved them, I just drowned. But the boys were watching, and for the first time since the fire began, their eyes held something other than pity or fear when they looked at him.

One of the older Scouts spoke softly. "Thanks, mister."

The words hit Henry like a stone to the chest. He opened his mouth, then closed it. His jaw trembled. Finally he muttered, "You're welcome."

The scoutmaster gave a curt nod, then turned back to the boys. "Now, stay put. Help's almost here."

The murmurs among the boys shifted. No more whispers about his failure. Just low, tentative conversations about home, parents, what they'd say when they saw them.

Henry hunched forward, hiding his face in his hands. His chest hurt, but not entirely from the cough.

The hum of helicopters grew louder overhead, steady now, inevitable. The TikTok crew scrambled to their feet, phones raised, voices pitched in excited stage-whispers: "Rescue incoming, baby! Hashtag HeroesInTheWild."

Henry wanted to laugh and cry all at once. He sipped the last of the bitter coffee, the warmth grounding him, and thought: Maybe the scoutmaster's wrong. Maybe I didn't save anyone. But maybe I wasn't completely useless, either.

The thrum of helicopters thickened until it shook the very rock beneath them.

There were helicopters from every agency imaginable.

Minnesota Air Rescue Team (MART), the Minnesota Department of Natural Resources (DNR), St. Louis County Sheriff's Office, and even private ambulance/helicopter services.

The Scouts lifted their heads, eyes wide. Relief swept the group like a collective exhale. Some boys cheered weakly, others just stared skyward, too wrung out to do more than watch. The scoutmaster stood tall, whistle raised to his lips, blasting three sharp notes in succession. The sound cut clean through the smoke.

Mark shielded his eyes, scanning the horizon. "There," he said, pointing east.

The TikTok crew erupted like fireworks. Phones aloft, grins plastered on their faces, they narrated over the roar.

"Choppers inbound, folks, this is it!"

"First on the scene, first to report — we got them here!"

"Scouts safe, rescue live — remember who showed you this!"

Their voices grated against Henry's nerves like sandpaper. Every syllable was a performance, every gesture angled for the invisible audience behind their glowing screens.

Henry clenched his fists. He wanted to shout, to expose them, to remind anyone who'd listen that these kids were alive because of sweat, fear, and grit — not hashtags. But what good would it do? Their story was already broadcasting across the world. His drowned face, his flailing arms, probably looped into a meme by now.

The helicopters circled once, then one dropped lower, hovering just off the shoreline. A loudspeaker crackled through the roar. "Stay calm. We'll extract in groups. KIds first."

The boys stirred, some clutching each other tighter. The scoutmaster barked steadying orders: "Buddies hold hands. Wait for direction. No rushing." His voice, even shredded, cut through panic.

Rescuers in bright jackets leaned out the helicopter's side, signaling. A sling was lowered, swinging in the rotor wash. The first pair of boys were guided forward by the scoutmaster and clipped in. They rose shakily, wind whipping their ponchos, until the helicopter hauled them up like awkward birds. Cheers erupted from the Scouts below.

The TikTok crew whooped louder, filming every second. "There it is! Real survival, guys! Subscribe for more!"

Henry groaned into his hands. "God help me."

Mark crouched beside him, steady as always. "Ignore them."

"I can't," Henry hissed. "They're rewriting it. Right in front of us."

Mark's gaze stayed on the helicopter, his expression calm. "Stories get twisted. But we know what happened. The boys know. That's enough."

Henry barked a humorless laugh. "Enough for who? Not for the internet. Not for my pride."

Mark finally looked at him, eyes steady. "Pride doesn't keep kids alive. You did what you could. That's the truth."

Henry bit the inside of his cheek until he tasted blood. He wanted to reject it, to curl deeper into shame. But then another pair of boys were hauled skyward, clinging to each other, faces pale but alive. The truth, whether or not it was recorded, was right there.

Extraction continued. Two by two, the Scouts vanished into the belly of the hovering machine, their neon covers bobbing like beacons until swallowed by the cabin.

This routine went on, for two hours, then finally the scoutmaster went last, his whistle still hanging around his neck, his shoulders squared even in exhaustion.

The helicopter rose higher, banking east with its cargo. Finally the next one droppled in, preparing for Mark and Henry.

The TikTok crew jostled for position, filming themselves in the rotor wash, hair whipping wildly, voices shouting to be heard over the roar. "We did it! This is history! Heroes in the wild!"

Henry stared at them, bile rising. He wanted to crawl across the rock, rip the phones from their hands, hurl them into the flames across the channel. He wanted the world to see them as parasites, not heroes.

But his body was spent, his lungs ragged. He couldn't.

Mark touched his arm. "Come on. Our turn."

Henry looked at him, then at the burning island. Flames still leapt skyward, consuming what little green had survived the storm. Black trunks fell, one after another, the fire advancing until nothing but glowing skeletons remained.

It should have been their tomb. Instead, it was just a backdrop now — content for strangers.

He rose unsteadily, leaning on Mark's arm, and let himself be guided to the sling. The harness clipped around him, snug and cold. As the line jerked, lifting him from the rock, Henry closed his eyes.

The outcrop shrank beneath him, the TikTok crew tiny dots waving at their cameras, Mark's figure steady as he waited for his turn. The fire stretched below, the lake gleamed gray, and the rotors thundered above.

Henry thought, I am alive. They are alive. And maybe that has to be enough, no matter who owns the story.

The helicopter carried him up, higher, until the smoke swallowed the view.

Chapter 17

Fly Like an Eagle

The helicopter dropped lower, rotors hammering the air, until Henry could see the clearing spread out below. It wasn't much: a patch of gravel and scrub at the edge of a ranger outpost, ringed by tall pines, smoke still drifting faintly from the west. Emergency vehicles dotted the clearing—trucks with flashing lights, a fire command trailer, ambulances lined in a hasty row. The scene looked both chaotic and organized, the way crisis always did in its second act: not the panic of survival, but the machinery of response grinding into motion.

The jolt of the landing, shook Henry.

"Got you, sir. Easy. Can you stand?"

Henry nodded, though his knees buckled. They caught him anyway, one on each side, half-dragging him toward a stretcher. He coughed, chest heaving, lungs still raw from smoke and lake water.

"Smoke inhalation," one medic called. "Possible near-drowning. Oxygen, blankets."

Henry tried to wave them off, but another cough doubled him over. A mask pressed over his face, plastic cool and snug. Oxygen hissed in his ears. His body rebelled at first, then gave in, greedy for the clean air.

The scouts already there, were already in trucks and police cars, being driven to town.

Henry turned his head, mask still hissing, and saw Mark climb he moved stiffly, his broad shoulders hunched with exhaustion, but he walked under his own power. A paramedic tried to pull him aside, but Mark shook his head, pointing at Henry. "Him first."

Henry wanted to laugh. Him first, as if Mark hadn't carried the whole damn rescue on his back.

The scoutmaster raised a hand, tired but steady. His whistle still hung around his neck, soot-streaked but gleaming.

"Alright, boys," he rasped to Mark and Henry, "we are safe"

Once in the ambulance. Henry heard them.

He wasn't sure if it was a nightmare or reality, but he head the TikTok crew arrived.

"Three million live, baby!" one shouted over the rotor wash. "We broke the record!"

Another swung his phone across the clearing, narrating. "You're seeing it live, folks—paramedics on the ground, scouts rescued after a devastating wildfire in the Boundary Waters. And guess what? We called it in. Without us, they'd still be out there."

Henry groaned into his mask. Of course.

The crew fanned out like anchors at a news desk. Bleach Hair, the ringleader, strode toward the scoutmaster, phone outstretched. "Sir, sir, can we get a word? You just led your troop out of a wildfire. How does it feel to be America's hero right now?"

The scoutmaster blinked at him, face blank. "My boys are alive. That's all that matters."

Bleach Hair grinned wider, turning the camera back on himself. "You heard it here, folks—humble hero, keeping it real. But don't forget, if we hadn't boosted the signal, if we hadn't gotten authorities on the line, who knows what would've happened?"

Laughter erupted from his crew. "Yeah, man, hashtag TrueRescue!"

A paramedic checked his pulse, scribbled notes on a clipboard. "You're stable enough. Sit tight, sir."

Henry leaned back on the stretcher, eyes half-closed, oxygen easing the fire in his chest. Around him, the clearing hummed with overlapping noise: paramedics calling vitals, radios squawking updates, boys murmuring into borrowed phones, the TikTok crew narrating every damn second.

He thought of the lake, of the ravine, of the fire swallowing the island. It already felt unreal, like a nightmare he'd half-woken from. And now here, in the floodlights of the rescue base, it was being rewritten in real time—edited, packaged, and streamed to millions who would never smell the smoke or taste the ash.

Henry's fingers curled in the blanket. He closed his eyes.

Alive. Embarrassed. Waiting for the next spotlight to swing his way.

Soon the doors shut, Mark and the scoutmaster rode together in a pickup tuck to the hospital to get checked out.

Henry more embarrassed then hurt, refused treatment, much to the anger of the paramedics, instead choosing to walk to the room where all the survivors were.

Inside the room, paramedics handed out bottles of water, packets of crackers, and spare blankets pulled from crates. The Scouts sat in one large room, hunched in their silver thermal wraps like foil-wrapped statues, chewing slowly or just clutching food they didn't have the strength to eat.

Soon a police team walked in, "Parents have been notified. You'll each get a chance to call. Quick check-ins only—we need to cycle through."

For the first time all day, real life cracked through the shock. The boys surged forward, hands trembling as they reached for the phones.

A boy no older than twelve held the phone to his ear, his lips pressed tight until a voice answered on the other end. His shoulders shook instantly. "Dad? Dad, it's me. I'm okay." The words dissolved into sobs, but the relief was palpable.

Another boy whispered "Mom" into his phone, then burst into hurried reassurances. "No, I'm fine. We're all fine. We got out. We're safe now. Don't cry, Mom, don't cry." His buddy sat beside him, waiting his turn, blinking furiously against tears.

Henry turned his face away. The rawness of it was too much. It reminded him of things he didn't want to touch—his own son, his own missed chances, the widening gulf between who he'd been and who he was now.

The TikTok crew, of course, saw an opportunity.

They swooped in with phones aloft, circling the clusters of boys like vultures around a carcass. "Look at this, folks," Bleach Hair narrated into his camera, his tone syrupy with faux emotion. "Raw survival. Kids calling their parents after escaping a fire. This is what resilience looks like."

Henry felt bile rise in his throat. He wanted to stand, to shout them down, to throw rocks at their stupid glowing screens. But his legs refused. His lungs wheezed. He sat pinned on the stretcher, forced to watch.

The scoutmaster cut across the clearing like a blade. He strode straight to the TikTok crew, shoulders squared despite the soot and exhaustion weighing him down. "Phones down. Now."

Bleach Hair blinked, grin faltering. "We're just showing the truth, sir."

The scoutmaster stepped closer, eyes burning. "No. You're stealing it. These boys are not props. Put the cameras down, or I'll have you removed."

For a heartbeat, the crew wavered. Then the one in the backwards cap smirked at his lens. "Scoutmaster mad, guys. Guess he doesn't like free press." Laughter followed, sharp and false.

But the boys were watching, and this time their eyes narrowed. One of the older Scouts stood, fists clenched. "Leave us alone," he snapped. His voice cracked, but it carried.

That did it. With the police officers looking on, they crew finally left the room.

Henry wanted to applaud the Scout's courage. But he stayed silent, gnawing on the inside of his cheek.

Mark appeared at his side, holding another bottle of water. "Here."

Henry took it reluctantly. "You see that? They're turning even this into content. Kids crying to their parents—and it's content."

Mark unscrewed his own bottle, calm as ever. "Let 'em. Doesn't change what happened."

Henry barked a bitter laugh. "Doesn't change? That's all it does. Three million people saw me drown today. By tomorrow it'll be thirty million. That's the story they'll know."

Mark drank, wiped his mouth. "And the boys will tell their parents something else. Their parents will tell their friends. That spreads, too."

Henry looked at him, incredulous. "You really think anyone cares about the quiet version?"

Mark's eyes didn't waver. "I do. They do." He tilted his chin toward the Scouts, still lined up at the phones, murmuring broken phrases of relief into static-filled connections. "That's who matters."

Henry wanted to argue. To rant. To let his fury spill out. But one of the boys caught his eye just then—a freckled kid, voice shaking as he said into the phone, "I thought I'd never see you again, Dad. But there was this man— he came into the ravine with us. He didn't quit. That's why we made it out."

The words weren't meant for Henry, but they hit him like a blow all the same. His throat tightened. He turned away, blinking hard.

The TikTok crew cheered suddenly ran back in, "Guys! Viral milestone! Three point two million live views. Trending number one nationwide!"

Their whoops cut through the fragile moment like glass breaking.

Henry groaned, covering his face with both hands. "God, I hate them."

Mark only said, "Then don't give them more space in your head."

But Henry couldn't stop. Every shout, every laugh, every glowing screen made his humiliation echo louder. He thought of tomorrow's headlines, the endless scroll of comments, the strangers dissecting his failure in thirty-second clips.

And yet, over it all, the sound of the Scouts calling home threaded through like a lifeline. "I'm safe, Mom." "I love you, Dad." "Don't cry." That sound mattered more than any camera.

Henry clung to it, even as shame gnawed at him.

Chapter 18

Ely

The police had arranged rooms, for everyone in Ely.

All except for the TikTok crew, who insisted on their own accommodations.

Outside the hotel, the police had stationed state patrol officers and DNR to keep the press away, until the parents could come to take the children home.

Henry and Mark, shared a room, just down the hall.

Getting into the room, the TV was already on.

How or why Henry will never know.

Maybe it was fate, or the devil or just someone at the hotel who left it on.

But on the screen was Henry, being pulled from the water his own ragged face on the screen above a tavern bar, grainy footage slowed to emphasize the moment he'd toppled into the lake. A red banner screamed WILDFIRE RESCUE IN BOUNDARY WATERS. The clip cut to the scoutmaster helping a line of boys onto a helicopter sling, his whistle flashing under floodlights. Then another cut: the TikTok crew standing proudly with their ring light, declaring into their phones that they had "saved the day."

Henry turned away, his stomach sour. He slumped against the bed clutching his borrowed blanket tighter.

Inside, the air smelled faintly of disinfectant and stale coffee.

He sat there for a long time, staring at the carpet, until the weight of exhaustion finally forced him upright. A shower. That was the next thing. A shower to scrub the ash and failure off his skin, even if it didn't come off inside.

The bathroom mirror was fogged over by the time Henry stepped out of the shower. He stood on the rubber mat, water still dripping from his hair, and swiped a hand across the glass.

For a second, he wished it had stayed clouded.

The face that stared back was battered by smoke and strain, eyes bloodshot, skin mottled red where branches had scraped him in the ravine. His hair stuck up in damp clumps. A bruise was forming along his temple, the faint outline of where he'd slammed into the canoe when he fell. His chest looked pale and slack, the belly soft where years of office work had dulled him.

The man in the mirror wasn't a survivor. He was a mess.

Henry gripped the sink and leaned forward. He half expected the glass to split open and replay the clip again—him thrashing, flailing, dragged like a sack of laundry into the boat. Instead, the only sound was the drip of the showerhead and his own rasping breath.

He shut the light off and walked back into the room in darkness, a towel cinched around his waist. The silence felt heavy, but not safe. He knew what waited if he picked up the remote again: more news anchors, more footage, more commentary.

Instead, he reached for the room's phone. His fingers hovered over the keypad, then pressed the number he'd known for decades.

The line rang once. Twice.

Then: "Henry?" Her voice. His wife. The tight coil in his chest loosened all at once, only to be replaced with something sharper.

"It's me," he said. His voice cracked. He coughed, cleared his throat. "I'm alright."

"Oh, thank God." Her breath hitched, like she'd been holding it for hours. "I've been glued to the TV. Everyone has. Do you have any idea—" Her words tumbled out too fast, then cut short. "You're really okay?"

"I'm banged up. Coughing up smoke. But yeah. Alive."

He heard voices in the background—female voices, chatter, laughter. Then his wife again: "I'm at Susan's. We've all been watching together. The whole neighborhood's here. The kids are with my sister."

Henry pictured it: a living room full of women, wine glasses in hand, eyes wide as they replayed the footage over and over. His fall. His shame. His rescue. He swallowed hard.

"They... saw me?"

"They saw everything," she admitted gently. "Henry, it's everywhere. National news. Social media. You're lucky, they keep saying. Lucky to be alive."

He let out a bitter laugh. "Lucky's one word for it."

Her voice softened. "Don't do that. Don't make it ugly. You scared me half to death, Henry. You scared all of us. You could've—" Her breath caught. "You could've died."

Silence hung a moment. He pressed the phone tighter to his ear. "But I didn't."

"No. You didn't." Relief surged in her voice. He heard muffled words behind her, someone else chiming in— something like 'Tell him the scoutmaster's adorable!' Laughter followed.

His wife chuckled awkwardly. "They've all been saying it. The scoutmaster—he's everywhere, too. Interviews, soundbites. They keep calling him the hero. And, well…" Her voice dipped, conspiratorial. "They also think he's… cute."

Henry's stomach knotted. "Cute?"

"Oh, don't get jealous." She laughed, but it wasn't unkind. "It's just girl talk. But Henry, listen to me—you should find him. Thank him. Really. Not just because of all this, not because the cameras are everywhere, but because he saved your life."

Henry shut his eyes. He could still feel the scoutmaster's grip on his lifejacket, dragging him up. The humiliation flooded back in a wave.

"I don't know if I can face him," Henry whispered.

"You can. You have to. Look—" her tone softened again, warm and steady. "I'm grateful to him. I don't care if the whole country's calling him a hero, if people are swooning. What I care about is that he pulled you out, that you're here to call me right now. So yes. Find him. Thank him."

Henry rubbed a hand over his face. "And then what? Pose for selfies? Let the whole town know I needed saving?"

"Henry," she said firmly, "being saved isn't shameful. Dying would've been. Don't you see that?"

Her words landed heavy. He wanted to argue, to push back, but his throat was too tight.

"I should let you go," she said after a moment. "They're calling again. News people. Susan's husband is saying they might try to come by here. It's crazy, Henry. But promise me you'll rest. And promise me you'll thank him."

He closed his eyes. "Alright. I promise."

They exchanged softer words—small reassurances, I-love-yous, the mundane check-ins that felt monumental now. Then the line clicked dead, leaving Henry in silence again.

He sat on the edge of the bed, towel damp against his skin, staring at the blank television. The scoutmaster's name echoed in his wife's voice, in the clerk's, in the reporters'. Hero. Cute. Savior.

Henry pressed his fists into his eyes until stars flared.

Lucky to be alive. Saved by another man. The whole country watching.

He exhaled, long and shaky, and let himself fall back onto the stiff motel bed.

The hotel television clicked on with a flat buzz. Henry hadn't meant to reach for the remote, but his hand had moved on its own, as if drawn by masochism. The screen blazed bright, the volume muted but subtitles marching across the bottom.

BOUNDARY WATERS WILDFIRE RESCUE: ALL SCOUTS SAFE

Behind the caption, footage looped: helicopters against a burning skyline, Scouts bundled in foil blankets, the scoutmaster's smoke-blackened face, his whistle glinting like a badge of honor. Then Henry himself—flailing, falling, dragged sputtering from the lake.

He turned the volume up just in time to hear an anchor's voice. "...and what many are already calling the 'Miracle of the Boundary Waters' ended with every child safe, thanks to the swift actions of their scoutmaster, a team of fellow campers, and quick-thinking livestreamers who alerted authorities in time."

Henry groaned. "Livestreamers. For Christ's sake."

A knock sounded at the door. Mark stepped in, holding a bag from the vending alcove. He tossed a soda and a packet of chips onto the bed. "Dinner of champions."

Henry muttered thanks, eyes still glued to the screen.

Mark followed his gaze. The channel had cut to an interview outside the rescue base. Bleach Hair was front and center, his arm draped around a reporter as though they were cohosts. "We were just doing what anyone would do," he said, grinning into the lens. "I mean, three-point-nine million people watched us make the call. That's history, right? Citizen heroes."

His crew cheered behind him, one of them flashing a victory sign.

Henry clenched the soda so hard the can bent. "Heroes. They're calling them heroes. They didn't lift a finger."

Mark cracked open his own drink. "They lifted phones. Different world now."

"Different world," Henry echoed, his voice sour. "A world where you can make millions laughing at some poor bastard drowning."

The broadcast shifted again—to the scoutmaster, standing stiffly behind a podium at a ranger press conference. His voice was hoarse but steady. "The boys stayed calm. That's why they're alive. I did my duty, no more, no less."

The anchor's voice came over the footage: "Already, the scoutmaster's story has struck a chord across the nation. Viewers are praising his humility, strength, and dedication. Social media users are calling him 'the real face of heroism.'"

Henry hurled the dented can into the trash. It clattered loudly, spilling soda down the inside of the bin.

Mark didn't flinch. He munched a chip, eyes on the screen. "He's not wrong. He did his duty."

Henry spun on him. "You sound like them. You're just gonna sit there and nod like this is fine?"

Mark met his glare with maddening calm. "What do you want me to say?"

"I want you to admit it's a joke! That I look like a fool! That the whole damn country thinks I'm some washed-up idiot who needed saving while the pretty-boy scoutmaster carried everyone out on his back!"

The words exploded out before Henry could stop them. They echoed in the cramped room, bouncing off the floral bedspread and the buzzing neon outside the window.

Mark set the chip bag down. "You done?"

Henry's chest heaved. His throat burned. "No. I'm not done. You know what my wife said? She said her girlfriends were watching it all. They think he's cute. Cute! Like this is some reality show where women get to swoon over the rugged hero while their idiot husbands fall on their faces."

Mark leaned back in the chair by the table, his arms folded loosely. "Maybe they're right. Maybe he is cute. Maybe he is a hero. Doesn't change what you did."

Henry laughed bitterly. "What I did? Fall in the water? Cough up my lungs in front of three million people?"

"You walked into that ravine," Mark said. His voice was quiet, but it carried. "You went where fire was falling and trees were snapping. You did what most men would've run from. Don't tell me that's nothing."

Henry shook his head, pacing. His bare feet slapped against the carpet. "It doesn't matter what I did. The story's written already. 'Scoutmaster saves boys and bumbling camper.' That's the headline. That's me."

Mark let the silence stretch. The only sound was the television—now showing clips of the Scouts boarding buses, reporters swarming, the TikTok crew waving like celebrities.

Henry stopped at the window. He pulled the curtain aside and looked out at the parking lot. News vans idled under the buzzing streetlamps, their satellite dishes pointed skyward. Cameramen smoked by the dumpsters, their laughter cutting sharp against the night air.

He pressed his forehead to the glass. "I spent thirty years in IT. Thought I mattered. Thought I was good at what I did. Then the company dumped me like old trash. A thousand job applications, nothing. And now this. Now my only claim to fame is being the guy who couldn't keep his balance in a canoe."

Mark didn't answer immediately. He poured the rest of his chips into his palm, chewed thoughtfully, swallowed.

Then he said, "Maybe you're focusing on the wrong part of the story."

Henry turned. "What part's left?"

"The part where you're alive."

Henry wanted to scream. To throw the TV out the window. Instead he slumped onto the bed, burying his face in his hands. His voice was muffled. "I don't know if that's enough anymore."

Mark's eyes softened. He didn't argue. He just sat there, steady as a stone, while the television blared with other people's versions of what had happened.

And Henry sat hunched on the bed, haunted by his own version: the fall, the water closing

The motel room smelled faintly of wet towels and vending machine salt. Henry lay sprawled on one bed, staring at the ceiling tiles as though they might spell out answers. The television still glowed faintly, volume lowered now, but the crawl of headlines was relentless.

BOUNDARY WATERS SCOUTMASTER CALLED HERO.

TIKTOK TEAM CLAIMS MILLIONS OF VIEWS.

SURVIVOR GRATEFUL TO BE ALIVE.

The last line made Henry snort. Survivor. As if the word meant anything when your survival was a punchline for strangers.

Mark turned off the set with a click and sat down on the opposite bed. He laced his hands in his lap, leaning forward. "You're burning yourself out, Henry. You're playing the same reel over and over in your head."

Henry covered his face with his hands. "Because it is the reel. That's all anyone will see. Me, coughing up lake water while some saint in khaki saves my sorry ass."

"You'd rather be dead?" Mark asked flatly.

Henry's hands dropped. "That's not what I'm saying."

"Sounds like it."

The words landed sharp, but Mark didn't flinch. His voice stayed calm, even, like a man reading from a manual he trusted. "You keep acting like being saved is shameful. It's not. It's part of being human. Sometimes we save, sometimes we get saved. The scoutmaster knows that. Hell, he said as much."

Henry barked a bitter laugh. "Easy for him to say. He's the one who looks good in the story. He gets to be the hero."

Mark's eyes narrowed. "You think he asked for that? You think he wanted cameras in his face, TikTokers shoving phones up his nose? He wanted to get his boys out alive. That's it. Same as you."

Henry shook his head. "Not the same. He pulled me out, Mark. Don't you get it? I'm the example of what not to be. He's the man everyone wishes their dad was. And me? I'm the idiot husbands joke about over beer."

Mark leaned back, exhaling slow. "You know what your wife asked you to do?"

Henry looked up sharply. "You heard that?"

"Thin walls," Mark said simply. "She told you to thank him."

Henry grimaced. "She also said her friends think he's cute. Like this is all some big reality show."

"So what if they do?" Mark's voice hardened. "What does that have to do with you? You're alive. You walked into fire with him. You helped keep those kids moving. And yes, he saved you when you fell. So maybe you owe him thanks, not resentment."

Henry opened his mouth, then shut it again. His throat tightened. "I don't know if I can face him. Not after... all of this."

"Then you'll stay stuck here," Mark said, gesturing at the motel walls, the muted television, the stale air. "Looping the same humiliation until it eats you alive. Or you get up tomorrow and you look him in the eye and you say thank you. Doesn't have to be more than that."

Henry stared at him, searching for cracks in the calm. But Mark was steady, as always—no judgment, no pity, just an unmovable truth.

He thought of the boy in the ravine who'd said, He didn't quit. He thought of the clerk in the lobby, gawking but still saying, You're lucky to be alive. He thought of his wife, her voice trembling with relief even as her friends teased about the scoutmaster.

Every voice pointed him toward the same place.

Henry rubbed his temples. "What if he hates me? What if he thinks I'm just some dead weight he had to drag?"

"Then you'll know," Mark said. "But I don't think that's who he is."

Silence stretched. Outside, a news van rumbled as its generator kicked on. The neon vacancy sign buzzed through the thin walls.

Finally Henry let out a long, shaky breath. "Alright. Tomorrow. I'll find him. I'll thank him."

Mark nodded once, satisfied. "Good." He stood, stretched, and moved toward his room. At the door he paused. "Get some sleep, Henry. You'll need it."

Henry lay back on the bed, staring at the ceiling again. His chest still ached, his pride still throbbed raw, but under it all was something new. Not relief, not pride. Just a fragile thread of resolve.

Tomorrow he would face the man who'd pulled him from the water. Tomorrow he would speak the words that had been choking him since the moment his head broke the surface.

Thank you.

Chapter 19

Home Ain't Sweet

The gravel crunched under the tires as Mark's truck rolled to a stop in front of Henry's house. It was just afternoon, but the sky still looked hazy, a dull gray film left over from the wildfire's smoke that had drifted miles south. The siding of the little rambler gleamed in the weak sun, freshly power-washed a month ago. The yard looked the same as it had before he left—same crooked basketball hoop, same plastic kiddie pool now deflated by the garage. Everything was the same, and yet Henry's chest tightened as if he were pulling up to a stranger's home.

His wife was on the porch. She sat with a glass of iced tea, hair brushed and shining, her posture easy in a way Henry hadn't felt in days. Beside her lounged a figure Henry recognized instantly, though he'd prayed he wouldn't: Backwards Cap. The TikTok kid who'd shouted into his phone while Henry nearly drowned. The same guy who had spun a joke out of every dangerous second.

Now here he was on Henry's porch, ballcap turned back, sunglasses hooked to his collar, holding Henry's wife captive in a stream of jokes. And she was laughing. Not the polite chuckles she sometimes gave Henry at his worst attempts, but deep, easy laughter. She covered her mouth, leaned into the armrest, eyes sparkling.

Henry froze halfway out of the truck. His pulse thudded in his ears.

Mark put a hand on his shoulder. "Take a breath."

Henry's mouth was dry. He didn't want to step forward, didn't want to make this real. But before he could retreat, the screen door banged open. Two figures exploded out onto the porch—his kids.

"Dad!"

They sprinted across the lawn, his daughter's hair flying, his son's sneakers slapping the sidewalk. They collided with him at once, arms tight around his waist, faces pressed against his smoke-stained shirt.

"You're okay!" his daughter cried, muffled in the fabric. "I saw you on TV! I thought—" She broke off, shaking against him.

His son clung tighter. "They said the fire almost got you. Mom was crying. I thought you were gonna die."

Henry dropped to his knees on the lawn, holding them as hard as his tired arms allowed. His chest ached with each breath, but he didn't care. He buried his face in their hair, breathing them in, alive and warm.

"I'm here," he whispered. His voice cracked. "I'm here."

They stayed that way for long minutes, until the trembling eased. Then his wife rose from the porch and walked toward them, her smile wide but her eyes glassy. She wrapped her arms around the cluster, pulling all three into one embrace. "We're so thankful," she murmured. "So thankful you're home."

For that moment, Henry let himself believe it could stay like this—his wife's arms, his kids pressed tight, the world shut out. But then Backwards Cap strolled down the steps, casual as if he belonged.

"Man, what a scene," he said, voice too loud. "Hallmark would pay for this footage. Glad you made it, dude."

And before Henry could react, the kid clapped him on the back—hard, too hard, like they were teammates celebrating a win.

The touch burned hotter than the wildfire. Henry clenched his jaw, forcing his face into a grimace that passed for a smile. He wanted to shake the hand off, to shout, You're the one who turned it into a joke, the one who made me into content. But the kids were watching. His wife was watching. So he nodded once, a stiff acknowledgment, and rose slowly to his feet.

Mark's eyes tracked the exchange. He said nothing, but his jaw tightened.

Henry's wife looped her arm through Henry's, guiding him toward the porch. "Come inside. You need rest, a shower, real food." She glanced back at the at backwards cap guy. "Thanks for dropping by."

"Anytime," Backwards Cap said smoothly. He tipped his hat backward another inch, flashing a grin. "We're family now, right? Survived the same story." He winked at Henry. "Catch you later, bro."

Henry's grip tightened on the railing until his knuckles went white. He blew air through his nose, the only outlet for his rage. Then he walked up the steps, his wife's hand still on his arm, and forced himself inside the house.

The familiar smell hit him instantly—laundry detergent, lemon cleaner, a faint trace of last night's spaghetti. The walls were covered with the same family photos, the same school portraits, the same souvenir magnet collection on the fridge. But it all felt sharper, brighter, as though the fire had burned away the filter he used to look through.

He dropped his duffel just inside the door. His wife kissed his cheek, lingering, then stepped back. "You've got calls, Henry. Your parents rang twice. Your brother. Even some of your old coworkers—Susan texted me about it. Everyone wants to hear from you. They're all saying how lucky you are. How blessed."

Henry rubbed his forehead, exhausted. He nodded without speaking.

"And…" she hesitated, then smiled. "They're saying the scoutmaster's a hero. They've been running interviews all morning. He's so humble, Henry. He gives all the credit to the boys, but you can tell—he's the one who saved them. And you."

Henry's throat closed. He forced a thin smile and said nothing.

She touched his arm again. "Go shower. I'll make lunch. We can talk after."

Henry walked down the hall, each step heavier than the last. Behind him, his wife's voice carried lightly as she told the kids to give Dad space, to let him breathe. Through the window, he could still see Backwards Cap leaning against his car, scrolling his phone, smirking at the world.

Henry shut the bathroom door harder than he meant to, stripped, and stepped into the shower, letting the water pound him like punishment.

The steam had barely cleared from the bathroom when Henry stepped out, a towel slung around his shoulders. He felt lighter in the way a man feels after shedding soot and sweat, but the heaviness in his chest hadn't budged. It followed him down the hall into the living room, where the television glowed softly.

His daughter was curled on the couch with a tablet, earbuds in, watching the same rescue clip for the hundredth time. His son sprawled on the floor, Lego pieces scattered in a half-built spaceship, his eyes flicking to the TV every few minutes to catch the latest replay.

Henry's wife was on the phone. She paced by the kitchen island, voice animated. "Yes, he's fine. He's right here. Yes, he looks tired, but he's home. ... No, no, the scoutmaster's the one who saved them. They've been replaying his press conference all morning. ... I know, isn't he amazing?"

Henry froze in the hallway, listening. She laughed softly at something the caller said, then lowered her voice. "I'll tell him you called. He needs rest now. Yes, yes, we're grateful. Bye." She ended the call, set the phone down, and exhaled.

Her eyes found Henry. "That was your mother. She's been frantic. You'll need to call her back soon."

Henry rubbed the towel over his hair, buying time. "Soon," he muttered.

His wife crossed the room, touched his cheek. "She cried when she saw the footage, Henry. She said she prayed harder than she's prayed in years. She's so thankful the scoutmaster was there."

There it was again. The scoutmaster. The word threaded through every conversation, every sentence, like punctuation.

Henry forced a thin smile. "Yeah. Thankful."

She guided him to the couch, nudging their son to scoot over. "Sit. Eat something." She pressed a plate of sandwiches into his hands, crusts cut neatly, just the way she always made them.

He bit in mechanically. The bread tasted like cardboard, his mouth too dry to chew, but he swallowed anyway. His kids' eyes tracked him, wide and solemn.

"You were brave, Dad," his son blurted. "Mom said you went into the fire too."

Henry swallowed hard. "I... I tried."

His daughter leaned against him, tablet balanced on her knees. "I saw you on TikTok. You looked scared. But you kept going."

Henry's stomach dropped. On TikTok. Even his daughter had watched.

His wife returned to the counter, rifling through slips of paper—messages jotted hurriedly. "Your brother called three times. So did Tom from church. Oh, and the neighbors. Everyone wants to hear from you. They're saying it's a miracle you're alive." She smiled over her shoulder. "And they all say the same thing: how blessed we are that the scoutmaster saved you."

Henry put the sandwich down, appetite gone. "Blessed," he echoed.

"Yes." She crossed back, perched on the arm of the couch, smoothing his damp hair with her hand. "You don't see it yet, but this will change things. People know your name now. They'll remember this. They'll remember him."

Henry flinched. "What about me?"

She hesitated, searching his eyes. "They'll remember you too. As the man who lived. Who came home to his family. Isn't that enough?"

Henry looked at his kids, their small faces pressed close, waiting for his answer. He swallowed the lump in his throat and nodded once. "Yeah. Enough."

But inside, the words curdled. The man who lived. Not the man who saved, not the hero. Just the one dragged from the water, lucky and nothing more.

He excused himself soon after, retreating to the quiet of the bedroom. The bedspread looked the same as when he'd left, but it felt foreign now, like stepping into someone else's life. He sat heavily, the phone on the nightstand buzzing with another incoming call. His mother again, probably.

Henry didn't pick up. He stared at the screen until it dimmed, then lay back and pressed the towel over his face. His wife's words echoed in the dark: The scoutmaster saved you. Blessed. Amazing.

Henry exhaled through his teeth, the bitterness coiling tighter.

Henry sat on the edge of the bed for a long while, staring at the silent phone. His mother's number glowed on the missed calls list—three, four, five times now. His brother's name, a coworker from years ago, even Tom from church who hadn't spoken to him in months. They all wanted the same thing: to talk to the man who had been saved.

The title thudded in Henry's skull. Not hero, not leader. Just saved.

He pushed himself up with a groan and drifted into the upstairs bathroom. The mirror over the sink was streaked with toothpaste and his daughter's handprints, smudged from reaching for the faucet. He turned on the faucet, splashed cold water over his face, and braced his hands on the porcelain.

He didn't want to look, but the reflection demanded it.

The same bloodshot eyes, the same bruise on his temple, the same sag of tired flesh along his jaw. No heroic gleam, no rugged scoutmaster aura, just a man who'd slipped, fallen, and been dragged to shore while millions watched.

His wife's voice looped in his mind: Blessed. Amazing. Thank the scoutmaster.

And over it, the memory of her laugh as Backwards Cap cracked another joke on the porch.

Henry squeezed the sink so hard his knuckles ached. He wanted to smash the mirror, to shatter the reflection into jagged shards until it didn't look like him anymore. But he didn't. He stood there, panting softly, until the anger softened into something worse: grief.

His throat tightened. His chest heaved once, twice, and then the sobs came. Silent at first, then ragged, ugly sounds that bounced off the tile. He pressed both hands over his face and let it happen, years of frustration spilling out—losing the job, failing to find another, watching neighbors laugh at his expense, now this: the final humiliation broadcast nationwide.

He sank to the floor, back against the tub, shoulders shaking. The sound of his kids' laughter downstairs floated up faintly through the vents, sharp against his unraveling. He hated that they'd seen him like this on a screen, hated that the first thing his daughter thought to say was, I saw you on TikTok.

He stayed there until his breathing slowed, until the tears burned themselves out. The anger still simmered, but the grief had emptied him.

Slowly, Henry pulled himself upright. He washed his face again, rinsing away the salt streaks, and studied the mirror once more. Still the same man, battered and tired, but at least now he could meet his own gaze.

"You're alive," he whispered, the words hoarse. "That's something."

He dried his face with a hand towel and walked back into the bedroom. His phone buzzed again, this time with a text from his wife: Lunch is ready. Kids want you downstairs.

Henry sat on the edge of the bed, phone in his lap. His fingers hovered over the screen. He thought of calling his mother, imagined her voice breaking with relief, imagined her saying the same thing everyone else had: how lucky, how blessed, how amazing the scoutmaster was. He couldn't bear it yet. Not tonight.

Instead, he typed back: Be down in a minute.

He slipped the phone onto the nightstand and stared out the window. The street was calm, sunlight slanting across the neighbor's yard. But in the driveway below, Backwards Cap's car was still parked, its glossy hood catching the light. The young man leaned against the fender, phone in hand, lips moving in a stream of commentary no one in Henry's house had asked for.

The sight sent a fresh ripple of anger through Henry's gut. He clenched his fists, but then exhaled. One battle at a time.

He forced himself upright, straightened his shoulders, and headed downstairs to his family.

The smell of grilled cheese and tomato soup met Henry halfway down the stairs. For a moment he almost smiled — the comfort food of sick days, the kind of meal his wife always made when the kids needed warmth. His stomach growled, but the hunger was shallow, the kind born of habit rather than appetite.

The kitchen table was already set. His daughter sat cross-legged on her chair, spoon clinking against her bowl, while his son slurped noisily and grinned at the steam. The television hummed in the background, volume low, but the captions marched on in relentless headlines.

BOUNDARY WATERS HERO: SCOUTMASTER TELLS HIS STORY.

VIRAL VIDEO APPROACHES FIVE MILLION VIEWS.

Henry's wife moved gracefully between counter and table, setting another plate down for him. She smiled when she saw him, but her eyes darted briefly toward the screen. "Come eat. You need it."

He slid into a chair, folding his long arms in his lap. His daughter immediately pressed against his side, leaning into him as if she needed to confirm he was real. He ruffled her hair, forcing a grin.

"You've got calls to return," his wife said between bites. "Your parents again, your brother. And Pastor Reynolds left a message. He wants you to come give a testimony once things calm down."

Henry nearly choked on his soup. "A testimony?"

She nodded, serious. "People are looking to this as more than just a story, Henry. They see it as a sign. Everyone's talking about how lucky you were to be saved. How God sent that scoutmaster at the right moment."

There it was again. The name like a drumbeat, never leaving the air: scoutmaster.

Henry's spoon clattered against the bowl. He took a breath through his nose, steadying himself. "Seems like everyone wants to thank him."

His wife smiled faintly. "And so should you." She reached across, touching his hand. "I mean it. He saved your life. That makes him part of this family's story now."

Henry stared at her, words catching behind his teeth. Part of this family's story. He wanted to protest, to say the family's story was his, theirs, not some stranger's. But the sincerity in her eyes stopped him. She wasn't taunting him. She wasn't laughing like her friends on the porch. She was saying it plainly, earnestly.

He pulled his hand back gently, wiped it on his napkin. "Maybe I will."

After lunch the kids went upstairs to play, their voices drifting down as a jumble of laughter and arguments about Lego pieces. Henry wandered into the living room. On the coffee table lay a pile of magazines and newspapers neighbors had dropped off: Duluth Tribune, Star Tribune, USA Today. Each one had a variation of the same cover photo — Scouts bundled in silver blankets, the scoutmaster's smoke-streaked face, his arm raised mid-instruction.

Henry picked one up, flipped it open. Halfway through, his own image appeared: a blurry frame of him being hauled into the canoe, mouth open mid-cough. The caption read: Rescued camper Henry Cole, moments after being pulled from the water.

He dropped the paper as if it had burned him.

From the kitchen, his wife called, "You should see the scoutmaster's interview tonight. He's on national TV. They said he turned down offers already, but he's willing to speak about leadership. Isn't that incredible?"

Henry gritted his teeth. He stared at the pile of papers, at his own face frozen in humiliation, and whispered, "Incredible."

He climbed the stairs slowly, each creak of wood carrying the weight of his thoughts. Back in the bedroom, he sat heavily on the mattress, phone in hand. The call log still blinked with missed numbers, but he didn't press dial. He stared instead at the black screen until his reflection stared back.

Finally he spoke aloud, voice low but steady. "I have to call him."

The words hung in the quiet.

He imagined the scoutmaster's face — tired, soot-streaked, steady. The hand that had dragged him out, the voice that had led boys through smoke. The man everyone now called hero.

Henry's pride recoiled, but something deeper pulled harder. Gratitude. Debt. A need to close the loop.

When his wife came in later, folding laundry into neat piles, he surprised himself by speaking. "I need to thank him. Face-to-face."

She looked up, eyes soft. "Good. That's the right thing." She smiled faintly, almost teasing. "Maybe you'll even like him. Everyone else does."

Henry didn't answer. He just sat there, staring at the folded shirt in her hands, feeling both smaller and heavier than he had in years.

But the decision had been made. Tomorrow, he would find the scoutmaster.

Not because the cameras demanded it. Not because his wife or the clerk or the neighbors wanted it. But because Henry couldn't keep carrying this weight without speaking the words himself.

Thank you.

Even if it killed him to say them.

Chapter 20

Thank You

Henry sat at the desk in the corner of the bedroom, staring at the slip of paper Mark had slid across to him the night before. The handwriting was blocky and precise: a name, a number.

Scoutmaster Daniel Hayes.

Beneath it, a phone number.

Henry turned the slip over in his fingers until it was soft at the edges. His stomach tightened each time he looked at the digits. He wanted to do it, to get it over with, but the phone on the nightstand felt heavier than a brick.

What would he even say? Thanks for saving me? Thanks for proving to the world that I can't even keep my balance in a canoe?

He rubbed his face, groaned, and finally picked up the phone. His thumb hovered over the keypad for long seconds before he forced it down. The line rang once, twice.

On the third ring, a voice answered. "Hello?"

Henry froze. It was the same voice that had cut through smoke and panic in the ravine, calm and steady while everything else fell apart. Hearing it now, in the quiet of his house, made Henry's throat tighten.

"Uh," Henry stammered. "Mr. Hayes?"

"Yes. Who's this?"

Henry swallowed. "It's... it's Henry Cole. From the Boundary Waters."

There was a pause. Then the voice softened. "Henry. I remember. You made it home alright?"

Henry coughed, suddenly aware of how small he sounded. "Yeah. I... I did."

Silence stretched, not unfriendly, just waiting. Henry could feel his pulse in his ears.

"I just—" He cleared his throat. "I just wanted to say thank you. For... for pulling me out. For... saving me."

The words stuck halfway, but he forced them out. They sat heavy in the air, as if he'd lifted something and set it down between them.

On the other end, Hayes exhaled slowly. "You don't have to thank me. Anyone would have done the same."

Henry gripped the edge of the desk. "That's not true. Not everyone would've jumped in. Not everyone would've—" He broke off, the image flashing again: the water closing over his head, his lungs screaming, then that hand dragging him back.

"I would've drowned," Henry said flatly. "If you hadn't—"

"You didn't drown," Hayes interrupted, calm but firm. "That's what matters."

Henry blinked, thrown by the simplicity of it. He opened his mouth, shut it again, then let out a shaky laugh. "You make it sound so easy."

"It isn't easy," Hayes admitted. "But it's simple. We take care of each other out there. You did your part too."

Henry frowned. "My part?"

"You kept those boys moving," Hayes said. "You went in with me. You didn't turn back. That matters more than you think."

Henry sat back in the chair, the words washing over him like cool water. He wanted to believe them. He wanted to believe that he'd done something besides embarrass himself in front of millions.

"Thank you," he said again, softer this time.

"You're welcome," Hayes replied. "But you don't owe me anything. Just live your life. That's enough."

Henry's throat tightened. He nodded even though Hayes couldn't see it. "Alright."

There was a pause, then Hayes added, "Take care of your family, Henry. That's the only real legacy."

Henry gripped the phone harder, the words digging deeper than he expected. "I'll try."

They exchanged a few more pleasantries, small talk that felt strange after what they'd shared in fire and smoke. Then Henry let the call end, the dial tone humming in his ear before he finally set the phone back down.

For the first time in days, his chest felt a little lighter. He'd said the words. The man had heard them. That weight was gone.

But as Henry sat back, breathing out slowly, a flicker of motion in the yard caught his eye. He turned toward the window.

On the porch below, his wife stood with a familiar figure: Backwards Cap. The young man leaned against the railing, talking animatedly, hands sketching shapes in the air. His wife laughed, head tilted back, one hand resting briefly on his arm as if steadying herself from the force of the joke.

Henry's stomach clenched again. The lightness he'd felt drained away in an instant, replaced by the sour churn he thought he'd washed down with gratitude.

And behind them, in the yard, his kids ran in circles, their voices shrill with play. One of them threw himself onto the grass, clutching his throat and fake-gurgling. The other stood over him, arms crossed, declaring in a mock-serious voice: "Don't worry, Scoutmaster Hayes will save you!"

They collapsed in laughter, rolling across the lawn.

Henry's fingers dug into the armrest of the chair. The phone still hummed faintly beside him, the words Just live your life echoing in his ears.

But outside, life was already being turned into parody.

Henry lowered the phone slowly onto the desk, careful not to let it clatter. The call had ended with polite words, promises to "catch up someday," but his mind hadn't been on them. It was fixed on the scene unfolding outside his window.

Backwards Cap leaned against the porch rail like it belonged to him, his sneakers balanced on the lowest slat, his whole body loose with confidence. He tossed his head as he spoke, the cap bouncing with the motion, and Henry's wife laughed again—her hand curling around her iced tea, shoulders shaking. Every so often, she reached out to steady herself against him, as if his jokes knocked her off balance.

Henry sat frozen, muscles tight, watching.

The kids were worse.

They ran across the patchy lawn, darting between the flower beds and the half-deflated kiddie pool, their voices high and bright. His son flopped onto the grass, waving his arms dramatically. "Help! I'm drowning! I can't swim!" He rolled onto his side, coughing fake water, spitting into the dirt for effect.

His daughter rushed to stand over him, hands on her hips. "Don't worry! The scoutmaster will save you!" She grabbed his wrist and tugged him up, both of them collapsing into shrieks of laughter.

Henry's heart seized. The sound should have been joy, ordinary sibling play. Instead it cut sharp, each giggle echoing the memory of his own thrashing in the lake. They weren't just playing—they were imitating him.

His son clutched his throat, groaned dramatically. "Henry Cole, helpless camper! Somebody help!"

His daughter doubled over, howling with laughter.

On the porch, Backwards Cap glanced at them, smirked, and shook his head as if in solidarity with the joke. He said something Henry couldn't hear, and his wife laughed harder.

Henry's chest burned.

He pressed both hands flat on the desk, leaning forward until his forehead nearly touched the wood. Breathe. Just breathe.

Scoutmaster Hayes' voice echoed in his head: You didn't drown. That's what matters.

But the words didn't land the same anymore. Not with his wife leaning into another man's jokes, not with his children mocking the most humiliating moment of his life.

He straightened and forced himself to look away. His hands shook as he tugged the curtains closed, blotting out the porch, the yard, the sight of them all. The room dimmed, mercifully, though the laughter still seeped through the thin glass.

Henry sat back on the bed, staring at the blank wall. His jaw ached from clenching.

He thought of storm winds in the Boundary Waters, trees catching fire, boys crying in the ravine. He thought of the scoutmaster's hand dragging him up, the TikTok crew's gleeful narration, his wife's friends calling Hayes "cute."

It all swirled together, one long humiliation reel.

A knock sounded at the door. "Henry?" It was his wife, voice casual. "You doing okay in there?"

He swallowed, forced his voice steady. "Fine."

"You should eat. Mark dropped off hotdish. I'll heat it up."

"Later," Henry said.

Silence. Then her footsteps retreated, and a moment later her laughter floated up again from the porch.

Henry rubbed his temples. He wanted to scream, to rip the curtains back open and shout down at them. But what would he say? That he hated being a punchline? That their laughter felt like knives? That his wife's smile at Backwards Cap was worse than any headline?

No. He stayed seated, letting the pressure build in his chest until it felt like a storm trapped under his ribs.

When he finally stood, it wasn't with a burst of rage but with a hollow resolve. He walked to the dresser, pulled his laptop from beneath a stack of bills, and carried it back to the desk. If he couldn't stop the world from laughing, maybe he could at least distract himself.

He flipped the lid open. The screen blazed with unread notifications.

104 new emails.

The bold number glared at Henry like a dare.

For a second he just stared, hands hovering over the keys, listening to the faint porch-laughter leaking through the window glass he'd just drawn the curtains over. His cursor trembled as if it could feel the pulse in his fingers. He drew a breath, clicked.

The first page of his inbox fanned open: subject lines like confetti, an explosion of attention he hadn't felt in years.

"Henry!! Oh my God — saw the news."

"Checking in — are you ok?"

"From your old team: praying for you."

"Media request: ABC regional wants a quick quote."

"Fox morning show pre-interview?"

"KARE 11: Can you hop on Zoom tonight?"

"Henry… we lost touch after the layoffs. Call me."

"Opportunity (maybe!) — contract role??"

"Boundary Waters survivor — partnership inquiry (TikTok)"

He almost laughed at that last one — a little strangled sound in his throat. Partnership inquiry. He hovered his cursor over the sender: a marketing address from a startup he didn't recognize. He did not click it.

Instead, his eyes homed in the way a damaged tooth finds the cold air: on the gray, cool sentences of obvious rejections that sat like stones among the exclamation marks.

"Re: Backend Engineer application"

"Re: Systems Administrator (Round 2)"

"Re: SRE Pool — Update"

"Re: Preliminary Chat"

He clicked the first rejection like a man pressing a bruise. The body of the email unfurled into boilerplate:

Dear Henry,

Thank you for taking the time to apply to the Backend Engineer role at Norling Data.

After careful consideration, we will not be moving forward with your application. While your background is impressive, we've decided to pursue candidates whose experience more closely aligns with our current needs.

We wish you the best in your search.

Sincerely...

The words were a lullaby for failure, familiar enough to hum. He'd read their cousins a hundred times this past year, the same phrases swapping places like chairs in a cheap living room. Impressive. Not at this time. More closely aligns. The sentences never bled, never stuttered, never admitted anything as messy as a human decision.

He closed it. Opened the next.

...thank you for your interest... we were fortunate to receive many qualified applications... we will keep your resume on file for six months...

Six months. Like he'd been put in a drawer.

He clicked another, then another, each one a matchstick scraped against the grain of his chest. Somewhere between the third and fourth he felt the old cold settle in — the knowledge that the world would always choose someone else, that he had become a placeholder men used to feel decisive.

A chime: another email arrived while he was reading. Subject line: "OMG HERO!" He looked at the sender — a woman from a project he'd once led, years ago. He remembered her desk plant more clearly than her face. He didn't open it. His cursor drifted back, homing again on what hurt.

He scrolled. The inbox became a map of his life's two dialects: Congratulations on not dying and Thanks but no thanks. Between them, a few neutral islands: Mom, twice. His brother. Pastor Reynolds (he read the preview text — testimony would bless the congregation — and moved on). A LinkedIn invitation from a recruiter he'd messaged four months ago and never heard back from until today. A PR person for a national radio show with bright, eager italics (we'd love to feature your survival story!). An email from "Team TrailCast"—the TikTok crew's handle—asking if he'd be open to "collab content to raise fire safety awareness" and "share the positive side of social media in rescue outcomes." His hand clenched into a fist so fast he nearly cracked the plastic of the trackpad.

He clicked Re: Systems Administrator (Round 2).

Dear Henry,

Thank you again for speaking with our team. We enjoyed getting to know you and appreciate the time you spent preparing.

Unfortunately, we will not be moving forward at this time. While we were impressed with your background, we've elected to move ahead with another candidate whose experience better matches our current stack.

This was not an easy decision.

Best wishes...

A laugh broke out of him, short and empty. This was not an easy decision. He imagined a slack channel where three avatars shrugged and clicked a template. He imagined the words stamped on a million digital foreheads: not at this time.

On autopilot, he opened a new tab and typed his own name into the search bar. His hands had done this to him before—gone wandering, seeking pain like dogs to a door. The results came up faster than he could brace.

There it was: a still image, his mouth open, water-slick hair plastered to his forehead. A caption he wish he hadn't read. A clip with the TikTok watermark, millions of views, the first comment pinned: "Man's out here speedrunning baptism." Laughter emojis stacked like confetti. Below it, a thread of strangers arguing whether he'd faked it for clout; someone claimed to know him and said he was "a sweet guy but clumsy as hell"; someone else called him a "tourist who had it coming"; a fourth linked the scoutmaster's interview, praising stoicism and "real men."

His finger twitched over the trackpad. He closed the tab so hard the browser hiccupped. Another chime: 105 new emails now.

He clicked a message from an old coworker with the subject line "You're a badass." The body: Dude. You went into a forest fire. I don't care if you fell in the lake—same here. Proud of you. Call me. He stared at it, unable to metabolize the words. Proud? The sentence couldn't attach to him, not when another rejection sat one line below.

He clicked the rejection instead.

Henry,

Thank you for interviewing with us. You clearly have strong experience; however, we decided to proceed with a candidate whose Kubernetes expertise is deeper.

We appreciate your time and wish you every success.

—

P.S. Saw the news. Glad you're okay.

The P.S. snagged him like a nail. He imagined them copying the sentence into every candidate's email who had suddenly become "that guy from TV." A PR patch on a refusal.

Outside, laughter burst again—his wife's warmer now, closer to the window. Henry's jaw clicked as he clenched it. He clicked back to the inbox and forced his eyes to the top where the subject lines still shouted friendship and life.

Henry!! Oh my God — saw the news. Another coworker. He hovered, then opened it.

Henry — My kids recognized you from the clip and we told them you're the bravest person we know for going in after those Scouts. Coffee on me any time. Seriously. We miss you at the office. I know these last couple years have been rough. Let me make some intros for you.

—Anita

He sat motionless, eyes fixed at the end of that line: Let me make some intros for you. The room shifted, a notch left. It felt like someone had set a glass of water down in a desert. He didn't touch it. He didn't trust it.

Another message from Mom: Call when you can. Dad is pacing. He pictured his father tracking grooves in the carpet, muttering about the news, about "those influencers," about "the Scout fellow being a real man."

The old ache flared—son as disappointment. Son as lesson.

He moved the cursor, opened one more. Subject: "Contract role??" From a guy he'd freelanced with years ago on a chaotic migration. The body was cautious, not quite an offer, but not a door slamming, either.

Hey Henry—

Saw your name everywhere today. Wild times.

This is out of the blue, but I might need a six-week contractor for a nasty cutover—nights, weird hours, decent pay. It's messy, which means it's your kind of thing. You game? No promises yet—depends on a budget meeting tomorrow—but thought of you first.

Ping me if interested.

His heart knocked once against his ribs. Thought of you first. It's messy, which means it's your kind of thing. He could feel the old part of himself stir, the one who'd thrived when systems screamed and no one else wanted to touch them. But overlaying it was a second skin of ridicule, the wet slap of that clip, the chorus shouting baptism and idiot tourist. What if they hired him because he was a novelty? What if he failed again?

He typed two words: I'm interested. Then stopped. Deleted. Typed again: Would love to talk. Deleted. He sat there, hands freezing in midair, as if a trapdoor might open beneath him the second he pressed Send.

A notification slid onto the screen, a calendar invite from a news producer for a segment titled "Saved Men: What It Feels Like To Be Rescued." He stared until the box timed out and slid away.

He clicked another rejection. He read it end to end, even the signature block, as if searching for a typo that would invalidate it. There was none. There never was.

His daughter's voice rose outside the door, closer now. "Mom, can we show Uncle Mike the video when he comes over? The funny one?" His chest seized. Funny one.

He slammed the laptop closed. The sound cracked the room, louder than he meant, like a gunshot muffled in carpet. He stood too fast, the blood going briefly thin in his head. Lines of text still burned behind his eyes: impressive… not at this time… another candidate… brave… proud… baptism… collaboration request…

The world inside the machine had stacked him like Jenga blocks—bravery balanced on humiliation balanced on indifference. He had one thought left that felt like his own: Get out of this room.

He tucked the laptop back under the bills, a rough shove that wrinkled the envelopes. The porch laughter rose, then faded; a car door thumped; a voice called goodbye. He didn't look to see whose. He moved.

Down the hall. Past the family photos (last year's school picture where his son's cowlick stood like a lighthouse, the beach trip where his wife had leaned into him under a sunhat, the framed print from their tenth anniversary dinner where he looked, he realized now, genuinely relaxed). Past the living room with the TV muted, a looping hero's jaw clenched mid-instruction on a news crawl. Past the kitchen, where the casserole Mark dropped off sat steaming on the stovetop, untouched.

He opened the door to the garage and let the smell hit him: old sawdust, motor oil, damp cardboard, the sweet metallic tang of tools that had been cleaned and put away by exactly one person in the house. The light flickered on with a thump. The cement floor was cold under his bare feet.

Here, at least, nothing pinged. Nothing refreshed. The pegboard still held the silhouette outlines of a hammer, two wrenches, a hand saw. The cheap metal shelving unit still sagged slightly in the middle where he'd overestimated its devotion and stacked too many paint cans in one spot. The jar of nails still sat clouded with dust like a snow globe that had given up on holidays.

He reached for the rag on the bench and drew a slow circle over the surface. The cloth came away gray-brown, satisfying in the obviousness of cause and effect. He wiped again. Again. It was not redemption; it was not a job. It was a small thing that obeyed him.

His phone buzzed in his pocket. He didn't look. He took the hammer down, simply to feel the weight of it in his hand—honest weight, almost refreshing after the weightless crush of pixels.

Another buzz. He imagined the subject line without seeing it: Boundary Waters Hero — booking request. Or We regret to inform you. He set the hammer handle-flat on the bench, palm against the smooth worn wood. The garage hummed with the house's lungs: the water heater clicking, the chest freezer sighing, the old radio on the shelf whispering static from a station it would never quite find.

He lined up the screwdrivers shortest to longest. He found a rogue hex key and set it with the others. He opened a drawer, found drywall anchors married somehow to guitar picks and a dead AA battery. He sorted them into old yogurt cups with a focus that bordered on prayer.

After a while—ten minutes, an hour, he couldn't tell—he realized he was breathing easier. It felt like bailing a boat with a spoon—ridiculous, doomed—but the point wasn't to keep the ocean out. It was to have something to do with his hands.

Through the door to the kitchen he could hear his wife's voice, soft now, telling the kids to pick up their plates. He heard the TV's new headline: Rangers praise citizen alerts. He imagined Backwards Cap's cap, jaunty, the ring light reflected in a window that wasn't his. The old fury flickered. He wiped the bench harder. The rag squealed faint on the wood, a sound not unlike the noise the canoe had made against rock.

His phone buzzed again, three times, a cluster. He thought of the contract email. He thought of Anita's Let me make some intros. He thought of Mom. Of the scoutmaster's voice: Take care of your family. That's the only real legacy.

He didn't pick up the phone. Not yet. He put the hammer back on its peg, handles aligned with the outline like a child coloring inside a line. He wiped the bench one more time as if the effort could erase a man flailing in a gray lake, as if order could be restored by torque and cloth.

When he finally straightened, his back cracked in a way that told him he'd been bent for a while. He looked around the square of the garage: bench cleaned, pegs tidy, the yogurt cups with their labeled tape — SCREWS, ANCHORS, ODDS — lined up like new recruits.

From the kitchen doorway his daughter's voice arrived again, smaller now, less sharp. "Mom? Where's Dad?" His wife's answer was muffled, then lighter: "Garage. He's cleaning the world."

Henry let a breath out that he didn't know he'd been holding. Cleaning the world. Maybe that was what this was. Not the world, but a square foot of it. Enough for tonight.

He reached for the light switch, then paused, hand hovering. The garage after he turned it off would go dark in an honest way: nothing glowed, nothing scrolled. He thought of the laptop upstairs with its mouth of a hundred open throats, all of them calling him by new names: brave, fool, survivor, content.

He clicked the light off. The dark came down, simple and complete.

Chapter 21

No Home For The Losing Team

Two months was long enough for the world to move on.

The news cycle had churned through the Boundary Waters fire, squeezed out every headline and clip, and spat it aside in favor of newer disasters. The viral video of Henry falling into the lake still floated around TikTok, resurfacing occasionally with a new caption or remix, but it no longer dominated feeds. Even the scoutmaster had disappeared back into obscurity after a flurry of interviews, politely declining offers to "brand himself" as a leadership coach.

But for Henry, the fire never really ended.

Every morning, he woke with the same knot in his chest. He padded downstairs, made coffee strong enough to strip paint, and opened his laptop to scan job boards. His inbox was clogged with auto-generated rejections. He had stopped clicking on most of them, only skimming the subject lines: Not selected... Thank you for applying... At this time... He sent out more résumés anyway, his fingers moving mechanically, like a man feeding coins into a machine that never paid out.

The afternoons were worse. The house was too quiet when the kids were at school and his wife was at work. He wandered the rooms aimlessly, straightening picture frames, picking up socks, wiping down already-clean counters. Sometimes he sat in the garage for hours, polishing tools he hadn't used in years. The hammer handles gleamed now, oiled wood as smooth as bone.

At night, silence hung heavier. His wife rarely spoke beyond logistics — what bills were due, what the kids needed for school, which groceries were running low. She answered his attempts at conversation politely but briefly, as if waiting for a meeting to end. She smiled at the children, at neighbors, at her phone when messages pinged. But rarely at him.

Henry felt it coming long before she said it.

One Tuesday morning, he came into the kitchen to find her already at the table, coffee untouched in her hands. The sunlight through the blinds striped her face. She looked calm, composed, like she had rehearsed this moment.

"Henry," she said, not looking up right away. "Can we sit down for a minute?"

He lowered himself into the chair across from her, heart steady but heavy.

She folded her hands, eyes finally meeting his. "I think it's time we talk about divorce."

There it was. The word he'd been waiting for, half-dreading, half-expecting.

Henry nodded slowly, the motion almost involuntary. "Alright."

No shock rose in him, no surge of anger. Just the quiet confirmation of what had already hollowed out between them.

She exhaled, relieved and sad all at once. "I don't love you anymore. I haven't for a long time. The last two months... they made it clear. We're just... not us anymore."

Henry rubbed his palms against his thighs. "I know."

Her voice softened. "I don't want this to be a fight. I don't want to make things harder than they already are."

"It won't be," Henry said. He meant it. He didn't have the energy left for battles.

She reached for her mug, but didn't drink. "My parents have agreed to help. They'll give you enough money to rent a small apartment out of town, just until you get settled. It's not charity, Henry. They want to make sure you're okay."

He looked at the steam rising faintly from her untouched coffee. His throat worked before he found words. "That's... thoughtful."

"I think it's the best way," she said gently. "For you, for me, for the kids. I want it to be amicable."

Henry nodded again. "Amicable."

The word felt like a verdict, final but painless in its delivery.

They sat in silence for a moment, listening to the hum of the refrigerator, the distant tick of the living room clock. Outside, the neighborhood stirred: car doors slamming, a lawnmower coughing to life. Ordinary sounds, steady and indifferent.

His wife's eyes softened with something like pity. "You'll be okay, Henry. You're stronger than you think."

Henry almost laughed at that, but the sound caught in his throat. Stronger? He hadn't felt strong in years. Not in the water, not in the news cycle, not in this house.

But he only said, "I'll manage."

She nodded, relief washing across her face. "Thank you. I didn't want this to be a war."

"No war," Henry agreed quietly.

He rose from the table, poured himself a cup of coffee, and sipped it while staring out the window. The yard was empty, the swing set still. The sunlight caught the edge of the lawn where the grass had burned brown in the July heat.

Behind him, his wife gathered her things for work, moving with quiet efficiency. She kissed the kids goodbye at the door a half-hour later, her voice bright for them. Then the door shut, leaving Henry alone again in the kitchen.

He sat back down at the table, the coffee cooling in his hands.

The end had come with no shouting, no tears. Just acceptance, like a curtain drawn on a play that had already finished.

Henry stared at the empty chair across from him and whispered, "Alright."

Henry sat at the table a long while after she said the word. Divorce. The syllables didn't echo or sting; they just landed like a stone in a pond and sank out of sight. He stared into his coffee, watching the thin film of cream swirl across the surface, and tried to feel something more than he did.

His wife stayed seated across from him, as if waiting for an explosion that never came. Her shoulders were tight, her eyes searching his face for sparks. But Henry had none to offer.

"I don't mean this cruelly," she said finally, her voice careful. "But I haven't loved you in a long time, Henry. I've been holding on because of the kids, because of the history... but I can't anymore. I feel like I'm lying to both of us."

Henry nodded once, slowly. He rubbed his thumb along the handle of the mug. "I know," he said.

Her brow furrowed. "You know?"

"I could feel it," Henry admitted. His voice was flat, but steady. "The distance. The way you look at me. Or don't. It's been a long time since we were... us."

Her lips trembled into something halfway between relief and sadness. "I didn't want you to think it was because of... what happened up there."

He almost laughed at that — a dry, humorless sound. "The whole country saw me fall into the water. I think it's safe to say that didn't help."

She winced. "Henry—"

"I'm not blaming you," he said quickly, holding up a hand. "I'm just saying... I know that moment didn't make me more attractive. To you, to anyone."

Her eyes softened. "It's not about that. It's about years, Henry. Years of us growing apart. Of me feeling like I was carrying everything alone."

He looked at her properly then, really looked. The lines at the corners of her eyes seemed deeper than they had two months ago. Her hair, once always carefully styled, now hung loose and practical. She looked tired, but certain.

"You probably were carrying everything," Henry said after a beat. "I let myself shrink. Let the job hunt, the rejections... all of it eat me alive. I stopped being a partner."

Tears pooled in her eyes, though she blinked them back. "I didn't want it to come to this. I wanted us to find a way back. But I can't do it alone. And you..." She hesitated, choosing words carefully. "You didn't fight for me."

Henry swallowed. The truth of it settled heavy. He had spent so much energy surviving humiliation, clawing through job postings, and retreating into silence that he hadn't noticed the marriage itself hollowing out. Or maybe he had, and he'd simply been too tired to stop it.

"I don't have a fight left in me," Henry admitted, voice almost a whisper.

She reached for her mug again, finally lifting it to her lips. She sipped, swallowed, then set it back down. "That's why this is the right thing. No screaming, no custody battles, no dragging the kids through mud. Just a clean end. Amicable. That's all I want."

Henry nodded. "Amicable."

She exhaled, shoulders sagging. "My parents have already offered some help. They'll give you enough to cover first and last month's rent, deposit, a little extra. You can get a small apartment out of town. Close enough to visit the kids, but… enough space for both of us to breathe."

Henry rubbed his temple. He should have felt insulted at the charity, but instead it landed like a strange relief. One less thing to figure out. One decision made for him.

"Alright," he said.

She blinked. "Alright?"

"What else am I going to say?" He gave a small, weary shrug. "You don't love me. I can't change that. At least this way, we don't have to destroy each other in the process."

For the first time all morning, she smiled. Not a joyful smile, but one of gratitude. "Thank you, Henry. For not making this harder."

He wanted to tell her it wasn't magnanimity, that he simply didn't have the strength left to fight. But he stayed quiet.

The silence stretched between them, heavy but oddly peaceful. Finally, she reached across the table, her fingers brushing the back of his hand. It wasn't affection, not anymore — just acknowledgment. "We'll tell the kids together, when the time is right. But for now… just start thinking about what you'll take with you."

Henry nodded again, his throat thick. "I'll pack while they're at school. No need for them to see."

"That's probably best."

The refrigerator hummed louder for a moment before kicking off. Outside, a dog barked. The world went on, steady and indifferent, while inside their kitchen, a marriage of nearly two decades ended without a raised voice.

Henry stared into his cold coffee, a hollow ache spreading through his chest. He wasn't surprised. He wasn't even angry. Just… sad.

Sad at how quiet the ending was. Sad that the storm of his life had blown itself out into nothing but silence.

He lifted the mug and drained the last of the coffee, bitter and lukewarm. Then he set it down gently, the sound of porcelain on wood like a period at the end of a sentence neither of them wanted to write but both had already read.

The house was unnaturally still the next morning.

The kids had left for school, their backpacks bouncing on small shoulders as they disappeared down the street with friends. His wife had left too, with a quick nod at the door that wasn't quite a goodbye, not yet. Henry stood in the hallway with his hands in his pockets, listening to the silence fill every corner.

It was the right time. No witnesses. No questions.

He started in the bedroom.

The closet smelled faintly of cedar and dust. His side was easy to distinguish: work shirts he hadn't worn in months, jeans frayed at the cuffs, a couple of jackets that still carried the faint scent of campfire. He pulled them down one by one, folding each into a cardboard box he'd dragged up from the garage.

As he worked, his mind wandered. Each shirt seemed to carry a memory — the blue one he'd worn on his first day at the IT firm, a day he'd thought would lead to decades of stability. The flannel he'd lived in during the Boundary Waters trip, now faintly stained and stretched. The collared shirt his wife once said made him look sharp, back when her compliments came without effort.

He folded them all the same way, efficient, methodical, trying not to let the weight of memory slow his hands.

The top shelf was worse. Boxes of old keepsakes: ticket stubs from concerts they'd gone to in their twenties, a faded Valentine's Day card with his clumsy handwriting, a photo album with snapshots of their honeymoon. He lingered over it, thumbing through the glossy pages — beaches, cheap cocktails, both of them young and laughing like the world was open wide.

He closed the album gently and set it aside. That would stay with her.

In the kids' rooms, he moved carefully, not wanting to disturb their worlds. He only picked up the things that were his: the baseball cap he wore to their little league games, a half-read paperback he'd abandoned on his daughter's desk, the broken wristwatch he'd been meaning to fix for his son. He set each item into the box like it was fragile, though none of them truly were.

By midday, the living room was filled with neat stacks of cardboard. His life reduced to boxes labeled clothes, books, tools, misc.

He sat on the couch and stared at them.

It didn't feel like loss so much as confirmation. The marriage had been slipping through his fingers for years; the divorce papers would only catch what had already fallen. Still, grief pressed at the edges of his chest. Not grief for what was ending — that part had ended long ago — but for what never became what he thought it would.

The afternoon sun shifted, laying new shadows across the floor. Henry rose again, moving into the garage.

The tools were easy. They belonged to him as much as the callouses on his hands. He packed them with care: the hammer with its worn grip, the screwdrivers lined shortest to tallest, the rag still stained from his long hours of "cleaning the world." These would come with him, a tether to something steady.

He found a shoebox at the back of the shelf, wedged behind a can of old paint. Inside were letters — not his, but his wife's, written during their first years of marriage. Sweet, awkward notes full of promises. He sat on the workbench, reading one after another, his chest tightening.

I love how safe I feel when you walk into a room.

You make me laugh like no one else.

I can't wait for the future we'll build.

He folded the letters back into the box and set it aside. Those weren't his to keep.

The clock ticked toward three. The kids would be home soon. Henry stacked the last box, taped it shut, and wiped his forehead. Sweat dampened his shirt, though the work hadn't been heavy. It was the kind of sweat that came from the inside, from nerves rather than labor.

He looked around the house one last time before the day reset itself with the sound of children's voices. The living room, stripped of his presence, looked oddly lighter. The kitchen, where they'd spoken yesterday, was spotless, the table bare. Upstairs, his closet held only her clothes now, the space beside them empty.

Henry stood in the quiet, his heart heavy but calm. There had been no fighting, no smashing plates, no last-minute declarations. Just packing. Just moving forward.

When the kids burst through the door later, flushed from the walk home, he greeted them with a smile and helped them with homework. They didn't ask about the boxes. Not yet. That conversation would come later, when their mother was ready.

For now, Henry let them chatter about their day, their voices filling the silence he had spent all morning inside.

And when they ran upstairs, he sat back on the couch, staring at the stacks of cardboard. Each one held a fragment of him, ready to be moved into a new, smaller space.

Grief whispered at the edges of his mind, but beneath it was a surprising flicker of relief. The charade was ending. The waiting was over.

All that was left was to go.

The next morning arrived with the same stillness as the one before, but Henry felt it differently. The boxes were already lined by the door, taped, labeled, stacked neatly.

His suitcase sat by the stairs, the zipper strained over its contents.

He had dreamed of fire again during the night — trees cracking in the Boundary Waters, the orange sky overhead. Only this time, when he stumbled into the water, no one pulled him out. He woke gasping, half expecting to taste smoke. Instead, he tasted the dust of cardboard.

His wife stayed upstairs with the kids, bustling them through breakfast and backpacks. Henry waited in the living room, listening to the muffled sounds of cereal bowls clinking, shoes being tied, the front door opening and closing. The kids shouted their goodbyes and raced toward the school bus.

When the house was quiet again, she came down.

She wore her work clothes: slacks, a blouse in a shade of green he used to tell her suited her eyes. Her face was calm, but her hands twisted at the hem of her sleeve.

"Are you ready?" she asked.

Henry nodded. "Yeah."

They stood in silence for a moment. There were no words left. Everything necessary had already been said yesterday.

She reached into her bag and pulled out an envelope. "This is from my parents. First and last month's rent, plus a little extra. It should cover you until you get settled."

He took it, the paper soft and heavy between his fingers. He wanted to argue, to insist he didn't need it, but that would have been a lie. So instead, he just said, "Thank you."

Her lips pressed into a thin smile. "You'll be alright, Henry."

He didn't answer.

Together, they carried the boxes to his car. The trunk groaned under the weight. The backseat filled with the overflow. The tools went in last, carefully arranged so they wouldn't rattle on the drive.

When the car was loaded, Henry stood by the open trunk for a long time, staring at the stacked boxes as if they might spell out the meaning of his life. Clothes. Tools. Misc. That was what it had come down to.

He shut the trunk gently and turned back to the house.

Inside, he walked slowly from room to room. The living room where the kids had built blanket forts. The kitchen where he and his wife once laughed while burning a first attempt at risotto. The hallway lined with school pictures, each year showing their children stretching taller, older, further away.

He paused at the bottom of the stairs, looking up at the closed doors of the bedrooms. He didn't want to disturb them. The house belonged to them now, not to him.

His hand skimmed the banister, the smooth wood polished by years of hands before his. He remembered sanding it when they first moved in, his wife teasing him for fussing over details. He smiled faintly at the memory, then let it go.

In the garage, he checked once more for forgotten things. Only dust and empty shelves remained where his tools had hung. He flipped the light off and stood in the doorway, listening to the hum fade.

Finally, he returned to the front door. His wife lingered there, arms crossed lightly, her expression unreadable.

"Well," Henry said softly.

"Well," she echoed.

They didn't hug. They didn't kiss. They simply stood facing each other for a moment, then nodded like business partners ending a meeting.

Henry opened the door. The morning air was cool, sharp with the scent of freshly cut grass from a neighbor's yard. He stepped onto the porch, down the stairs, and into his car.

As he pulled away, he glanced once in the rearview mirror. His wife stood at the door, framed by the house that had been theirs. She raised one hand in a small wave. He lifted his fingers from the wheel in return.

Then the house disappeared around the corner.

The drive out of town was quiet. His car rattled faintly under the load, the boxes shifting with every turn. Fields stretched on either side of the highway, golden with late summer sun. The radio stayed off. He didn't want songs, didn't want voices. He wanted the sound of the tires on asphalt, steady and certain.

An hour later, he pulled into the lot of the apartment complex.

It was plain — two stories of beige siding, narrow windows, cars parked bumper to bumper. No lawns, no porches, just concrete and gravel. But it was clean. Anonymous. Exactly what he needed.

Henry parked, sat for a moment with his hands on the wheel, then let out a long breath. He opened the door and stepped out, stretching his stiff back.

A manager in a polo shirt appeared, clipboard in hand. "Mr. Cole? We've got your unit ready. Second floor, end of the hall. Keys are here."

Henry took them, the metal cool against his palm. "Thanks."

The man pointed toward a narrow staircase. "Stairs are a little creaky, but the place is solid. Let me know if you need anything."

Henry nodded and turned toward the trunk. He lifted the first box — Clothes — and carried it toward the stairs. The cardboard dug into his arms, but he held it steady.

Inside, the apartment smelled faintly of fresh paint and empty air. Beige carpet, white walls, a small kitchenette with appliances that hummed louder than they should.

Sunlight streamed through a narrow window, landing on a blank wall.

Henry set the box down in the middle of the floor and stood there, breathing hard.

This was it. His new beginning.

Not heroic, not glamorous, not even hopeful. Just a small apartment out of town, four walls and a key. But it was his.

He closed the door behind him and let the silence settle in, clean and sharp.

Chapter 22

New Home

One week into his new apartment, Henry finally knew where everything was.

The place wasn't much — beige carpet, thin walls that carried the sounds of neighbors' televisions, a kitchenette barely big enough for one person to stand in. But it was his. No wife tiptoeing around silences. No kids looking at him with confusion he couldn't fix. No boxes scattered like accusations. Just four walls, a key, and a kind of peace.

He'd set up a rhythm. Mornings started with coffee brewed in the cheap Mr. Coffee machine he bought at a thrift shop, its burble the only cheerful sound in the place. He checked job boards until his eyes blurred, sent out applications into the void, then filled the silence with small chores. Laundry. Sweeping. Rearranging the handful of things he'd brought with him — tools in the closet, books on the single shelf, clothes folded neatly in drawers.

There was no dishwasher here. The first time he realized that, he'd stood at the sink with a plate in one hand, sponge in the other, and laughed softly. Another thing to do by hand. Another reminder that the conveniences of his old house were gone. But after a week, the dishes had become oddly grounding. Hot water, suds, a rhythm of scrub and rinse. Something he could finish, unlike the endless job search.

That evening he stood at the sink, finishing the last of the day's dishes. A pot, a plate, two forks. The window above the sink looked out over the parking lot, where the sun was setting behind rows of cars. The sky glowed pink, the kind of color that would've had his daughter running for her phone to take a picture.

The thought made him smile, and he dried his hands on a towel before picking up his phone.

He called them every evening, and tonight was no different. After a few rings, his son's voice came on, breathless and excited. "Dad! Guess what? Coach says I might get to pitch next game!"

Henry chuckled. "That's great, buddy. You been practicing?"

"Every day! Mom says I'm gonna wear out the glove."

"I'll buy you a new one if you do," Henry said. His chest tightened at the thought — not knowing if he'd really be able to afford it, but wanting to promise anyway.

Then his daughter came on, voice high with happiness. "Hi, Daddy! I made a picture for you. I'll bring it next time."

Henry leaned against the counter, eyes closed. "I can't wait to see it."

They talked about school, about their friends, about the dog down the street they wanted to adopt if their mother would say yes. It was all ordinary, and it was all precious. By the time the call ended, Henry felt both full and hollow — full from their laughter, hollow from the silence that returned when the line went dead.

He set the phone on the counter, sighed, and turned back to the sink. The last plate gleamed, stacked neatly in the drying rack. The apartment smelled faintly of dish soap and coffee.

Then came the knock.

Henry froze. He wasn't expecting anyone. He barely knew his neighbors. For a second, his heart thudded — a landlord complaint? A delivery to the wrong door?

The knock came again, firmer this time.

He wiped his hands on the towel and walked to the door. The peephole was useless — warped glass that showed nothing but a blur of color. So he unlocked it and pulled it open.

Standing there was a woman unlike anyone he expected.

She was in her late forties, maybe fifty, but carried herself with the confidence of someone younger. Blonde hair fell in careful waves to her shoulders. Her blue eyes were sharp, framed by makeup that only highlighted their brightness. She was slim, her blouse cut neatly, her posture straight. And yes, Henry noticed — her figure drew the eye, the kind of presence that turned heads in any room.

"Mr. Cole?" she asked, her voice clear, professional but warm.

Henry blinked. "Yes?"

She smiled. "You don't know me, but I know you. My name is Claire Whitaker. I'm the mother of one of the Scouts you helped in the Boundary Waters."

Henry's mouth went dry. "Oh."

She extended her hand. "May I come in for a moment?"

Henry hesitated, then stepped aside. She entered with the ease of someone used to being welcomed, her heels clicking against the apartment floor. She looked around briefly — the bare walls, the boxes still unpacked in the corner — but didn't comment.

"I've been looking for you," she said, turning back to him. "I wanted to thank you in person. My son, Tommy— he told me what you did. That you didn't leave them. If not for you, he might not be here."

Henry swallowed, suddenly unsure what to do with his hands. "The scoutmaster did the saving. I just—"

"No," she cut in gently. "You went in. You didn't run. Tommy said you were the first one he saw after the fire started. He remembers your face in the smoke. You mattered, Henry. More than you realize."

Henry stared at her, stunned. Praise felt foreign, almost painful. He opened his mouth to deflect again, but she pressed on.

"I own a boutique law firm here in town," she said. "We represent the local news station. And I want them to tell your story —on air. Not just the fall, not just the TikTok clip. The truth. What you did for those boys."

Henry's heart hammered. "On the news?"

She nodded, her smile unwavering. "Yes. You deserve recognition. And I want to help make that happen."

Henry took a step back, shaking his head. "I... I don't know. I'll need to think about it."

"Of course," Claire said smoothly. She reached into her bag, pulled out a card, and placed it on the counter. "Here's my number. Call me when you're ready. But please, Henry — don't hide from this. The world should know who you really are."

She gave him one last smile, then walked to the door. Her heels clicked softly against the floor until the door shut behind her, leaving the apartment silent again.

Henry stood there staring at the card, his pulse still racing.

For the first time since the fire, someone had told him he mattered.

And he had no idea what to do with it.

The apartment was silent after Claire set her card on the counter. Henry stared at it as though the ink might rearrange itself into something less terrifying than his own name scribbled in neat type.

He cleared his throat. "I don't know about this," he muttered.

Claire tilted her head. "Don't know about what?"

"Any of it." He gestured vaguely — the card, her, the mention of cameras. "I'm not someone people want to see on TV. I already made a fool of myself in front of millions once."

Her expression softened, but she didn't back off. Instead, she set her bag down on one of the two kitchen chairs and sat, crossing her legs with a calm confidence that made Henry acutely aware of how bare his apartment looked. "That video? That wasn't the truth. It was a moment — one moment taken out of context. My son told me the whole story. He said you were there in the smoke, shouting for them to keep moving, helping them scramble down into the ravine. That you were coughing as hard as they were, but you didn't leave."

Henry's chest tightened. "The scoutmaster did the heavy lifting."

"Yes," Claire agreed. "He pulled you out of the water. He guided the boys. He deserves praise. But Tommy told me what he saw too. He said you were the first adult face he recognized through the fire. That you didn't turn back when the flames cracked the trees. That matters, Henry. Children remember who stood with them when things got ugly."

Henry rubbed his palms over his jeans. His skin prickled as if her words were a draft blowing through the room. "He's just a kid. Kids remember things wrong."

Claire leaned forward slightly, her blue eyes unwavering. "I'm his mother. I know when he exaggerates. And I know when something imprints on him. He told me you kept saying, Don't stop. Keep moving. We'll get through this. Do you remember that?"

The words flickered back into Henry's mind like a spark: his own voice, hoarse with smoke, shouting into the chaos. He had barely remembered them himself until now.

"I..." He hesitated. "Maybe. I don't know."

"You did," Claire said firmly. "And it helped him. He said he kept repeating your words in his head until the fire was behind them. That's not nothing."

Henry sat heavily in the other chair, staring at the countertop as though it could anchor him. "I don't know how to accept that."

Claire's voice softened. "You don't have to accept it. Just hear it."

For a long moment, neither spoke. Outside, a car pulled into the lot, headlights sweeping across the blinds before fading. Somewhere upstairs, a child cried briefly, then was hushed. The ordinary life of the building went on while Henry sat with praise that felt too big for him.

Finally, Claire reached into her bag again and pulled out another card, thicker this time. She slid it across the table. "My firm represents Channel 7. They'd love to have you on. Not to make fun of you, not to twist anything — but to finally tell the story right. The scoutmaster has already had his moment, and deservedly so. But you deserve one too."

Henry blinked at the card, words blurring. Partner, Whitaker & Jameson Law. Her name printed bold across the top.

"I don't deserve—" he started.

She cut him off, gently but firmly. "You don't get to decide what you deserve alone, Henry. Sometimes other people see it clearer than we do. My son would not forgive me if I didn't thank the man he says helped save him. And I intend to do more than just thank you in private."

Henry rubbed his face, exhaustion sweeping over him. "I can't just sit in front of cameras. I don't have anything to say."

Claire leaned back, considering him. "Say what you said to those boys. 'Don't stop. Keep moving. We'll get through this.' That's more powerful than any lawyer could draft."

He looked at her then, really looked. She wasn't joking. Her eyes held conviction, the kind that came from years of advocating for others.

Henry shook his head slowly. "I'll… I'll need time. To think about it."

"That's fair," she said, standing smoothly. She gathered her bag, slipped her extra card back inside, but left the first one on the counter. "Take all the time you need. But don't let fear make the choice for you."

Henry walked her to the door, unsure whether to be relieved or more unsettled when she smiled warmly at him before stepping into the hall.

"Goodnight, Henry," she said. "And thank you. From a mother who knows what could have been lost."

The door closed behind her with a soft click.

Henry stood in the quiet again, the card gleaming on the counter under the kitchen light.

For once, it wasn't rejection mail. It was an invitation.

And it scared him more than all the rejections combined.

Henry didn't move for a long time after Claire left.

The card sat on the counter, neat black lettering on white stock, as if it had been waiting for his whole life to arrive. Whitaker & Jameson Law. Claire Whitaker, Partner. A phone number gleamed in the corner.

He poured himself another cup of coffee just to have something to do with his hands. The taste was bitter, too strong, but he swallowed it anyway. His chest buzzed with nerves, the way it had the morning he walked into his last job interview and saw the interviewer's eyes flicker at his résumé gaps.

Finally, he picked up the card and read it again, forcing himself to really see it. A door, wide open. The kind of door that had been slamming shut in his inbox for two years.

And still, all he felt was dread.

When the knock came a second time, softer this round, he nearly jumped out of his chair. He set the card down, heart hammering, and opened the door.

Claire hadn't left after all. She stood there again, her expression apologetic but determined.

"Sorry," she said. "I realized I was rushing you. But I want to be clear before I go."

Henry blinked. "Clear?"

She nodded. "Yes. The station doesn't just want to film you in some short clip. They want you live. A sit-down, ten minutes on air. To tell your side. Not TikTok's version. Yours."

Henry's stomach lurched. "Live? Absolutely not."

"Why not?"

"Because…" His words stumbled over each other, desperate to get out. "Because I'll make a fool of myself. Because I'll freeze. Because people will laugh again."

Claire tilted her head. "Do you think people laughed at you because you were weak, Henry? Or because they only saw half the story?"

Henry slammed his palm against the doorframe. "They laughed because I fell in the damn water!"

The outburst echoed down the hall, startling even him. He pressed his hand to his mouth, shaking his head. "Sorry," he muttered.

But Claire didn't flinch. She stepped closer, her voice quiet but firm. "You fell, yes. But your body, was exhausted from saving my son. That's the story people need to hear."

Henry laughed bitterly. "People don't want to hear that. They want clips. Jokes. Memes."

She crossed her arms. "And yet, millions still tune into the news. Millions want more than a punchline. Let us tell them."

He shook his head again, retreating into the apartment. She followed a step, but stopped at the threshold. "I'm not ready for that," he said.

"No one is ready to be seen clearly," Claire said. "But you can't hide forever. Not if you want to live again."

The words hit him like a splash of cold water. Not if you want to live again.

He turned his back to her, staring at the counter where the card still lay. His shoulders hunched, his breathing shallow.

Finally, he managed, "I really don't think so."

Claire nodded once. "I understand. But lets do this, let me buy you dinner as a celebration."

"You really don't have to do that." Said Henry.

"I insist." State Claire. "I will have my assistant arrange it."

Stunned with the forwardness, Henry simply smiled.

"I look forward to seeing you there Henry." Stated Claire, walking away.

Then the door closed behind her.

Henry paced the apartment in circles, the walls closing in. He replayed the scene over and over: her son in the fire, Claire's voice steady, the promise of being seen not as a fool but as someone who tried.

But louder still was the echo of online laughter, the baptism joke pinned at the top of the clip, the endless stream of comments. He pressed his hands against his ears as if that could muffle the memory.

Finally, exhausted, he collapsed onto the couch. The card sat on the counter, a white rectangle glowing in the lamplight, daring him to pick it up.

He didn't. Not yet.

He just whispered into the empty room, "What if they're right? What if I am the fool?"

The silence answered back.

Henry left the card on the counter and turned off the kitchen light, but its white rectangle still burned in his mind. He couldn't shake the image of Claire's eyes —

steady, blue, unwavering — as she told him he mattered. It unsettled him more than the laughter ever had.

He tried distracting himself. He flipped through the handful of books on his shelf. He checked the job boards again, though it was after nine and no one was posting at that hour. He even took a rag to the tools he'd unpacked, wiping at wrenches that didn't need cleaning. Nothing dulled the hum of her words.

Finally, he picked up his phone and called his kids.

They answered on speaker, their voices overlapping in the way siblings do when they've both got news to share. His son talked about practice — "Coach says I'm pitching Saturday!" — while his daughter described a science project that involved a papier-mâché volcano. Henry listened, laughing in the right places, nodding though they couldn't see him.

When their voices softened and they asked, "How are you, Dad?" he hesitated. The truth sat heavy on his tongue. He almost told them about Claire, about the offer, about the terrifying idea of being seen live on air. He wanted to hear them say he should do it, to hear faith in his voice reflected back.

But when he opened his mouth, all that came out was, "I'm proud of you both. You sound happy."

They giggled at that, embarrassed but pleased. His daughter promised again to bring him her drawing on Sunday. His son asked if Henry could come to the game. Henry said yes to both, his heart aching with the thought that they still wanted him there, even if their mother didn't.

After they hung up, the apartment felt even emptier.

Henry sat on the couch, staring at the muted glow of the TV across the room. He hadn't turned it on since moving in. News still felt radioactive. He imagined flipping it on now and seeing himself — soaked, coughing, eyes wide with panic — replayed once more as background to a punchline. His stomach clenched.

He stood, restless, pacing the length of the apartment. Back and forth, bare feet whispering over carpet. The card waited on the counter like a dare. Each time he passed, he glanced at it, then looked away, then circled back again.

Claire had said: Don't let fear make the choice for you.

But fear had been making his choices for years. Fear had shrunk him from husband to roommate, from worker to applicant, from man to meme. He rubbed the back of his neck, sweat prickling though the room was cool.

"What if they laugh again?" he whispered.

No one answered. Not the walls, not the tools, not the ghosts of his mistakes.

He walked to the window and looked down at the parking lot. A couple argued softly near their car. A teenager in headphones skateboarded past, oblivious to everything but his music. Ordinary life. No cameras. No viral videos.

Henry envied them all.

He went back to the counter, picked up the card, and turned it over in his hands. The cardstock was thick, expensive, the kind of detail people like Claire lived in. Her number was crisp, her name bold. His fingers traced the letters as though they might anchor him.

He thought of Tommy— the Clarie's soon who looked up in the smoke and seen him there, who had remembered Henry's cracked voice saying, Keep moving.

He thought of Claire's words: Children remember who stood with them when things got ugly.

He sat at the table, the card flat in front of him. He didn't dial the number. Not yet. But he didn't throw it away either.

Instead, he whispered the smallest rebellion against his own doubt.

"What if?"

The words barely stirred the air. But they were there, fragile and trembling, the first crack in the wall he had built around himself.

Henry leaned back, staring at the ceiling, the card still under his fingertips. The apartment was silent, but the silence no longer felt empty. It felt... paused. Waiting.

And for the first time in months, Henry didn't feel like a man waiting to be forgotten. He felt like a man on the edge of a choice.

Chapter 23

The Restaurant

The restaurant sat on a quiet corner downtown, its windows glowing golden against the night. Cars lined the street, and Henry had to circle twice before finding a spot half a block away. He killed the engine and sat for a long moment, staring at the entrance. A doorman in a dark coat opened the door for couples as they arrived, each one looking polished, purposeful, confident.

Henry glanced down at his suit — the shoulders too tight, the lapels too wide, the tie knot crooked despite three attempts to fix it in the rearview mirror. His shoes, though polished, still carried faint creases that spoke of years. He rubbed his palms on his thighs, already sweating.

You don't belong here.

The voice was sharp in his head. He imagined the maître d's raised eyebrow, the whisper of who let him in? from other diners.

But then he pictured Claire's face — the way she had spoken about her son, the conviction in her voice when she said he mattered. That steadied him, enough to open the car door and step into the cool evening air.

Inside, the restaurant was softly lit, chandeliers casting a warm glow over white tablecloths. Waiters moved like shadows, efficient and silent. The low hum of conversation filled the air, punctuated by the clink of glassware.

Henry approached the host stand, clearing his throat. "Reservation for Whitaker."

The young host smiled professionally. "Of course, sir. Right this way. She hasn't arrived yet, but we'll seat you."

The sir startled him. He followed, shoulders stiff, as they wove between tables. Diners glanced up briefly — women in dresses, men in tailored suits, laughter soft but sure. Henry felt each look land on his old jacket, each one confirming what he already believed: he was out of place.

The host led him to a small table near the window. "Your guest should be here shortly. May I bring you water?"

"Yes, thank you," Henry said, his voice dry.

He sat, hands folded tightly on the table, staring at the empty chair across from him. The tablecloth was crisp, the silverware gleamed, and the glass of water the server set down soon after reflected the chandelier above. He took a sip, throat tight.

Every minute felt stretched. He adjusted his tie again, tugged at his cuffs. He thought about leaving, making some excuse, texting Claire later with an apology. He imagined the relief of slipping back into his car and driving to his quiet apartment, alone but safe.

Then she walked in.

Claire moved with the confidence of someone used to being noticed. Her blonde hair caught the light, her blue eyes scanning the room until they landed on him. She wore a deep navy dress that skimmed elegantly along her frame, understated jewelry that caught just enough light. The conversations around them seemed to hush as she crossed the floor, heels clicking softly.

Henry started to rise, fumbling with his chair, but she waved him down with a warm smile. "Henry."

"Claire," he said, his voice catching.

She sat gracefully, setting her bag by the chair. "I'm so glad you came."

Henry tugged at his tie, self-conscious. "I wasn't sure I'd... fit in."

Her eyes softened. "You fit in fine. Don't worry about that suit — I think it suits you."

He huffed out a nervous laugh. "This old thing? It's been in the closet for years."

"Well," she said, folding her napkin across her lap, "then it's about time it saw the light again."

Something in her tone — warm, unbothered — loosened the knot in his chest. The waiter arrived with menus, and she glanced at hers briefly before setting it aside. "Order whatever you like. My treat."

Henry shook his head. "No, I can pay—"

"Henry." Her voice was gentle but firm. "Let me. This is dinner to thank you, remember?"

He nodded reluctantly, eyes dropping to the menu. The prices made his stomach flip. He scanned quickly, searching for something modest. Claire noticed but didn't comment, only ordering a glass of wine with casual ease.

Once the waiter left, she leaned forward slightly. "So. How have you been settling in?"

Henry shrugged. "The apartment's… fine. Quiet. I keep busy."

"With job hunting?"

"And dishes. And laundry. And staring at the ceiling some nights." He tried to make it a joke, but it landed flat.

She didn't flinch. "Transitions are hard. Give yourself some grace."

Grace. The word sounded foreign in his ears. No one had offered him that in years.

The conversation started cautious, but as the minutes ticked by, Claire's steady presence drew him out. She asked about his kids, about his hobbies before everything fell apart. He found himself telling her about the garage projects he used to tinker with, the long bike rides he once took, the Saturday nights at the rink playing hockey with friends in his twenties.

"Hockey?" she said, eyebrows raised, genuinely curious.

Henry smiled faintly, almost sheepish. "Yeah. Local league. Nothing serious. But I loved it. I was a defenseman — not fast, but I could hold the line."

Her eyes lit. "See? That's the Henry I want people to know. Not just the man who fell in the water, but the man who played hockey, who raised kids, who worked hard."

For the first time in months, Henry didn't feel like a fool. He felt like someone worth listening to.

The steaks arrived sizzling, filling the air with a rich, savory aroma. Henry's plate looked almost too polished to touch — a perfectly seared cut beside a swirl of potatoes and greens he couldn't identify. He picked up his knife and fork carefully, feeling like he was performing surgery instead of eating dinner.

Claire, by contrast, was at ease. She leaned back in her chair, wineglass in hand, her expression open. "So," she said, "tell me about hockey. You lit up when you mentioned it."

Henry's knife paused. "Lit up?"

She nodded. "Yes. You've been careful with your words tonight, Henry. A little guarded. But when you said hockey, your whole face changed. Tell me about that."

Henry cleared his throat, pushing a piece of meat around his plate before cutting it. "Well, it wasn't much. High school mostly. Then a local men's league after. We played on Saturday nights at the rink by the river. No crowds. No scouts. Just a bunch of guys trying not to break their ankles."

Claire laughed softly. "Did you win?"

"Sometimes," Henry admitted, a small smile tugging at his lips. "We weren't the fastest, but we played tough. I was defense. My job was to keep people honest. If someone came barreling toward our net, I'd be there to slow them down."

Her eyes sparkled. "So you were the wall."

"The wall?"

"Yes," she said. "The one everyone relied on, even if you weren't the star scorer. That's a kind of heroism too, you know."

Henry blinked, surprised by the word. Heroism. No one had called him that before — not seriously.

He took a sip of water, trying to hide his reaction. "Mostly it was beer league chaos. Guys tripping over the blue line, pucks flying into the stands, goalies swearing under their breath. But..." He paused, his fork halfway to his mouth. "It felt good. Being part of something. Knowing the guy next to you had your back."

Claire leaned forward slightly. "You miss it."

"Every day," Henry said, the words slipping out before he could stop them.

The admission hung in the air, startling in its honesty. Henry hadn't even told his wife that — not in the years when he still laced up skates, or in the years when the games faded into memory.

Claire didn't rush to fill the silence. She let him sit with it, her gaze steady, patient.

Finally, Henry chuckled ruefully. "My kids don't even know I played. Not really. I never talked about it. Maybe I thought it sounded silly. A grown man chasing a puck around."

"It doesn't sound silly at all," Claire said. "It sounds like a piece of you. And pieces like that are worth remembering."

Henry stared at her. She said it with such conviction that for a moment he believed it.

They ate quietly for a few minutes, the clink of silverware and hum of conversation around them filling the gaps. Henry found himself watching Claire when she wasn't looking — the way she smiled at the waiter, the way her fingers curved lightly around her glass, the way she carried herself as if the room belonged to her.

She turned back suddenly, catching his gaze. "What?"

He flushed, looking down at his plate. "Nothing."

She tilted her head. "Henry, you've spent years hiding. From jobs, from people, maybe even from yourself. But tonight, you're here. You're sitting across from me in that suit that probably has stories of its own. That means something."

He let out a shaky laugh. "You make it sound noble. It's just dinner."

"Nothing is just anything," she said softly.

The words struck him. He thought of the Boundary Waters, of the moment he'd fallen into the lake. Just a stumble. Just a fall. But it had followed him for months, a shadow he couldn't shake.

Now here he was, in a nice restaurant, talking about hockey with a woman who actually listened. For the first time in years, he felt safe — not like a joke, not like a burden, but like a man with something to share.

Henry found himself telling her more. About the time he scored his only goal, a clumsy rebound that still earned him cheers. About the locker room after games, the smell of sweat and cheap beer, the camaraderie that made the bruises worth it. About skating under the old arena lights, the ice gleaming, the sound of blades carving turns.

Claire laughed in all the right places, eyes bright, leaning in as though each story mattered. And the more she laughed, the more Henry remembered details he hadn't thought about in years.

By the time the plates were cleared, Henry realized he had been talking freely for nearly an hour.

And for once, it felt good.

The dessert menus arrived, leather-bound and heavy for something that listed five choices. Henry waved his off, still full from the steak and potatoes. Claire, however, ordered a crème brûlée with the ease of someone who knew exactly what she wanted.

When it came — the sugar crust cracking neatly under her spoon — she slid the dish across the table. "Share with me," she said, matter-of-fact.

Henry hesitated, then dipped his spoon in. The custard was rich, smooth, sweet in a way he hadn't tasted in months. He closed his eyes briefly, savoring it.

Claire smiled. "See? Better than eating alone."

The words landed with quiet force. Better than eating alone. Henry felt the truth of it deep in his chest.

They lingered over dessert, the hum of the restaurant softening as tables slowly emptied. The wine bottle on their table stood nearly finished, Claire's glass still half full, Henry's long abandoned after a few cautious sips. Conversation had ebbed into comfortable pauses, the kind that didn't demand filling.

Finally, Claire set her spoon down, folded her hands, and looked at him with a steadiness that made Henry sit a little straighter. "Henry," she said, "I need to ask you something directly."

He braced. "Alright."

"Will you do the interview?"

The words hung between them, sharp and clear. Henry's first instinct was to recoil, to reach for the old excuses

— I'll look foolish, they'll laugh, I'll freeze. He could feel them bubbling at the back of his throat.

But then he thought of the last two hours. Her laughter at his hockey stories. The way she had listened without pity. The crack of the crème brûlée shared across the table.

For the first time in years, he hadn't felt like a failure. He'd felt like a man worth sitting across from.

Henry exhaled slowly, the air trembling out of him. "Yes," he said, almost surprised at himself. "I'll do it."

Claire's smile spread slowly, not triumphant but warm, like sunlight breaking through cloud. "Good," she said simply. "Not because I asked, but because you're ready."

Henry shook his head, chuckling nervously. "I don't know if I'm ready. But I'll try."

"That's all anyone can ask."

They lingered a few minutes longer before she checked her watch. "We should go before they start stacking chairs around us."

Outside, the night air was cool, a faint breeze carrying the scent of rain on pavement. The streetlights glowed against slick asphalt, cars hissing past. Henry walked beside Claire toward their cars, feeling the weight of the evening settle into him — not heavy, but grounding.

At her car, she turned, touching his arm lightly. "Thank you for tonight. Not just for saying yes. For sharing yourself. It matters."

Henry swallowed. "Thank you. For... not laughing."

Her hand squeezed his arm gently. "Never."

For a moment, neither moved. The city hummed around them, but Henry felt suspended in a bubble of quiet. Then she opened her door, slid in gracefully, and with a last smile, drove off into the night.

Henry stood for a moment in the lot, hands in his pockets, the old suit jacket tugging at his shoulders. He felt foolish for wearing it, but at the same time, strangely proud. It was what he had. And tonight, it had been enough.

He drove home in silence, headlights carving the road ahead. The apartment was dark when he arrived, the counter bare except for Claire's business card. He picked it up, turned it over once more, and set it on the table by the couch.

For weeks, it had been a weight — a demand he wasn't ready to answer. Now, it was a promise.

Henry sat down heavily, shoes still on, tie loosened. He leaned back, staring at the ceiling. His chest was tight, but not with dread this time. With something closer to anticipation.

For the first time since the fire, he let himself believe: maybe he wasn't just the man who fell in the water. Maybe he was someone worth listening to.

And maybe, just maybe, tomorrow would not feel quite so empty.

Chapter 24

Morning Revival

Henry woke before dawn.

He lay on his back in the dim light of the apartment, staring at the ceiling where faint shadows stretched across the plaster. His alarm hadn't even gone off yet, but sleep had abandoned him hours earlier. Every time he drifted close, his mind conjured images of cameras, lenses like unblinking eyes, and the roar of unseen laughter.

By five thirty he gave up. He rose, shuffled into the kitchen, and made coffee. The machine gurgled loudly in the silence, filling the apartment with the bitter smell that always reminded him of his old office. He poured himself a mug and stood at the counter, staring at Claire's card.

Today.

The interview was today.

He could still call, cancel, fake a stomach flu, say he wasn't ready. The thought crossed his mind a dozen times before the phone rang.

Claire.

Henry swallowed hard, wiped his palms on his pajama bottoms, and answered.

"Morning," she said brightly.

"Morning," he muttered, his throat gravelly.

"You sound like you didn't sleep."

"Didn't."

There was a pause. "Henry," she said gently, "you're going to be fine. I'll be right there next to you. And Tommy too. It's not going to be an interrogation. It's a conversation."

He let out a shaky laugh. "A conversation broadcast live to half the state."

"Maybe," she said. "But think of it this way — it's not for them. It's for Alex. For the boys. For yourself. You've been hiding too long."

Henry rubbed his eyes. "I don't know if I can do this."

"You can," Claire said firmly. "I'll be by to pick you up at nine. Wear whatever makes you feel steady. That old suit, if you want. Or jeans and a shirt. Just come as yourself."

Henry hesitated. "Alright."

When she hung up, the apartment felt less suffocating.

———————————————

By six- , Henry stood in front of the mirror, adjusting the same old suit he'd worn to dinner. It still didn't fit quite right, but at least now he'd already survived one evening in it. He tugged the tie straight, polished his shoes again for good measure, and tried to steady his hands.

The knock came right on time. When Henry opened the door, Tommy bounded in first. The boy was all energy, his backpack bouncing, his grin wide. "Hi, Mr. Cole!"

Henry blinked. "Hey, kiddo."

Claire followed, elegant as always in a tailored jacket, her blonde hair shining even in the dull hallway light. "Ready?" she asked.

"Not really," Henry admitted.

"Perfect," she said with a smile. "No one ever is."

They drove in Claire's SUV, Henry in the passenger seat, Tommy chattering from the back. The boy talked about school, about how all his friends couldn't believe he was going to be on TV. "They think I'm famous," he said proudly. "But I told them it's Henry who's the hero."

Henry's chest tightened. "Don't—" he started, but Tommy cut him off.

"It's true," the boy said simply. "You didn't run. You came in after us."

Henry stared out the window, unable to answer. The autumn trees blurred by, gold and red against the clear blue sky.

Claire reached over, squeezing his hand briefly on the console. "Listen to him," she said softly.

The station loomed larger than Henry expected. A low, sprawling building with tall glass doors, its parking lot already busy with cars. A banner above the entrance read: Channel 7 – Your Community, Your News.

Henry's stomach dropped. He wanted to turn back, to feign illness, to melt into the seat. But Tommy had already unbuckled and was bouncing out of the backseat. Claire parked, cut the engine, and turned to Henry.

"You're not alone," she said, meeting his eyes.

He nodded, swallowing hard. "Okay."

Inside, the lobby buzzed with activity. People in headsets carried clipboards, rushing past with a practiced urgency. The air smelled faintly of hairspray and coffee. A receptionist greeted them, led them down a hall plastered with framed photos of past anchors, reporters smiling under bright lights.

Henry felt smaller with each step.

They reached the prep room, where a makeup artist bustled forward. "Mr. Cole? Right this way."

Henry flinched. "Makeup?"

"Just a little powder," the woman said cheerfully. "The lights are brutal. We don't want you shining like a disco ball."

Before he could protest, she had him seated in a chair, brushing lightly across his forehead and cheeks. He caught a glimpse of himself in the mirror — pale, nervous, but suddenly less haggard.

Claire sat nearby, calm and poised, chatting easily with a producer. Tommy swung his legs in another chair, grinning at Henry's discomfort. "You look good, Mr. Cole," he teased.

Henry groaned. "I feel like a mannequin."

"Better than looking like one," Claire said with a wink.

The producer clapped his hands together. "Alright, folks, five minutes until you're on. We'll get you miked up and seated. Just relax — our host will guide you through."

Relax. The word felt impossible. Henry's heart thundered as they clipped the small microphone to his lapel, the wire running under his jacket. He tugged at the cord nervously until the technician patted his shoulder. "Don't worry, we've got you."

They led him onto the set, and Henry nearly stumbled.

It looked both smaller and larger than he'd imagined: a polished desk under glaring lights, cameras on rolling tripods, a backdrop of the city skyline lit in artificial twilight. The air was cool, the silence heavy with anticipation.

He sat where they pointed — center seat, Claire on his right, Tommy on his left. The reporter, a woman with kind eyes and a practiced smile, sat across from them. She leaned forward, whispering, "You'll be fine. Just breathe."

Henry nodded stiffly, hands clenched on his knees.

The red light on the camera blinked to life.

And Henry realized there was no turning back.

The red light above the main camera glowed like an alarm. Henry's throat closed, his palms slick against his knees. Every instinct screamed at him to run — out of the chair, out the doors, into the cool morning air where no one was watching.

But he couldn't. Not with Claire sitting beside him, her calm presence anchoring him, and Tommy swinging his legs lightly in the other chair, excitement radiating off him.

The reporter leaned forward, smile warm but controlled. "Good morning, and welcome back to Your Community, Your News. Today we have a very special segment. You've all heard about the fire in the Boundary Waters two months ago. You've read the headlines, seen the TikTok clips, maybe even caught the national coverage. But today we're joined by two people who lived it — Claire Whitaker, whose son was among the Scouts rescued, and Henry Cole, who was there in the smoke with them."

Henry's heart lurched as his name echoed through the studio speakers. The applause sign flashed and the small in-studio audience clapped politely. He forced a tight smile, his chest stiff.

The reporter turned to him. "Henry, thank you for being here."

Henry coughed to clear his throat. "Uh, thank you for having me." His voice came out rough, thin.

"Now," the reporter continued, "we all saw that viral clip. You've probably heard the jokes. But what people may not know is the full story. Claire, why don't you start?"

Henry glanced sideways, relief flooding him as Claire took over. She smiled at the reporter, her voice steady. "That clip doesn't show what really happened. My son, Tommy, walked into the woods looking for a way out. During the walk, he got disorientated, lost and confused. Smoke and fire all around.

That's when Henry showed up.

Henry braved the water, the strom to cross across the water to the island, to resuce the boys who were trapped.

Upon learning of my son, not being with the group. Henry fought through fire, burning his hands fighting to get to my son.

Then grabbing him, he push and pulled him out to the other scouts. Once there Henry and his friend Mark, pulled the kids to safety across the water, where they were rescued."

The camera panned to Henry. He shifted uncomfortably. "I… I just did what anyone one would do, Between Mark, the Scoutmaster and myself we worked together"

Claire shook her head gently. "Henry, don't sell yourself short. You chose to run into the fire, when others ran from it."

The reporter turned back to him. "What was going through your mind that day?"

Henry opened his mouth, but nothing came. His mind flashed to the fire — the trees cracking, the smoke burning his throat, the panic of boys stumbling behind him. His hands clenched.

"Honestly?" he said finally, his voice trembling. "I was scared. I thought… I thought we might not make it. But those kids — they were looking at me, and I couldn't just… stop. I had to keep moving."

The reporter nodded, her expression softening. "That's bravery, Henry. Acting even when you're scared."

Henry swallowed hard, eyes dropping to his lap. "I don't know about bravery. I just didn't want them to die."

There was a hush in the studio. Even the cameramen seemed still.

Then Tommy leaned forward, small hands clutching Henry's arm. "But we didn't. Because of you."

Henry turned, startled. The boy's eyes were bright, his face earnest. And before Henry could react, Tommy slid off his chair and hugged him tight around the middle.

Henry froze, stunned by the sudden warmth. He glanced at Claire, who was already blinking back tears.

Into the microphone, Tommy said, clear and certain, "No one would be alive without Henry."

The reporter's eyes glistened. She reached across the desk, placing a hand over Claire's. "That's powerful, Tommy. Thank you." She turned back to Henry, her own voice trembling. "How does it feel to hear that?"

Henry's throat tightened. Words tangled, useless. Finally he managed, "It feels… more than I deserve."

Claire whispered, just loud enough for the microphones to catch, "It's exactly what you deserve."

The audience clapped again, this time louder, not the polite opening applause but something warmer. Henry felt it ripple through him, unfamiliar and overwhelming.

The reporter smiled gently. "We'll take a quick break, and when we come back, we'll talk about Henry's life before the fire — including a little-known fact: he used to be a hockey player."

The red light dimmed. The producer signaled a commercial break. Henry slumped back in his chair, shaking his head.

Claire touched his hand under the table. "You're doing great."

Tommy beamed up at him. "Told you, Mr. Cole."

Henry exhaled, for the first time since the cameras turned on, a faint smile tugging at his lips.

Maybe, just maybe, he could survive this.

The red light blinked back on, and Henry straightened in his chair, the echo of Tommy's hug still wrapped around him. His shirt felt warm where the boy's arms had been, and somehow that warmth steadied him.

The reporter smiled brightly, her voice smooth and practiced. "Welcome back. If you're just joining us, we're here with Henry Cole — a man whose bravery during the Boundary Waters fire helped save a group of Scouts — and with Claire Whitaker, the mother of one of those Scouts. Before the break, we heard Henry's powerful account of that night. Now, we'd like to get to know him a little better."

Henry's heart sank. Get to know him meant dredging up pieces he had kept locked away for years.

The reporter leaned in conspiratorially. "Claire, you mentioned earlier that Henry has an athletic past. Care to share?"

Claire smiled slyly, her eyes twinkling. "Henry used to play hockey."

The reporter gasped in mock surprise. "Hockey! Now that explains the broad shoulders."

Henry's face flushed crimson. He laughed nervously, rubbing the back of his neck. "I wasn't any star, just college. "

"Don't let him fool you," Claire said, teasing. "He told me he was the wall — the defenseman everyone counted on."

The audience chuckled. The reporter grinned. "The wall, huh? That sounds like a nickname worthy of an NHL highlight reel."

Henry shook his head, but for the first time, his smile reached his eyes. "More like the guy everyone yelled at when I missed a check."

The room laughed with him, not at him. The sound washed over Henry, strange and freeing.

The reporter leaned forward again. "Tell us, Henry, what did hockey mean to you?"

He hesitated, the seriousness of the question cutting through the humor. He thought of the nights under the rink lights, the smell of ice and sweat, the camaraderie of teammates who trusted him to hold the line.

"It meant..." He searched for words. "It meant belonging. Being part of something bigger than me. Knowing I had a job to do, and if I did it, the team was stronger. I miss that."

Claire's hand brushed his on the table. "You gave that same feeling to those boys in the fire. You belonged to them, Henry. They counted on you."

Henry blinked rapidly, throat tight. "Maybe," he murmured.

The reporter smiled, eyes glistening again. "You see, folks? A humble hero on the ice and off."

Henry chuckled dryly. "Hero's a big word. Mostly I just tried not to fall down."

Claire smirked. "That part didn't always work out."

The audience roared with laughter. Even the cameraman chuckled. Henry groaned, but a grin spread across his face despite himself. "You're never going to let me live that down, are you?"

"Never," Claire replied, laughing too.

For the next several minutes, the questions stayed lighter. Henry talked about his one and only goal, a rebound that surprised even him. He told a story about tripping over his own skates and crashing into the penalty box, sending a stack of Gatorade cups flying. Tommy giggled so hard he nearly fell out of his chair.

The reporter kept the tone playful, encouraging Henry to share little details. "Did you ever get into fights?"

Henry laughed outright now. "Not good ones. I swung once and missed. Hit the ref instead. Got tossed for three games."

The studio erupted. Claire covered her mouth, laughing until tears gathered again, this time from humor instead of sorrow.

For the first time in years, Henry's laughter wasn't cautious. It wasn't defensive. It was free, rolling out of him in a way that surprised even himself. He felt lighter, as if each laugh loosened another chain he'd carried.

The reporter leaned back, clearly pleased. "See, this is why we wanted you here, Henry. Not just the viral clip, not just the fire. People deserve to know the whole person. And I think they'll like what they see."

Henry sat back, breathless from laughter, his chest warm. For once, he believed her.

The red light above the camera blinked again, signaling the final segment. Henry sat a little straighter, still flushed from laughter. He hadn't expected to enjoy himself, yet here he was, cheeks warm, heart beating with something closer to excitement than dread.

The reporter leaned forward, voice softening. "Henry, before we wrap up, I want to say something on behalf of everyone watching. We cover a lot of stories on this show — tragedies, triumphs, viral clips that come and go. But what we've seen today isn't just a headline. It's a man who showed up when it mattered."

Claire dabbed her eyes with a tissue, smiling through tears. Tommy leaned against Henry's arm, his small hand gripping tightly.

"You are a hero, Henry Cole," the reporter said firmly. "And our community should be proud of you."

Henry shook his head instinctively. "I—" His voice cracked. He swallowed, tried again. "I don't feel like a hero. I was scared out of my mind. I stumbled more than I stood."

Claire reached over, covering his hand with hers. Her voice carried, soft but sure. "Heroes aren't the ones who feel fearless, Henry. They're the ones who act even when they're terrified. That's what you did."

Henry's vision blurred. He blinked rapidly, fighting the sting in his eyes. The cameras, the lights, the audience — they all faded, leaving only Claire's hand, Tommy's grip, and the quiet truth of her words.

The reporter's voice thickened with emotion. "And as if that weren't enough, we wanted to give you something."

She gestured toward the side of the set. A stagehand walked out carrying a sleek black box, polished and gleaming. He placed it on the desk in front of Henry. Not just any skates but a new set of Bauer Vapor FlyLite Skates.

Henry frowned, bewildered. "What's this?"

"Go on," the reporter encouraged.

Henry lifted the lid. Inside lay a brand-new pair of ice skates, shining under the studio lights. The steel blades gleamed, untouched. His throat tightened as he lifted one out, the weight familiar yet foreign in his hand.

"We've also reserved ice time at the community rink for you next week," the reporter continued. "It's yours, Henry. A chance to skate again."

The audience clapped, cheers rising louder than before. Even the cameramen grinned.

Henry stared at the skates, his hands trembling. Memories crashed over him — the chill of the rink, the echo of skates carving ice, the laughter of teammates. He hadn't thought he'd ever feel that again.

"I don't..." His voice broke. He pressed a hand to his mouth, unable to continue.

Claire squeezed his hand harder. "Say thank you, Henry. That's all you need."

He swallowed, nodding. "Thank you. I—thank you. More than I can say."

The studio erupted in applause again, the kind that rolled like a wave. Henry felt it wash over him, not ridicule, not mockery — but recognition.

The reporter smiled, blinking away her own tears. "You've given us all a reminder today, Henry. That courage doesn't always look perfect. Sometimes it looks human. And that's what makes it real."

Henry couldn't speak. He just nodded, holding the skate close, Tommy's arm still wrapped around him.

The segment wound down, the reporter signing off with practiced grace. "That's all for today's special edition of Your Community, Your News. Join us tomorrow, but for now — let's give one more round of applause for Henry Cole."

The audience rose, clapping, some even cheering.

Henry sat frozen in the noise, overwhelmed. He had dreaded this day, feared it would destroy him. Instead, it had given him something he thought he'd lost forever: dignity.

When the cameras finally cut, Claire turned to him, eyes shining. Tommy launched himself into another hug. "You did it, Mr. Cole! You were awesome!"

Henry let out a shaky laugh, ruffling the boy's hair. "Couldn't have done it without you, kid."

Claire leaned in, pressing a quick kiss to his cheek. "I told you you mattered."

Henry swallowed hard, still clutching the skate. "I'm starting to believe you."

They walked together to the parking lot, the studio crew waving as they passed. Henry felt every handshake, every clap on the shoulder, like proof that he was still here, still standing.

Outside the studio was his friend Mark.

"Hero huh, what's that about." Teased Mark.

"Did you have something to do with this to?" asked Henry.

"Nah it was all her idea." Henry said pointing at Claire.

"Lets go get a cup of coffee." Said Mark.

"You two go, call me later." Said Claire.

Smiling Henry hugged Tommy goodbye and walked over to Mark.

Chapter 25

Flying On Ice

The box sat on the passenger seat like a living thing.

Henry glanced at it every few seconds as he drove, knuckles white on the steering wheel. Inside was the brand-new pair of skates, sharper and cleaner than anything he'd ever owned. They caught the light even through the cardboard — bright, gleaming, almost mocking in their perfection.

It had been years since he'd stepped onto a rink. Longer still since he'd felt confident on the ice. He was heavier now, softer in places that used to be muscle, and the idea of skating under the fluorescent lights of the community arena made his stomach twist.

When he pulled into the lot, the building looked the same as it had decades ago — squat and brick, a curling banner above the double doors reading Community Ice Center. He sat in the car for a long moment, the engine ticking as it cooled, watching kids in sweatshirts and carrying sticks stream through the doors. Their laughter echoed faintly, sharp against the crisp morning air.

Henry exhaled slowly, grabbed the box, and forced himself out of the car.

Inside, the rink smelled the same: cold air, faint popcorn from the concession stand, the sharp tang of ice and Zamboni fuel. The sound of blades carving against ice reached him even from the lobby. For a second he was sixteen again, lugging a bag half his size, hair dripping sweat into his eyes.

He shook his head. That was a lifetime ago.

The attendant at the desk looked up. "Mr. Cole?"

Henry nodded. "Yeah."

"Rink's all yours until eleven. Ice was cut fresh fifteen minutes ago. You need a locker?"

"No, I'm good."

He carried the box to the benches by the rinkside and sat down heavily. The cold from the concrete floor seeped up through his suit pants — he'd dressed neatly without really thinking, still wearing the jacket from the interview as though armor.

Opening the box, he pulled the skates free. They gleamed in the dim light, laces crisp, blades shining with that fresh, untouched edge. His hands trembled as he threaded the laces, tugging them tight the way he used to, double-knotting the ends out of habit.

Standing was awkward. The weight of the skates shifted him forward, ankles stiff, calves protesting. He shuffled toward the gate and placed a hand on the cool metal frame, staring down at the sheet of ice before him.

It stretched out smooth, gleaming under the overhead lights, a perfect canvas.

Henry took a breath, pushed the gate open, and stepped onto the ice.

His first glide was clumsy. His ankles wobbled, his knees bent too far. He flailed for balance, catching himself before toppling. The ice felt both familiar and foreign, like meeting an old friend whose name you suddenly can't recall.

He pushed again, tentative, each stride shorter than it should have been. His body protested, the extra weight dragging him off center. Sweat beaded on his forehead after only two laps.

He almost quit then. He could already imagine the cameras, the laughter, the clip of him stumbling replayed endlessly online.

But something stubborn in him pushed back.

He remembered the scoutmaster's voice in the smoke: Keep moving.

He remembered Tommy's hug in the studio: No one would be alive without Henry.

And he remembered Claire's eyes, steady, believing.

So he pushed again. Harder this time. His left leg extended, his right followed, the blades cutting deeper into the ice. His breath came ragged, but his body began to remember.

By the fifth lap, his strides lengthened. By the seventh, his shoulders loosened. He wasn't flying — not yet — but he wasn't stumbling either.

And when he leaned into a turn, the ice whispering under his blades, a jolt of recognition shot through him.

It was still there.

The muscle memory. The rhythm. The quiet power of gliding over ice, weightless for a heartbeat with every push.

Henry let out a breathless laugh, startling himself. The sound echoed in the empty arena, bouncing off the boards. He pushed harder, faster, his legs aching but steady. He carved wide circles, then tighter ones, testing himself. The stiffness didn't disappear, but beneath it lay something strong, waiting to be uncovered.

For the first time in years, Henry wasn't just moving. He was skating.

Henry was halfway through another shaky lap when he spotted movement in the stands.

At first, he thought it was just a parent waiting for a kid's practice, but then he recognized her immediately. Claire. Even in jeans and a simple cream sweater, she carried herself with that same presence, a kind of quiet authority that made the rink suddenly feel smaller. She had a coffee in one hand, her other tucked into her pocket, eyes fixed on him.

Henry's chest tightened. He nearly stumbled on his next push.

She waved lightly, lips curving in a smile, and mouthed something he couldn't quite make out. He straightened, tried to smooth the wobble in his stride, and pushed harder down the straightaway.

Then he noticed the cameras.

Two people in Channel 7 jackets had set up near the boards, one with a shoulder-mounted camera, the other fiddling with a boom mic. A producer he remembered from the studio waved cheerfully at him, like this was all just another extension of the interview.

Henry's stomach lurched. His first instinct was to head straight back to the bench, rip the skates off, and bolt for the door.

But Claire walked down the bleachers and leaned casually against the boards, her eyes locked on him. She mouthed again, clearer this time: You're fine.

The producer gave a thumbs-up. The camera whirred, tracking Henry as he circled the rink.

His strides faltered. His shoulders hunched. He imagined how it looked through the lens — an aging man, soft around the middle, puffing for breath, wobbling like a rookie.

He nearly stopped.

But then Claire clapped. Just once, sharply, the sound echoing through the half-empty arena. Tommy wasn't there this time, but Henry could imagine the boy cheering too, that unshakable faith in his voice.

Henry pushed again. His blades cut a little deeper. His balance steadied.

And then something clicked.

It wasn't dramatic — no sudden burst of speed, no miraculous trick. Just the subtle, sure return of muscle memory. His legs remembered how to glide, how to dig in, how to shift weight from edge to edge. His arms loosened, swinging with the rhythm. The clumsiness melted with each stride, replaced by something smoother, more natural.

He rounded the far corner and accelerated down the straight, the cold air rushing past his face. For the first time in years, the rink wasn't just a place — it was a stage, and he belonged on it.

The cameraman followed his every move, but Henry stopped noticing. He leaned into the turn, carving tight arcs, the sound of steel on ice ringing like music. His breath came hard, his legs ached, but exhilaration burned through him.

Claire clapped again, louder this time, her smile wide and unguarded. "That's it, Henry!" she shouted, voice carrying across the rink.

Henry grinned despite himself, pushing harder. Faster. He crossed the rink in long, steady strides, his chest heaving, sweat prickling under his jacket. The ice felt alive beneath him.

The producer leaned toward Claire, whispering something, and she nodded, eyes never leaving Henry.

He finished another lap, then coasted toward the bench, bending over his knees to catch his breath. His chest burned, his legs throbbed, but he was smiling — really smiling.

Just then the rink doors opened and 13 kids came barreling out onto the ice.

Henry shocked, stopped and stared.

It was the scouts from the fire.

Surrounding Henry, they each went and skated over giving him a hug. The cameras rolling nonstop.

Clarie now also on the ice, but brining a stick with her.

"How about a pickup game. " asked Claire.

At this the kids cheered.

An hour later, the cameras started to shut off, the crew stated to pack up, the kids parents now in the stands, filming while the news stations cameras were shutting down.

Henry skated over to the side, and each parent came down to say Thank You, to Henry.

The thanks yous, lasted longer then Henry felt comfortable with, but Henry stayed till the last parent left.

Finally Claire came over. "Sorry about surprising you today, the other parents wanted to thank you and the news station wanted a puff piece. But you did wonderful."

"Wells it better than laying on the ground with your pants around your ankles." Joked Henry.

"Yea, lets not talk about that again." Said Claire.

Henry smiling simply shook his head yes.

Chapter 26

My Life Is Not Over.

The apartment knew all his habits. It knew where he'd put his keys when he remembered—on the little saucer by the door—and where he'd drop them when he didn't—on the counter, next to the coffee maker that took twice as long as the box promised. It knew the sound of him settling into a chair like a man easing into a cold lake, one inch at a time, and the shape of his evening laps around the living room when his legs had too much worry in them to hold still. It knew the pauses between one breath and the next when he read job postings and pretended not to care, and the way the refrigerator motor could fill a room if the room was empty enough.

Tonight, the apartment could have been a cathedral. That's how large the quiet felt.

Henry's phone lay on the table, facedown so he wouldn't watch it not ring. He had a half-done grocery list on a sticky note and an unopened envelope with his health insurance COBRA information turned into a coaster. The TV was muted; closed captions crawled across a hockey highlight reel of last season's playoffs—angles of ice like clean paper, the quick black hyphen of a puck, cheering that you could feel through the screen even with the sound off. He had not played hockey in a long time, not for real, but the body never forgets its geometry. The eyes follow, the ankles tense, the heart anticipates the moment before contact. He could still almost smell the rink: cold air, sharpened steel, tape, the faint burr of rubber.

He told himself he was not waiting.

The phone buzzed.

A small scuff of vibration against wood, the kind of tremor you could talk yourself out of hearing if you wanted to. He didn't. He flipped it and squinted at the caller ID.

Unknown number. New York, NY.

His hands went colder than the room. Telemarketer, he thought. Or another recruiter with a commission smile and a "we'll keep you on file." He almost let it go to voicemail out of habit, out of self-defense. But the New York sat on the screen like a dare.

He answered. "Hello, this is Henry."

"Hi, Henry. This is Allison from the National Hockey League. Is now a bad time?"

He sat down because standing would have made him say something dumb. "No—uh—no, not at all." His voice came out formal, like a jacket with the tag still on it. "Hi."

"We saw your segment this morning," she said gently, as if the sentence might scare. "On KMSP. Claire Jensen's piece. Our comms team circulated it around the office. First for the story—what you did up there. Then... well, someone in tech noticed your profile floating around LinkedIn. IT leadership. Infrastructure, vendor management, legacy modernization. And, um, a bit of hockey in the résumé too."

He thought of the highlight reel still moving silently on his TV. He thought of the years he'd swallowed down like pills, chalky and reluctant, telling himself he was too old to want anything more than a paycheck that cleared. He thought, foolishly, of his skates in the hall closet, blades wrapped in a towel. "Yes," he said, because it was the only thing that would come out.

"Are you open to a conversation about an IT Manager role at league headquarters?" Allison asked. "Hybrid in Manhattan. Core focus on enterprise systems and broadcast-adjacent workflows. Some travel. We'd need someone comfortable in both the hands-on pieces and the calm-the-storm pieces. The team's good. We've been looking for steady."

He swallowed. There was a moment when the apartment seemed to tilt and then right itself. The refrigerator clicked off in the kitchen and the room's hum changed pitch, as if the building were listening. "I'm open," he said. "Very open."

She told him about the role. Not the PowerPoint version—he could tell she'd done those conversational rounds where the other person is allergic to corporate nouns. She talked in specifics: ticket backlogs that looked like geological strata, a CMS integration that had grown like ivy, vendors with excellent slides and complicated scopes, an analytics initiative that wanted a grown-up. He asked the questions that had become the tightrope under his feet these last months: budget authority, headcount, decision rights, whether "agile" meant sticky notes or executive backup. Allison answered without overselling. He knew the difference now; six hundred days of interviews will teach humility to both sides.

"Could you do a video call tomorrow?" she asked. "Initial panel. Two directors and me. Nothing adversarial. We'd like to move fast."

He almost laughed because the word fast in his life had lately meant a slow bleed. "Yes," he said. "Absolutely."

"Great." The smile in her voice was a small, bright thing. "And, Henry—one more thing. This is off-script. The segment... it came at us in a week when we needed a story about somebody doing a hard thing and not asking for anything back. People here were... moved. It's not a hiring criterion. But I wanted you to know it mattered."

He looked at the muted TV. A winger broke free up the boards and the camera cut too late; the captions tried to keep up with names and speeds that didn't fit inside the white rectangle. The old ache rose in his chest and then softened into something he couldn't name. "Thank you," he said, and meant it harder than any two syllables he'd spoken all month.

They set the details: the time tomorrow, links, a pre-read. He gave an email address that, weeks ago, he'd considered canceling because it felt like a mailbox behind a house that was no longer there. They said goodbye. He hung up.

Silence.

Not absence. The kind of quiet that follows a bell.

He stood in the center of the living room, phone still in his hand, the blue notification bubble like a small, tame star. His brain did the math without asking permission: rent in New York, winter coats, transit passes, the cost of a city where people decide things quickly and talk about it slowly. He saw an office with glass conference rooms and an old team photo of men he'd watched as a kid, stern in their suits, foreheads like polished wood. He saw server rooms and people who said "we" and meant it. He saw a badge on a lanyard and a first day.

He didn't see anyone to tell.

The apartment went back to being a room. The refrigerator started up again, bravely. A car door thumped in the street and someone shouted goodnight across the lot. The TV rolled to a commercial about insurance with a fake family pretending not to be grateful for coverage.

He sat down and placed the phone in the saucer as if it could be contained that way. He looked at his hands. The bandages on his palm were newer than his brain wanted them to be; the skin underneath felt tight, tender, pink with newness. He turned the hand palm up, then down. He imagined shaking hands with a new team tomorrow and laughed once, softly, at the gallows formality of his own imagination. He had never been precious about hands when he worked. You typed. You carried a stack of laptops. You tore down a patch panel at midnight and built something that would hold. But now one had held a boy's shoulder through fire, and the other had dialed into luck. They felt like the same hand.

There were people he could call.

His kids were two towns over with their mother, who had become a woman he could talk to about the weather like a conscientious neighbor. He pictured calling his daughters and trying to explain that a league they knew mostly as logos on hats wanted to pay their dad to fix the systems that ran the league's pulse. He pictured their immediate, unvarnished joy—children don't negotiate their happiness for you—and then the echoing after: the details, the logistics, the questions about school years and plane tickets and how often he'd be back. He had been trying to hold them steady for months; he could not put flight under their feet tonight, not without a plan.

His father would pick up and say "what's wrong?" before hello, because older men learned the shape of a late call as if bad news had a fragrance. But his father lived with the old maps in his head: you worked for a thing with a name that would fit on the side of a building and you stayed. The NHL wasn't a factory but it had that heft. His father would love that. But then the other conversations would begin—about moving, about money, about whether this was chasing a story because a story had finally chased him. He didn't have the answers yet, only the yes.

He reached for the phone and did not pick it up.

In the kitchen he poured water and drank it standing up, the glass cool along his lower lip. He turned the tap to cold and held his bandaged palm under it without removing the gauze, just to feel the idea of coolness soaking through. He set the glass down and leaned into the counter until it bit a line across his abdomen that made him feel anchored.

You're allowed to be happy, he told himself in the same tone he used with kids on the lake who needed permission from someone taller. You're allowed to feel this.

The happiness came like weather. Not a thunderclap. More like a front moving across the plains, the way the light changes on a highway in the middle of an afternoon with no plans. All at once the room had edges again. The couch was not just a place where he'd fallen asleep by accident but a place he could imagine falling asleep on purpose after a day of work where someone would say "goodnight, Henry" and mean "see you in the morning."

He grinned. It surprised his face. He felt the shape of the grin in his ears.

The phone chimed; his email had already populated with a calendar invite and a bare-bones JD that did not do the job justice. He opened it and scanned. He recognized acronyms like old teammates. He saw lines where his brain automatically filled in the missing pieces: risk registers, rollout communications, the particular language you use with business partners so they will come with you through a migration and not just watch. He knew which dashboards should be useful and which would be pretty.

He caught himself beginning a list. On the back of the sticky note under the grocery list he wrote, without asking permission, three words at the top: Day One Checklist. He drew a square box to the left of each line because checking boxes has always made the animal brain purr.

- Learn names. Real ones, preferred ones.
- Ask the team what's broken that we say isn't broken.
- Walk the racks. (Know where the bodies are buried.)
- Buy coffee. Listen more than I speak.

He stopped and laughed at himself again. It was either laugh or burst. He folded the note in half and slid it under the phone as if tucking it into bed.

The temptation came then, bright and clean as a whistle: call someone who will understand the size of this without needing a diagram. Someone who had been with him when the room had been smaller and the humiliation had been louder and the nights had been longer. Someone who had looked at him on live television when his throat tightened and, with a professional's mercy, held the silence until he found air again.

He thought of Claire.

He could still see her across the studio floor that morning, the way she listened like a person who knew that listening is not the pause between speeches. The way she bent the interview toward dignity and then toward humor and then toward something that felt like relief. The way, afterward, off-camera, she squeezed his arm at exactly the pressure that makes a man remember that his body is his home. He had thanked her and she had said the kind of thing a good reporter says—"you did the hard part"—and he had wanted to argue that the hard part is being alone with the after.

He stared at the phone and tried, unsuccessfully, to think of a cooler way to dial a number.

"Call her," he said aloud, as if the apartment would hold him accountable.

He did not. Not yet. He took a small tour of the room, touching objects like a blind man learning a map he'd drawn himself. The back of the chair. The worn spot on the arm of the couch where denim had polished fabric into something smoother. The window latch that grit stuck in each spring. At the bookshelf he let his fingers fall on old paperbacks not because he'd read them lately but because they had traveled with him through leases and fights and babies learning to stand. He paused at the framed photo of his daughters on the lake, two sets of cheeks bright with cold that year it froze early. He closed his eyes.

You are allowed to be happy.

It was not his style to pray. But he found himself making a simple bargain with the ceiling: If this job comes through, I will show up like a man who remembers gratitude, even when the printer jams and the budget shrinks and someone writes an email that makes me want to walk into traffic. I will be steady. I will be kind. I will carry coffee and not mention that I carried it.

When he opened his eyes, New York was in the room with him. Not literally. But the noun had shape now. He could see the first morning: the train he would miscalculate by one stop and then pretend he meant to be early; the lobby with a security desk where someone would ask for an ID without looking up; the elevator ride where he'd read the list of floors twice. The conference room with the view you don't look at during a meeting because people who belong don't turn their heads at glass. He saw himself in a chair that rolled too easily and heard himself ask, in the tone of a person who intends to do the work, "What do you need most from me in the first ninety days?"

The word we slid into his skull like a key. We need. We're going to. We'll try. He could feel the pronoun loosening knots he had not known were there.

He took out his wallet and, without meaning to, felt for the old photo tucked behind his health insurance card: him in his twenties, uniform dark with melted ice, grin reckless, hair not yet defeated by weather and money. He looked ridiculous and lucky. He looked like a boy who would laugh at a future where an IT job could feel like a door swinging open to the rink. He slipped the photo back and let his fingers rest on the edge of the leather long enough to hear it creak.

Call Claire.

He sat, picked up the phone, and scrolled to her number without having to hunt for it. He had not saved it under "Claire KMSP," even though that would have been like adult camouflage. He had saved it under Claire Jensen because that's who she was in his head: a person with a name, not a job.

His thumb hovered.

It was 8:17 p.m. She had a life. She had probably already filed her piece and was halfway through cold pad Thai with her laptop angled like a second dinner partner. She might be at the gym; she might be in pajamas; she might be on a different call with someone else holding a shock that needed a place to land. He did the thing men do when they are more polite than brave: he rehearsed an apology for interrupting a person who had not asked for their schedule to be considered.

He hit the call button before his courage could argue itself into smaller parts.

The ring sounded different once. Once on TV he had watched a show where the ring tone gained echo for dramatic effect. This was a cheap phone. It did not care for drama. It was flat and ready.

One ring. Two.

"Henry?" Claire's voice, picking up on the third like a person who keeps their promises to their contacts list. Professional warmth, then a quick turn toward concern. "Are you okay?"

He closed his eyes because kindness is its own heat. "I am," he said, and heard how strange that sounded in his mouth.

"Good." He could hear her smile turn audible. "You sounded surprised to hear yourself say that."

"I got a call," he said, and then his voice came apart at the edges with laughter he hadn't planned. "From the NHL. Headquarters. IT manager role. They saw the segment. They want to talk. Tomorrow."

There was a silence that wasn't silence; it was the noise made by a person holding words in both hands long enough to see which were the right ones to give away. Then she exhaled. "Henry. That's... that's wonderful."

"I didn't know who to tell," he said, like a confession he didn't mean to give.

"You told the right person," she said, and anything after that was gravy.

He was not a man who cried easily in front of other people. He did not cry now. But his body loosened the way the world loosens after a storm finds its exit. He found a chair with his free hand and sat.

"Tell me everything," she said, light entering the room through the phone. "What they said, what you said, whether you asked the budget question, because if you didn't I'm going to be mad on your behalf."

He told her. He told her about Allison and the voices in his head and the sticky note with the checklist that had started all on its own. He told her about seeing the office in his mind and his children at the lake and the photo in his wallet like a ghost with better posture. He left out nothing that would make her job easier to narrate later if she wanted to, and nothing that would cheapen the private glow he was trying, with both hands, to hold.

"Do you want to celebrate?" she asked, as if the word celebrate were a simple kind of labor two people could share. "Tonight? It's only Thursday. I know a place that pours a dangerous old-fashioned and makes pretzels as long as your arm."

He looked at the room to make sure it wasn't shrinking again and felt it steady. "I would like that," he said. "Very much."

"Good" She paused. "I'm proud of you. I know that's corny. I don't care."

He swallowed and the water glass on the counter across the room looked like a lake you can startle with a thrown rock. "Thank you," he said.

"Text me the address," she added. "Thirty minutes?"

"Thirty." He ended the call and the apartment, which had been large with quiet, felt briefly too small for the size of the next hour.

He stood. He looked down at his shirt—clean enough—and then at the shoes by the door. He reached for a jacket he hadn't worn since the last time he believed a night might end with a story worth telling. He put his wallet in the inner pocket and, with a thoughtfulness he wouldn't have managed yesterday, slid the old photo into the front of the billfold where it might see a little light.

He stopped by the bathroom mirror, and the face there startled him with its brightness. Not handsome—he was too tired for that lie—but awake. The kind of awake that doesn't beg the day to be merciful. He smoothed his hair. He considered shaving and then did not. A man should look like the day he had, he decided; tonight he had a day worth recognizing.

He grabbed his keys from the saucer. They chimed against the ceramic and he liked the sound. He thumbed a quick text with the address and a joke about pretzels being a religion he could join.

On his way out, he turned back and scanned the room the way you do when you know you're about to step into a different version of your life and you want to remember the museum of the old one exactly as you left it: the muted TV still broadcasting joy without sound, the grocery list with "eggs" and "coffee" and "apples" written like talismans, the glass on the counter with a thumbprint halfway up the side, the phone charger coiled like a small sleeping animal, the bandage scissors on the table, the folded sticky note tucked beneath the phone with a box waiting to be checked.

He locked the door and went out into the long hallway that led to the stairwell and then down, toward a night that belonged to him again.